More Than a Passing Shot

TOMI TABB

 Formatted with Vellum

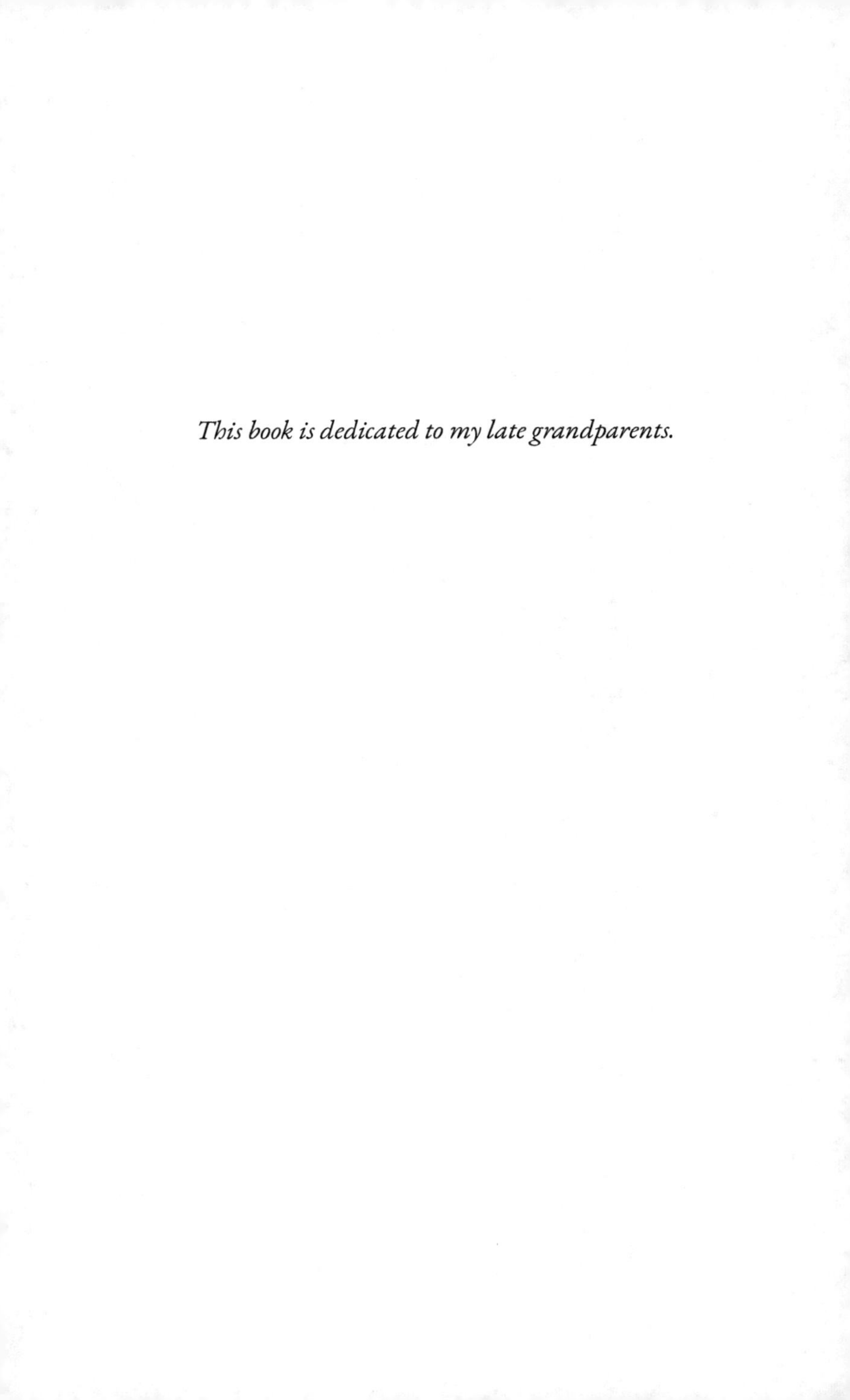

This book is dedicated to my late grandparents.

Pressure is a privilege.
-Billy Jean King

CHAPTER 1

A Wish Fulfilled

SIX YEARS AGO

Twenty-year-old Olive Nakamura tiredly closed her eyes. The warm hand of her longtime coach, Paul, rubbed her back as she rested her head on his shoulder. "It's almost over. No matter the outcome, I have never been prouder of you."

The soft cotton fabric of his jacket rubbed against her cheek. Her heart beat wildly in her chest. There was nothing more she could do except wait. Olive opened her eyes. Over and over again, she visualized the last eight routines she had performed over the course of the Olympic trials. She saw herself sticking the landing of her difficult double-twisting Yurchenko on vault, tumbling higher than ever before on her double-layout on floor, and for once, making it through a beam routine without a single wobble.

But have I done enough? She'd put her entire life on hold for the last four years and even deferred going to college. What if she was named as an alternate yet again? Would she be able to handle the disappointment? What about all the time and money Coach Paul and Mom and Dad had invested into her? She bit her lip and bounced her right leg up and down.

The sold-out crowd above the athletes' room in the arena clapped in anticipation. In the distance, Olive could hear the MC of the Olympic trials announcing that a decision was close at hand. Suddenly, the door creaked open. Olive's stomach lurched. A waiting television crew was ushered into the room from the hallway.

A reporter quietly said, "And we're back with our live coverage of day two of the US Women's Gymnastics Olympic Team Trials. The team has now been selected. Here we go…"

The members of the Olympic selection committee filed into the athletes' waiting room and stood with rigid shoulders. Their facial expressions were unreadable. Coach Paul and Olive gripped one another's hands tightly. Her breathing shortened. The names on the paper they held in their hands decided who would represent the United States in two weeks' time in Paris.

The committee chair cleared his throat and slipped a pair of oversized black glasses on his face. "I would like to thank all of the athletes and coaches for putting in a tremendous effort over the last few months. Our decision was very difficult. In no particular order, the first two members of this year's Olympic team are Leah Simmons and Margot Maldonado…"

No surprise. Leah and Margot finished first and second and guaranteed themselves a spot.

The two girls bounded out of their seats, hugging one another. The committee chair handed them a large bouquet of flowers. Time was moving slowly. She scooted toward the edge of her seat.

"Joining Leah and Margot will be… Scarlet Parker, Aleksandra Kovaleva, and…"

With each name announced that wasn't hers, Olive's hopes dimmed a bit more. Screams and ugly crying resounded across the room. She dropped her head. The committee had one more name to announce. Who would it be?

"...Olive Nakamura."

Olive's head shot up. A camera was pointed directly at her face. *Have they just called my name?* She gulped and glanced from the program director to Coach Paul. They both jumped to their feet. Coach Paul embraced her fiercely and whispered into her ear, "You *did* it! *You* are an *Olympian,* Olive." Tears of joy fell. She wiped her face with the sleeve of her red, white, and blue tracksuit jacket.

"The two traveling alternates will be Lana Osipova and Elsa Schreier. The non-traveling and third alternate will be Samantha Lifen. Congratulations to you all."

Olive was passed a bouquet of flowers. Clutching them closely, she savored the fresh scent of the roses. Sandra, her closest friend on the national team, squealed. She nearly tackled Olive. They grabbed hands and jumped up and down. Her ice-blue eyes gleamed with joy. "I *told* you that you would be on the team this time around."

At the same time, Olive was not immune to the sniffling and sobs of bitter disappointment emanating across from her. *That was me four years ago.* Excusing herself, she slowly approached the three younger girls whose dreams had just been crushed. She offered them a few encouraging words and hugs, though nothing, at the moment, would dull their pain.

At the urging of her coach, he pointed for her to line up beside her fellow Olympic teammates. He promised her that the disappointed girls would be looked after. *I hope Paul is right. Last time we were left without our coaches in the room. It took me so long to overcome the letdown.*

In the background, the reporter stood in front of the camera. "In a surprise move, the selection committee has left off the reigning World Balance Beam champion and event specialist, Samantha Lifen, from the team—"

Olive didn't have any further time to reflect on what was happening inside the room. The director of the selection committee led the members of the team and the alternates down a tunnel leading to the full arena.

The MC in the arena bellowed, "It is my pleasure to be the first person to finally introduce you to the five incredible athletes who will wear the red, white, and blue, in Paris... They are...Leah Simmons..."

Each gymnast sprinted out of the darkened tunnel and onto the floor exercise mat as their name was called out. Her muscles shook with nervous energy. When it was her turn, Olive bounded out onto the floor. Bright flashes from hundreds of cameras nearly blinded her. The crowd cheered her on, feeding her some much-needed energy.

She smiled brightly, waved, and blew them kisses. Goosebumps appeared on her arms. She squared her shoulders and stood tall. This was *her* moment to shine. Olive wasn't sure if any moment would ever match this in exhilaration or excitement. To this point in her life, she'd learned the valuable lesson that with hard work and determination, dreams could come true.

Four years after being named an alternate to the Olympic team and enduring a series of two surgeries, she was an Olympian. No one would ever be able to take that moment of triumph away from her. The years of training and sacrifice had paid off. Her entire life had centered on chasing one dream, and now she'd done it and could finally be at peace with herself.

For the next two weeks, she wouldn't take any part of her Olympic experience for granted. She visualized the team's arrival in the Olympic village, pin trading with other Olympic athletes, and the national anthem playing aloud as they received the gold medal. Just what else would unfold over the coming weeks?

CHAPTER 2

A New Beginning

PRESENT DAY

Twenty-two hours of travel had taken its toll on Olive's body. She eagerly awaited the moment she could disembark the plane and stretch her appendages. To her left, a middle-aged man wearing oversized headphones snored with his arms splayed across both armrests. His legs stuck out on either side of him at an awkward angle. The woman in the aisle seat held a baby whose lungs reached a new octave.

Olive pulled up the window shade and grinned. The vast blue water and white clouds of Hawaii had been replaced with golden fields of scattered trees and rows of neat farming plots. Slowly, the empty spaces transformed into clusters of buildings growing steadily closer together until all Olive observed was the gray concrete jungle of modern-day Athens. *More than half of the Greek population lives in this single, ancient city.* She pinched herself. She was really here.

Within thirty minutes, the plane landed, taxied, and pulled up to the gate. Olive stood the moment she was given

5

the go-ahead and nearly collapsed back into her seat. Had the compression sleeves under her jeans done anything? The muscles in her legs refused to listen to her body. They cramped and gave off a sensation of pins and needles. Next time, she would splurge on business class regardless of if her flight was paid for by her friend's fiancé or not.

Passengers in the rows ahead of her stood and blocked the aisles. Cabin bins were snapped open. The air filter changed from freezing cold air to warmer, stagnant air. Over the speaker system, the Pacific Skyways theme song played aloud. Finally, it was her turn.

Rising up onto her toes, however, she was confronted with a problem. The man standing behind her chuckled. Her cheeks flushed. "Would you mind helping? I am a little vertically challenged."

"Of course. Which bag is yours?"

"The champagne-colored rolling bag with the Hello Kitty luggage tag."

The man retrieved her luggage. Olive thanked him and wobbled off the plane. Her muscles and tendons crackled and acclimated themselves to movement. Walking off the plane and into the airport, there were teal, pink, and yellow signs in both English and Greek.

First thing's first. Olive swung her backpack to her front and strode over to the nearest trash can. From the front zipper pocket, she pulled out a silver envelope featuring her name in fancy script. Setting her rolling suitcase beside her, Olive gave the envelope a satisfying tear and ripped its contents to shreds. As the pieces fluttered down into the bin, a huge weight lifted itself off of her shoulders.

"Good riddance," she exclaimed. Why would anyone in their right mind invite an ex to their wedding? She held her hands up and happily danced in place.

She entered Greece with a blank slate. From here on out,

there was only what stood ahead of her not behind. *I can finally give Clara's wedding the focus it deserves and enjoy this once-in-a-lifetime trip.*

~

From the airport, Olive caught a taxi and arrived at her hotel situated in the quiet, residential Koukaki district of Athens. She tapped her fingers against the black quartz countertop of the front desk. She blew a stray lock of hair out of her face.

The concierge of the Olympus Hotel sighed. "I'm sorry, ma'am, but there is an ongoing national strike involving nearly all the workers of the Ministry of Culture. The Acropolis, Delphi, Olympia, and all other archaeological sites run and maintained by the Ministry are closed until further notice. It was just announced earlier today."

Olive's mouth opened and closed. She gripped the rim of the countertop and leaned forward. Her hands turned white. "Is there any word of when this might end? I'm only here for a few days before I leave for Venice."

The man with dark, curly brown hair wore a name tag that read Nikko. He refreshed the screen of his computer, then shook his head. "According to the tourist bureau website, the earliest update will be tomorrow morning." He patted her hand. "Strikes here in Greece can end just as quickly as they begin. Don't give up."

Her shoulders hunched. She breathed deeply and pinched the bridge of her nose. There was no use in becoming upset. The strike was beyond her control. The best she could do was to find another way to enjoy Athens. She rubbed her temples. Tension and lack of caffeine were not helping the situation. She peered over to the rack of brochures opposite the desk.

Nikko followed Olive's line of sight. "If you are interested, I can recommend several islands you might enjoy taking a cruise to. Poros, Hydra, and Aegina can all be seen in a day. Or perhaps you might consider an excursion to the ski resort city of Arachova."

"You can ski in Greece? I didn't think it grew cold enough." Olive rubbed the back of her neck.

Nikko chuckled. "Mount Parnassus is covered in snow from December to May. You can even view the sea on a clear day."

"Go figure." She let out a low whistle.

Nikko stepped out from behind the desk at the same time as a sure-footed, orange-striped tabby cat sprung itself onto the counter and meowed at Olive. She offered her hand for inspection. The tabby sniffed it and immediately began butting its head against her, while purring wildly. Her mood instantly lightened.

"So sorry, Miss Nakamura." Nikko frowned. He placed his hands on his hips and reached over to move the cat.

"Leave him. This is his home. I'm the intruder." Olive scratched under the cat's chin. "What's this fella's name?"

"This spoiled feline is Hermes. He belongs to the hotel owner. He has a habit of finding himself as the center of attention with our guests," Nikko said.

On cue, Hermes sat atop Olive's signed registration card. "He likes you." Nikko returned behind the desk and lined up three brochures on the counter. "These are just a few to get you started."

She thanked him. She neatly gathered up the brochures, and Hermes placed his front paw on the one labeled Hydra. Olive inclined her head. "I will keep your recommendation in mind, Hermes." Olive laughed.

Nikko handed Olive the keys to room 418. "Please call me if you have any other questions. I am more than happy to assist. Welcome to Athens."

"Thank you, Nikko. Thank you, Hermes," Olive said. The tabby yawned and curled up on the desk for a nap.

Nikko shook his head and spoke to the cat in Greek, absently petting him. Olive picked up her backpack and rolling luggage and ascended the four flights to her room. The wooden floorboards creaked each time her feet moved up one stair. The stairs were narrow and could accommodate only one person at a time. The keys to her room jingled in her hand.

Reaching 418, she inserted the key into the lock and pushed the door open. She gasped. Her luggage clattered to the floor. Olive rushed to slide open the balcony door and step outside. A gust of wintery air greeted her flushed face. Her pulse raced.

In true splendor, the Parthenon rose above the city of Athens with its long, white, elegant colonnades on the hill before her. Air left her lungs. She could just make out the arched outline of the theater known as the Odeon of Herodes Atticus, its Roman-style architecture a perfect complement to its Greek sister. Lush green trees filled in the empty space. *This* was what she had flown around the world to see. She shivered in delight.

I've waited so long for this moment.

She leaned out over the railing onto her elbows and stared, a goofy grin on her face. On the street below, a car honked. A motorbike whizzed by. A dog barked. The entire city was built around this one hill. Empires had risen and fallen, and yet the Parthenon still stood.

Goosebumps formed on her arms. She eventually managed to break away from the balcony and return inside. She rubbed her hands over her forearms. Curled up in the center of the king-sized bed, with its tail flicking, Hermes meowed at her. Olive laughed. "My own fault for leaving the door wide open." Quickly, she picked up her fallen luggage and placed it on the luggage rack near the entryway. She left the door slightly ajar. "Stay as long as you want."

The room held a rustic, wooden desk and chair set, a matching dark brown armoire, and a mini fridge. The bathroom, decorated in a nautical theme, contained a small shower, sink, and mirror. The room was small but airy. Several vases of flowers brought a freshness to the room and a semi-sweet aroma of vanilla and citrus. Questionable art on the walls depicted cats as Greek gods. Olive's favorite art piece showcased a cat with a mermaid tail.

After sending her parents an email indicating she had safely arrived at the hotel, Olive itched to explore. She changed out of the clothing she had worn on the plane and into a fresh pair of jeans, a baby blue button-up top, and her new shoes. "Shall we see what adventure awaits?"

The marmalade-colored cat jumped off the bed and ran out of the room. Olive slipped a light white windbreaker jacket on and locked the door behind her.

To the right of the hotel, local residents lazily reclined at the outdoor tables of a tavern, chatting under blue-and-white-striped umbrellas. She smelled the scent of freshly baked bread from the bakery at the intersection near the closest subway stop. To the left, the street ran uphill, twisting up and out of her sight line. She wondered just how far it extended. *The only way to find out is by exploring.*

Her shoes squeaked with every step she took. Twenty minutes into her walk, the nagging ache on the back of her heels was too much. Her new shoes may have matched her outfit, but they weren't yet broken in like her trusted Converse. If she didn't take care of her newly formed blisters now, walking for the remainder of her trip would be miserable.

Across the street was a luxury hotel with stained-glass windows depicting Greek nymphs and other mythological animals. Water rushed from a massive outdoor fountain surrounded by five-foot-tall shrubs and equally tall trellises covered in vibrant orange, pink, and red bougainvillea plants. It would be the perfect place to sit for a few minutes, figure out the shoe situation, and grab a much-needed cup of coffee.

To one of the two door attendants, she decided to test out one of the few Greek phrases she knew. "Kalispera Do you know where I can find the best coffee in the area?"

The closer of the two men pointed to the illuminated cafe sign. In a deep, crackling voice he said, "Ask for Leonidas."

They pulled open the glass doors. "Thank you," Olive said, entering the lobby.

Bright crystal chandeliers hung from mirrored ceilings. Glass windows let in plenty of natural light, and at the same time, revealed the spectacular views of the front gardenscape. As she followed the black, cream, and gold mosaic-patterned "catwalk" floor past the front desk, deeper into the lobby, Olive passed a white grand piano and yet another pond adorned with lilies and small fish. Ancient Greek-inspired pottery held fresh bouquets of flowers.

I could live here forever. Are the rooms as fancy as the lobby?

The cafe was nestled across from the hotel gift shop. She studied the chalkboard menu of displayed items listed in both Greek and English, distracted by the aroma of freshly roasted coffee beans and cinnamon.

"Kalispera, how may I assist you today?" the barista, a man with a broad chest, shaved head, and a beard, asked. He placed a fresh sheet of rolls into the pastry display case.

Olive bit her lip. "A coffee, please."

"In Europe, we don't have American-style coffees." The barista surveyed Olive. "We have espressos, lattes, and cappuccinos."

Olive glanced at the barista's black apron and the name Leo embroidered on the upper right-hand corner in green. She resisted the urge to face-palm. "I'll take whatever has the strongest caffeine."

"That I can do." He winked and spoke in a soothing melodic voice, with the barest hint of an accent. "Leave everything to me. Strong drinks are my specialty. In the meantime, I recommend the seating area by the fountain."

Olive moved to find her wallet, but the register opened and closed without a payment being processed. "Your first beverage is on the house. *My* confections are an *experience.*" Leo busied himself with the espresso machine. "I'll bring this out to you in a few minutes." He whistled and pulled the levers on his espresso machine as if he were a well-practiced wizard performing magic.

Was everyone in Greece so kind? Olive slowly shuffled to the recommended seating area with dark, cherry-colored tables. The plush fabric of the seat, cool air, and soothing music relaxed her. Two men chatted at the table directly next to her. She slipped off her jacket and placed it on the back of the chair. Under the table, she rubbed the back of her heels.

The exhaustion was taking hold. She closed her eyes and listened to the sounds around her. Her breathing slowed.

"Miss? Miss?" Leo asked.

Olive's eyes fluttered open. "I must have dozed off." She yawned and covered her mouth with her hand. "Sorry."

His brown eyes danced with mirth. "Once you have a sip of *this,* you will be wide-awake." A customer at the register claimed his attention. "I'll check on you in a moment. Let me know your thoughts on the drink." He placed the tray on the table and wiped his hands on his apron, jogging back to the register.

Olive stared down at the ceramic white espresso cup and biscotti. It smelled strong, yet rich. There was a thin layer of brown, frothy foam at the top. She counted to three and then drank the coffee as a shot, pouring the entire contents of the cup into her mouth.

Her taste buds were not ready for the bitterness or the heat. She coughed. Coffee dribbled down her face and onto her shirt. The men sitting behind her observed the entire failed experience and abruptly ended their conversation.

The sandy-blond-haired man sitting closest to her jumped out of his seat and rushed over to her table with several napkins. He exclaimed, "Alex… you see, I'm not the only one who isn't ever prepared for the strong flavor!"

Olive frantically patted at her clothing and the table. She grimaced. The coffee stain was in the worst possible spot—right on her chest.

The sandy-haired man's companion, a tall man with shoulder-length, dark brown, curly hair gingerly stood. "Are you alright? Did you burn yourself?" He unbuttoned his green linen dress shirt to reveal a white tank undershirt and long sculpted arms. He draped the dress shirt around her shoulders. "It's a little large but should cover up the stain." Alex's shirt smelled of fresh bergamot and oranges.

"I'm fine." Olive swallowed hard and attempted to hand the shirt back to the man. "I just need my jacket."

He chewed on his lip. "Your jacket didn't escape the coffee spill unscathed." He picked up the white jacket dripping with coffee from the floor.

"Of course it's on my jacket." She pulled the man's shirt around her small frame and inclined her head. "I am so embarrassed."

"Don't be. As Drew mentioned, he had the *exact* same reaction, but his shirt was white." She cracked a tight smile. "Was this your first time trying Greek coffee? Leo makes them scalding hot. I'm Alex, by the way."

Olive's entire face turned bright red. "That coffee had such a kick to it." She stared into the man's chocolate-brown eyes. The thin fabric of his undershirt contoured to his sculpted abdominal muscles as he moved. He crossed his arms.

He looks like a Greek statue, and he speaks with a British accent!

"Eyes up here…" he teased.

Leo, the barista, arrived at the scene of the mess. "What happened?" His playful tone had vanished and was replaced with concern.

Alex answered for her. "*Somebody* forgot to warn this lovely lady how strong and scathingly hot his creations can be."

Leo frowned. "Alexander," he warned. "Now is *not* the time to be funny. The coffee was scalding hot. Did you ensure she wasn't hurt from it?"

Olive let out a shrill whistle to capture the men's attention. "I promise the only thing that is bruised is my ego. I am jet-lagged, cranky, and humiliated, but otherwise no worse for the wear. I *really* needed a jolt of caffeine in my system."

The blond man played peacemaker. "Leo, what if you prep another coffee?"

"Is that too much to ask?" Olive whispered.

"Of course not." Leo's body relaxed. "I am *more* than happy to make another drink. Leave the mess. I'll take care of it in a few minutes."

"I'm Drew. Nice to meet you." He offered his hand to Olive. She hesitated but shook the hands of the two men. She could feel a set of thick callouses on Alex's hand, his grip firm.

Something about the names Alex and Drew is so incredibly familiar. Have I met them before?

"Why don't you join us?" Alex held her gaze. She chewed on her lip. "Leo can vouch for us if you are concerned."

Olive admitted, "It's not that. I don't want to interrupt you two. I should head back to my hotel."

"Coffee first. All the locals will tell you there is *always* time for a coffee." Alex pulled over an extra chair to their table for Olive. He signaled for her to sit. "We're here, waiting for Leo to finish his shift, anyhow."

"Only if you're certain." Olive settled herself next to Alex. "I'm Olive."

Drew remained standing. "Do you mind terribly if I leave you two alone? I really should go up and change. I have a dinner date at seven with Penny."

Alex glanced at his wristwatch and raised an eyebrow at Drew. "Is it really going to take you three hours to prep?"

"I haven't actually made any reservations yet." Drew scratched the nape of his neck. "Not to mention, I still need to pick up flowers and run out to buy some piece of expensive jewelry. I, uh, may have forgotten it's our wedding anniversary tonight."

Alex closed his eyes and shook his head. "Penny's favorite stone is blue sapphire. Have the hotel concierge assist you. That's the only way you'll be able to manage your way out of this mess."

Drew blew a chef's kiss to Alex. "Thank you, mate. I owe you one." He waved to Olive. "It was nice to meet you. So sorry to have to cut this meeting short." Drew jogged in the direction of the front desk.

"Like clockwork, every year for the last three years, Drew has managed to forget." Alex combed his hair out of his face with his fingers.

"You were kind to hint at a gift." She pulled the dress shirt around her body tighter and shimmied in her seat. The linen was incredibly light and soft to the touch.

"Penny is not exactly subtle when it comes down to what she wants to be given as a gift." Alex laughed. She admired its musical quality. She studied the dimples and laugh lines around his mouth.

They sat in silence for a few moments. Alex scratched his chin. "So, um, Olive—" He hesitated. "How long have you been in Athens? Have you been to the city before?"

"I haven't seen much of anything yet. I've been here two hours and, so far, all my plans are ruined because of the national strike."

"Oh, the strike is a bit of a joke."

She huffed. "I've waited my entire life to visit Athens, and it's like fate is against me."

"We can't have you starting off your vacation like that." Alex shot her a sympathetic glance. "How about this. I can—"

Leo approached the table and placed three drinks and an assortment of cookies on the table. "Where's Drew?"

Alex just shook his head. "Working his way out of the doghouse."

"Never mind. Forget I asked." Leo took the extra coffee for himself. "This time, please promise me to sip it." Leo untied his apron and drank from the cup. "I just have to reconcile the till, then I'll be ready."

Leo stepped away.

Olive reached for the coffee, but Alex placed a large, warm hand on top of hers, sending an electric current buzzing through her body. "You know what to expect this time around. Before you drink it, smell it. Take a small drink and a bite of this chocolate biscuit." He released her hand.

Blindly following Alex's directions, with her fingers still tingling, she grasped the cup, swirled the drink, sniffed it, then sipped. Biting into the cookie, the semi-savory chocolate melted in her mouth, neutralizing the bitter, nutty taste. "Yum…" she uttered. The mixture was pure bliss.

"Better, yes?" he asked.

"Much." She licked her lips.

"You have an interesting accent. Where exactly are you from?" Alex asked. He leaned back in his chair.

"Hawaii. The Big Island to be exact." Had her pidgin English slipped out? It didn't usually, unless she was home.

Alex snapped his fingers. "I should have guessed."

"Have you been there before?" Olive enjoyed another taste of her coffee and finished her biscuit.

"A handful of times, but I've never strayed outside of the Waikiki area of Honolulu," he confessed.

"I can't say that I blame you. Waikiki has pretty much everything a tourist needs in one central place." She wiped her mouth with the napkin and leaned her elbows onto the table.

"You know," Alex said. "I dabble in photography, and I'm planning to play in my first tourn—"

Leo's sudden appearance caused Olive's heart to drop. She was only just beginning to enjoy and settle into chatting with Alex. Leo collected their empty plates and in his other hand, he carried a white helmet. "What did you think of the Leo special?"

Olive cleared her throat. "Oh, it was delicious."

Leo pointed to his smartwatch. "Sorry to interrupt you two, but Alex, we have to leave now if we are going to make it to your appointment only a few minutes late."

"I'm so sorry, Olive." Alex tapped his forehead. His neck flushed. "This is one appointment I can't risk missing."

Both Olive and Alex stood. She slipped Alex's shirt off of her shoulders and folded it up. "Thank you for letting me use this. I think my own jacket is dry enough now." Olive and Alex both glanced at the large brown splotch. She reached for her jacket, shaking off droplets of coffee.

He shook his head. "No. Keep it. I have another shirt in my room that I can run up and throw on."

Olive hesitated. "Won't that make you even later than you already are?"

Alex shrugged. "If I'm going to be late, a few more

minutes do not make all *that* much of a difference. With Leo driving, I am in expert hands."

Leo puffed out his chest.

Olive covered her mouth with her hand, hiding a smile. "I promise, I'll return it to you tomorrow then. Do you have a shift, Leo? I can drop it off at the café."

"No." Alex was quick to jump in. He patted his trouser pockets and pulled out a scrap of paper. "Leo, do you have a pen?"

"A pen? No. But like any good barista, I have a sharpie." From the upper-front jacket pocket, he removed the afore-mentioned item. Alex rolled his eyes and stretched out his hand. He scribbled down a few numbers. Leo walked the dishes over to the café.

"This is my room number here at the hotel. Have the front desk ring me, and I can come down and collect it."

Olive raised an eyebrow. "You aren't worried about what I'll do with this information? What if I am a crazy lady?"

Alex snorted. "That is a risk I am willing to take."

Leo returned and crossed his arms. "If Alex gives you any trouble, you can come and find me at the café." He was about an inch shorter than Alex.

"Duly noted." Olive giggled. "Thank you for the chat and for the coffee. I'll leave you two here."

"It was our pleasure," Leo and Alex said at the same time. They stared at one another in disbelief.

Leo tapped his watch. "Alex, you have two minutes while I bring the bike around front."

"I'm going. I'm going." Alex shoved his hands into his pockets and slowly walked to the elevators. Leo sighed.

"Now my cousin is moving at a snail's pace just to spite me." Leo shook his head. "I'll walk you to the doors on my way out."

"Thanks."

They parted at the doors. She wandered back down the cobblestone streets the way she had come, her feet, for the moment, no longer bothering her. Olive was grateful to have a few quiet moments to herself. More than ever, she was confused. She was positive she'd heard Alex's voice before. The information was on the tip of her brain.

He was too tall to be a gymnast and definitely not a friend from the University of Washington. Had they crossed paths in Hawaii? She rubbed her temples. *I'll have to let my brain figure this out once it's had some sleep.*

CHAPTER 3

Learning to Fly Again

Olive soaked her feet in the bathtub. Sweeping her dark brown waist-length hair into a low ponytail, she began to braid it just as the soft rock music she was listening to faded out and her phone rang. She glanced down. It was one of her two closest friends, Amanda Collins.

She dropped her hair, reached for the phone, and swiped to accept the video call. A redhead with curly hair, green eyes, and freckles appeared on the screen. "Hi, Olive! I didn't actually expect you to pick up! I just wanted to check in with you."

"I was just thinking about you." Olive laughed.

"It's my superpower. What can I say?" Amanda joked.

She removed her feet from the tub and reached for one of the fluffy white towels stacked on the rack to her left. "Here, I'll give you a quick tour of the room." She dried her feet and picked up the phone, switching the camera from the front view to the back camera. She panned the phone around the room, showing off all of its highlights.

"Wait until you see this—" Olive pulled back the drapes from the balcony.

Amanda let out a long whistle. "Stunning." The sky was a purple and orange color right above the Parthenon.

"I'll keep this conversation short and to the point," Amanda said. "I have been dying to know… did you *actually* follow through on what we talked about yesterday?"

Olive solemnly nodded and sat on the bed. "Sean's wedding invitation is history."

Amanda squealed. "I am soooooo proud of you, Olive."

She rubbed the back of her neck. "Three years is too long. Honestly, the cheating jerk has been fully out of my system for over a year."

"The gall he and his fiancée had to send you an invite." Amanda clicked her tongue. "You are an amazing person, and I know the right man is out there waiting for you. You deserve to be treated like the queen you are."

A sandy-haired man with blue eyes popped into Amanda's screen. "I thought I heard you say something about my mother."

Amanda rolled her eyes. "No. I'm not speaking about your mother."

"How was I to know?" Amanda's boyfriend held his hands up. He spied Olive on the screen, and waved. "Nakamura! Good to see you. Only a few more weeks until you can officially meet me in the flesh." Amanda's boyfriend winked.

"She isn't coming *just* to meet you, Princey. She's here to be put to work as a bridesmaid," Amanda reminded him.

Olive giggled. "Hi, Eddie. I'm excited to finally meet you. I'm going to hold you to your word to teach me how to ride a horse. By the time my ten-week London stay is over, you are going to be so tired of me."

If Eddie were an animal, he'd definitely be a cat of some sort. He's curious about everything and always has to be at the center of attention.

"Me? Grow tired of your company? Never!" Eddie took

control of the screen and held the phone up to his face. "Any friend of Collins's is an automatic friend of mine."

"Princey and I are counting down the days until the entire gang is together again." Amanda playfully pushed Eddie out of the screen. "I'll let you go. Get some rest."

Olive yawned. "I'm going to bed as we speak." Her eyes grew heavy.

"Brilliant. We'll chat tomorrow. If you need anything, don't hesitate to call."

Eddie's disembodied voice added, "What Amanda said. Bye, Nakamura."

"Bye, you two." Olive clicked the disconnect button, dropped her phone onto the side of the bed, and lay down. She closed her eyes.

I wasted so much time pining over a man who couldn't have cared less about me. Will I be lucky enough to meet someone like Eddie? It's been a long road for me to understand and accept that I do not need to change myself to be happy.

The thick foam mattress of the bed conformed to her body. Her breathing slowed. After an exceedingly long day, she could no longer deny her body the rest it so desperately needed.

Olive didn't awake until the sun was well risen the next morning. She stretched and rubbed her eyes. Her bed was so comfortable, a warm cocoon. She turned her head. The red numbers of the bedside clock glared back at her. A jolt of energy coursed through her body. "It is already ten a.m.?"

Readying herself for the day in record speed, she dressed in a light green, Hawaiian-pattern, floral top, black leggings, a tan overcoat, and a black pair of Converse shoes. Her gaze settled on the dress shirt hanging in the closet. Alex's dress shirt. She reminisced on her mishap with the coffee the day before. Olive's face turned warm. She was not about to encounter him again. Once was more than enough. Shirt in hand, her first stop would be Alex's hotel.

~

Olive reviewed the plan in her head several times: enter the lobby, leave the shirt with the concierge, and sneak away. It sounded simple enough. Unfortunately for her sake, the moment she entered the facility, her plans went awry. Speaking to the concierge, and dressed in a pair of figure-hugging dark wash jeans, a burgundy crew neck sweater, and a charcoal gray overcoat, was Alex.

She ducked behind the closest pillar. The pitter-patter of her heart raced against her chest. *So much for having a plan.* Could she sneak out without being seen? Why did she suddenly care so much?

She held her breath and counted down from ten. Poking her head out and around the pillar, Olive chanced a glance.

"Is there a reason you are reduced to hiding behind this colonnade? Or is there a secret meeting memo I have missed out on?" Alex's voice whispered into her ear.

Olive jumped and squeezed her eyes shut. *I wish I was invisible right now.* Her body grew hot. She opened her eyes to see Alex casually leaning against the pillar, one leg crossed over the other. His eyes danced in amusement.

She swallowed hard and, with as much dignity as she could muster, slipped her tote bag off her shoulder. She reached in and passed the neatly folded clothing item to him.

"I wanted to return this to you." Her voice came out higher pitched than intended. She cleared her throat. "Your appointment went smoothly?"

Alex raised an eyebrow and accepted it. He slipped it under his arm. "The visit with the physio?" He ran a hand through his hair. "It was fine."

"That's great to hear." Olive crossed one arm in front of her body and rubbed the other. She lowered her gaze and stared at the sidewalk. Yesterday it had been so easy to speak with Alex. Their conversation flowed. Today, every single movement or word seemed awkward. "I'm just going to slip away now." She took two steps backward.

"Wait! Don't leave yet, Hawaii," Alex exclaimed. "I've been waiting around the lobby area all morning, hoping I might cross paths with you. Do you have any plans for today?"

Olive's racing pulse set a new record for beats per minute. "Excuse me?" Her head whipped up.

"I wanted to ask you yesterday." Alex winced. "I'm sorry if that came across as too forward." He stood up straight and rigid. "I thought I could be your tour guide in Athens."

"You? Play tour guide?" Olive's mind grew fuzzy.

"Well, I had me in mind. Unless you might prefer someone like Leo?" Alex chuckled. "I just wanted to be the nice bloke for once."

"Why would you want to spend time with me?" Olive stared, open-mouthed.

"When you said, and I quote, 'I have waited my entire life to see the city,' I was intrigued."

A red-alert sound blared in her mind. Nice men did not exist in the world she inhabited. From experience, they always wanted something in return.

If he is telling me the truth, it would be a fabulous way to see the city without a big-bus kind of tour. I want to say yes. Olive bit her lip. Could she trust a near stranger? *What if I treat this like a test? What if I see if I truly have moved on from Sean?*

The words were out of her mouth before she could rescind them. "I'll go with you. My only plans today were to see the Acropolis and whatever isn't closed."

"Brilliant." Alex flashed Olive a dazzling, pearly white

smile. Butterflies inside her stomach performed flip-flops as if they were tumbling down a four-inch-wide balance beam.

I hope I am making the right decision.

They walked out of the double glass doors from the lobby toward the front drive of the hotel. Alex excused himself to speak to the valet. She pulled out her phone from her pocket and sent off a quick text message.

Olive: *I am sharing my location with you just in case anything strange happens to me. I'll explain everything to you later.*

Three dots lingered on her phone. Amanda always had her mobile at her disposal.

Amanda: *Just what are you up to, O?*

Olive: *Learning how to fly again.*

Amanda: *In that case, good luck! I can't wait to hear what this is about :)*

Keys jingled. The valet jogged off to the opposite end of the hotel's parking lot. Alex rejoined her. The valet revved the engine of a green Vespa and expertly pulled it up to the hotel's entrance. He tossed the keys to Alex, who caught them and confidently strode over to the back of the bike.

From the storage compartment on the side, he located two helmets and shoved the returned shirt inside. "This is Leo's, but he won't mind if we borrow it for a few hours."

Slowly, she backed away. Her mouth grew dry. All her courage from moments ago fled her body. "Um… I don't think this is a good idea," she sputtered.

Alex placed a hand on her arm. Her hands trembled. "If you are uncomfortable with the Vespa, I can ask the hotel for their courtesy car."

Olive's mind relived her horrifying second date with Sean. *He scared the living daylights out of me with the bursts of speed and dangerous, almost reckless driving on his motorcycle. I nearly suffered a coronary embolism, and all he could do was laugh and call me a wet blanket.* She clenched her hands into fists.

The old Olive swore never to set foot near a motorcycle or Vespa again. The new Olive she was building up had to be different. Facing her fears was one way to overcome the past.

"Have you ever driven one of these things before?" She inspected the Vespa from top to bottom, pretending to know what she was looking for.

"Since I was old enough to drive." Alex attempted to reassure her. "This Vespa is better suited to navigate all the sites I wanted to show you, but"—Alex stopped himself midsentence and unstrapped the helmet from atop his head—"I'll have the valet retrieve the car."

"No. I *have* to do this." Fire burned in the pit of her stomach. Olive forced the helmet from Alex's hands, popped it onto her head, and positioned herself on the back of the bike. "Let's do this."

Alex let out a deep breath. "Once I start the engine, lean into me. Grab my waist and don't let go." He climbed to the front of the Vespa and tested the gears.

She wrapped her arms around his waist. The wool of his overcoat was thick. Even through the layers, however, she could feel the strong muscles beneath the coat at work. Alex definitely was no stranger to physical activity.

"If you are frightened, we can turn around at any point during the tour." He flipped the visor down on the helmet.

She shook her head. "I'm ready."

"Welcome to your personalized scenic tour of Athens." The motor revved. Alex turned them out of the hotel drive and onto the main street.

～

Adrenaline coursed through her veins. Leaving the quiet neighborhood of the Koukaki district, they passed street after street of identical, three-story, concrete apartment blocks. The road transitioned from bumpy cobblestones to smooth city streets. They joined a dizzying array of buses, cars, and other motorbikes.

Slowly, the buildings became the more traditional white-washed with blue roofs. They were built in two stories with arched openings. Potted plants lined the front steps. The wind rushed through her helmet and through her jacket.

Alex shouted over the noise. "This is the edge of the Plaka district, the soul of the ancient city. If you like to shop, I'd start here. Any Greek souvenir you could ever dream up is guaranteed to be sold in some of the stalls."

Alex pointed to an open-air fast-food stand. She smelled freshly cooked meat and spices. The workers carved the meat and slopped it into pita bread rolls with lettuce, cucumbers, and onions before they slathered on the sauce. "Gyros are the best deal around."

They passed the palm trees of the botanical gardens. At the next signal, Alex gestured to an ivy-covered chain-linked fence. She didn't see much until she looked up and saw three towering white marble Corinthian columns. Olive's stomach fluttered in excitement.

"The Temple of Olympian Zeus," she mumbled.

"That's right." Alex wolfishly grinned. "At one time this was the largest temple in the ancient world. Let's get closer."

Alex slowed the Vespa and turned onto a quieter side street. They passed the remains of a freestanding Roman arch, en route to the deserted entrance to the grounds. Alex stopped. Olive quizzically tilted her head to the side. It was almost out of place amidst the busy street and modern buildings. "Why did they choose to preserve this archway?"

"The Roman Emperor Hadrian had this built to declare Athens as his city. It marked the entryway into the old city."

Olive nodded. "Hadrian built a fair few monuments to himself, didn't he?"

"Indeed. He was a lover of all things Greek, a philhellene." Alex pulled the Vespa into a parking slot and turned off the engine. Olive climbed off the bike. She took a moment to regain her balance.

The white columns were even larger than Olive imagined. *They must be fifty feet tall.* She walked up to the locked hunter-green gates to the historical site and looked through the slots.

"I am at a complete loss for words. Too bad we can't get any closer."

Alex unsnapped his helmet. "Your wish is my command."

Olive gaped. "We can't *sneak* into the temple ruins!"

"And who is going to stop us?" Alex gestured to the empty space around them. "Answer me this, Olive. When are you going to be in Athens again? What if the strike continues for the entire duration of your stay here?"

Alex had her again. She shifted her weight from foot to foot. "I am not the type of woman who gets into trouble. I am a model citizen."

Alex jiggled the gate. The metal groaned and slid open wide enough to grant a person access if they squeezed through. Alex pulled his stomach in and wiggled through the opening. An impressive feat for a six-foot-two man. "If there are any problems, I will take full responsibility."

Olive threw her head back. She groaned. "Why am I even *considering* this?"

The amount of trouble breaking and entering into a historical site could get her into frightened her, but on the other hand, being in Alex's presence brought out the thrill-seeking, daredevil side of herself. The part of herself that had been dormant since her retirement from gymnastics. *I will probably only be here once.* She badly wanted to see an ancient Greek temple up-close. *I'll take the risk.* Biting her tongue, Olive reluctantly joined Alex on the other side of the barrier.

CHAPTER 4

Wonders of the Ancient World

No alarms went off. No workers shouted at them. The police did not materialize out of thin air. They were left alone. The deserted Temple of Olympian Zeus was their own private sanctuary. A gravel pathway circumnavigated the ruins with an American football-field-sized grass area in the center.

They walked in silence, the dampness from the grass cutting through the thin fabric of her Converse. Approaching the temple ruins, Olive got as close as she could to the barrier protecting it. She marveled at the flower-like curves and scroll tops of the columns. They were giants among men.

"In total, there are fifteen columns left standing." He put his hand on the small of her back. "Can you see the metal bits sticking out of the top there?" Alex pointed to the collapsed column lying in pieces on the ground.

Olive moved closer. She could just make out a thick iron pin. "That's inside the column?"

"When temples were built, the architects used those to align and hold up the individual column sections. An amazing piece of engineering."

Olive had always thought the columns were one continuous piece of marble, but it made so much more sense thinking about it being assembled in more manageable sections. "And inside was a large statue of Zeus?"

"Whatever gave you that idea?" Alex chuckled. "There were two statues inside the temple. One of Zeus and one of our favorite Emperor Hadrian."

Olive opened her jaw. "You're joking."

Alex crossed his arms and raised an eyebrow. "It's true." She was impressed with the depth of knowledge he held in his brain. So far, he was proving to be quite the informed tour guide.

As they explored the remainder of the area, Olive lamented, "I wish I had my camera on me, but I left it in my tote bag in the Vespa's storage bin."

Alex patted his jacket pockets. "Use mine. I never go anywhere without my compact camera or my larger DSLR." He passed her a gray camera case. Olive opened it to reveal a top-of-the-line Canon G7X Mark II. "This camera is better for taking videos but, for a compact camera, captures photos well enough."

She wracked her brain. Alex had said something about dabbling in photography yesterday. "What are you going to use?"

"My other camera is also in the Vespa's bin if I need it. I've been here before. It hasn't changed at all since my last visit."

She powered up the camera and took a few snapshots zoomed in on the columns. She had Alex take a photo of her standing in front of the towering set of columns. Alex pointed out several other points of interest, such as areas where smaller temples might have once sat on the grounds. No matter where Olive stood, she could always make out the Acropolis from the corner of her eye. It was never too far off, always at the city's center.

They returned to the Vespa. Olive strapped the helmet to her head. "Do you have any favorite subjects to photograph?"

"Candid photos and landscapes. Nature is best when it speaks for itself, but with humans, it's the in-between moments of life that are often overlooked that interest me. It's fascinating to capture photos of people when they don't realize anyone is watching them; they're most at peace with themselves."

Such a deep answer for someone who seems otherwise carefree.

Five minutes away from the Temple of Olympian Zeus, Alex stopped at the Panathenaic Stadium, the site of the first modern Olympic Games. The flags of Greece and of the Olympics waved in the breeze at the visitor's entrance.

A burly security guard lazily said in English, "No visitors. Closed for the strike." The small groups ahead of them left disappointed. Alex waited until the coast was clear and spoke a few words to the guard in Greek. She wandered up to the gate, placed her hand on it, and surveyed the rows upon rows of empty seats. Being in an Olympic stadium brought Olive back to her time in Paris.

We weren't allowed to march in the Opening Ceremonies with the other athletes. I have never even set foot in the Olympic stadium.

Regret filled her stomach. Their coaching staff had opted for them to stay in a hotel so that the team might be better focused. A stray tear escaped down her cheek. In her head, she could hear the roar of thousands of spectators and picture athletes waving to the crowd.

We experienced the crowd inside the gymnastics arena, but this is so much grander. Aside from winning a medal, it's the one experience I wanted above all others.

Alex tapped her shoulder. "The security guard said he can only grant us access for five minutes. Just enough time to take a lap around the track and perhaps stand atop the victor's podium. Are you alright?"

Olive rubbed her eyes. "Just emotional. The Olympics are near and dear to me." They entered the stadium.

"If we had the time, I would take you underground. There is an actual spring of water the stadium was built atop, and the actual torch and mirror used to light the Olympic flame on display."

"It just means I'll be due for a return trip once everything is fully open again," Olive said.

The rubber of the track brought a spring to her step. Two thrones were carved into the stadium seats for the disposed king and queen of the country. In the center of the stadium, not only was there a balance beam, but to Olive's amusement, there was also a trampoline. Its springs, however, contained a few telltale signs of rust.

Alex glanced at his watch. "Our five minutes are just about up, but before we go, would you like a photo on that beam?"

Nothing seemed to escape Alex's attention. "If you wouldn't mind playing photographer." Olive coyly smiled. Butterflies filled her stomach. What type of pose should she do? Something simple? Or should it be fancy?

Olive rubbed her hand reverently over the rough, weathered leather of the balance beam. It was her least favorite event, but it was also the one she was most well-known for. She could still recall performing one of the best routines of her life during the women's team finals.

It was like magic. My body knew exactly what to do. When I opened up from my two and a half twists, my feet were literally glued to the landing mat. Olive had clinched a silver medal for the American team.

"You are just the right height for a gymnast," Alex joked.

She removed her coat, handed Alex the compact camera, and mounted the beam. "Growing up, that was my sport."

Olive bent her knees and jumped up and down. The beam clattered. *Not super secure for a back handspring, but it should be strong enough for a handstand.*

"I can see why." Alex backed up and focused the camera. He directed her to stand so her shadow would not appear in the photo. "Have a go when you are ready. I'll just continue clicking away. That way you'll have a variety of action shots to choose from." She gave him a thumbs-up.

Kicking up and onto her hands, Olive held a sideways handstand and positioned her legs into a stag split where one leg was bent and one was straight. She arched her back and looked at Alex. She thought she heard him let out a low whistle. Upside down, she could see him move around the beam to capture her from the side. With a ghost of a smile on her lips, she put her legs together and came down to her feet.

"How did it turn out?"

He appraised her with a look of respect. Olive's heart fluttered.

"Oh, great." He offered her the camera. "See for yourself."

She slipped her jacket back on. On the back of the camera's display screen, she scrolled through more than a dozen photos. "They're all nicely centered and not blurry. You *do* have some photographic skills."

"You are an easy subject to work with." The corners of Alex's mouth curved upward.

"I'm a little rusty, and I'll probably pay the price tomorrow." She rubbed her lower back. "Some skills never leave your muscle memory."

Alex's hands twitched. He cleared his throat. "One last photo atop the medal stand, and we'll leave."

"Only if we can make it a selfie. Your arms are longer than mine, so you're in charge here." He laughed from his belly. Its tone was light and joyful, not forced and cynical as Sean's had always been.

Alex's presence was relaxing her. She could feel the heat from his arms wrapping around her body to take the photo. His musky scent intoxicating. *When was the last time I was confident around a man? Not since my breakup.*

Alex thanked the security guard when they departed. The scenic route passed through the center of the modern city and Syntagma Square. Masses of tourists waited to watch the Changing of the Guard Ceremony in front of the neoclassical Greek Parliament building. Alex pointed out the special costume worn by the guardsmen. "There are over four hundred pleats in their fustanella, the kilt-like garment they wear. One for every year the Greeks were under Ottoman occupation."

The Vespa glided through the city streets and around the market district Alex called Monastiraki. She made a mental note to return for their weekly flea market. Near the main square, she saw many more outdoor cafes and captured her first glance of the brown stones and rounded dome of a Byzantine church.

"Technically this is a part of the Acropolis slope." Alex secured their helmets and her tote bag in the storage bin of the Vespa. The Parthenon, covered in scaffolding, peeked out just above Alex's head. She had never noticed just how thick the walls surrounding the slope of the Acropolis were. This was the closest she had ever been, and yet it remained just out of reach.

They walked to the pedestrian pathway. Olive saw the large, modern New Acropolis Museum building with rows of glass windows at the end of the footpath. Three men stood at its entrance dressed in Hercules-style short tunics. They held gold helmets, swords, and a club. A queue of lingering tourists jumped at the opportunity to take photos with them. They flexed their muscles.

Alex snorted. "This area is always lively. You never know what to expect around these parts."

They followed the signs to the open plaza area containing the ticketing office, an empty café, restrooms, and a postal office. "I've seen photos of the queues in summer. This plaza is normally crawling with tourists," Olive said. "It is so eerie to see this so empty."

Alex agreed.

They walked along a dirt footpath that led up to the Acropolis's entrance. The tree cover grew thick, engulfing them. Olive could hear the whistles of several different bird species. It was as if they were walking through a great forest just as in ancient times. She imagined an ancient Greek procession to the temple, laden with carts full of offerings.

Closer to the top, the path turned to marble. They slowed their pace to avoid the puddles from the overnight rain. Both Alex and Olive stumbled a few times.

"Consider this practice for atop the hill. It's made of marble too," Alex said. His face was red and covered with perspiration. He breathed heavily.

For a man in fine physical shape, Alex shouldn't have this much difficulty walking. He didn't have any trouble at the stadium. What was making him so exhausted?

She attempted to lighten the mood. "What are the names of the other temples up there?" She pointed to the Acropolis. Her mind had always conjured an image of the Parthenon standing alone.

Alex stopped to remove his coat and his crew neck sweater. He wiped his brow on its sleeve. "Not counting the Parthenon, there are also the Temple of Nike and the Erechtheion Temple."

The trees cleared and, suddenly, Olive could see the

towering gate of the Propylaea extended out overhead. Were it open, tourists would be climbing the zigzagged mixture of modern wooden and ancient marble steps to reach the entrance that led to the temples atop the Acropolis. Squinting, Olive could clearly see just how the hillside had been carved out over millennia.

"There must be one hundred million more marble steps up there," Olive said.

Alex locked eyes with her. He blinked slowly. "A hundred million steps, huh?" His tone was dry. "If that were the case, like Odysseus, that would take us nearly ten years to traverse."

Her gaze settled upon the off-white-, brown-, and orange-toned bricks of the majestic Temple of Nike, dedicated to the goddess of victory. The smallest of the temples. It still left her breathless to see it standing tall and proud, jutting out on a ledge above modern Athens.

I'd give anything to stand up there.

The pathway leveled out. Her pulse quickened. Deep down, Olive hoped they might be able to "sneak" atop the Acropolis as they had at the Temple of Olympian Zeus. Yet this time their luck did not hold. A metal gate was padlocked and labeled "closed" in English and Greek. A few workers with official lanyards around their necks lingered about, advising and assisting stray tourists.

Alex's body deflated. "What a waste of our time." He placed his hands on his head. He breathed sharply. "It's all my fault."

"Don't blame yourself. I would've wanted to come up here regardless of if it was open or not. At least I can take some more photos up here." Alex shoved his hands into his pockets, kicking softly at the dirt. She took her time enjoying the scenery and the hushed chatter of people.

"Mind acting as my official photographer again?" Brow

furrowed, he followed through with Olive's request while she made silly poses.

He breathed in sharply. "Why didn't I think of it earlier?" He handed the camera to Olive. His countenance immediately shifted. He placed his hands on her shoulders and, spinning her around, he pointed to a distant set of hills. "Areopagus Hill is only a short walk from here. It's just about level with the Acropolis and has a surreal view. I'd wager it's one of the best alternatives to being up there." He pointed to the Parthenon.

"Really? And it's open to the public?"

Alex nodded. "Yes. I've been up there a few times to photograph the sunset."

Olive's stomach let out a growl. She placed a hand on it. Her cheeks colored. "Can we pick up some food on the way? I um … may have forgotten to eat breakfast."

Alex chided her. "Breakfast is the most *important* meal of the day. Any athlete should know that." He glanced at the large silver watch on his wrist. "It's two in the afternoon now. Let's grab lunch. There should be just enough daylight afterward to climb Areopagus. It doesn't grow as dark here as it does in London."

Olive chuckled. "At home, even in winter, it is never dark before six at night."

Olive leaned her elbows on the white table and propped her chin atop her hands. Soft jazz music played in the background. The inside of the taverna across from the New Acropolis Museum was warmly lit, with highly-polished wooden floors and sea foam-teal walls containing modern art. A small vase adorned each place setting. Only one other couple sat across from them, dining.

"Kalispera," the waiter greeted them. "Are you ready to order?"

"I will have the grilled artichokes and steak with a glass of water, please. Oh, and an extra side of chips," Alex rattled off.

"The Portobello mushroom burger with tzatziki sauce and a water, please." The server recorded their choices and left them to their own devices.

Alex offered a half smile. "No coffee today?"

Olive coughed. "Not yet. Water first. Then maybe a coffee and dessert."

Alex's pallor was nearly back to normal when the waiter returned with a small basket of fresh bread.

"Dessert is always one of the first menu items I review, followed by the entrees." Olive helped herself to a piece and passed the basket to Alex.

"Interesting. It's never crossed my mind." Alex added a roll to his plate and unpacked his cutlery from the napkin at his place setting. "When I think about it, I *do* always glance at the beverages side of the menu first."

Olive considered which direction she wanted to take this conversation. There were so many questions she wanted to ask Alex. Yet, she was hesitant to ask him anything too personal. Despite having spent almost half of the day together, he was still a stranger. There were many pieces of her past she was still only comfortable speaking about with her close friends.

Olive played with her water glass. "Not including your personal tour of the city today, do you have any other places that you can recommend for me to add to my itinerary? The concierge at my hotel has me booked for a one-day cruise to the islands of Aegina, Poros, and Hydra tomorrow."

This is a nice, safe, neutral topic.

Alex ran a hand over his goatee. "Nafplio, Greece's first official capital, is one of the more underrated cities you'll find in the country. It is an easy half-day trip from Athens."

Olive tilted her head to the side. "Is it smaller than here?"

"By far. It only has a population of thirty-three thousand." Alex laughed. "Nowadays, Nafplio serves as more of a pit stop for tourists on their way to the ruins of Mycenae. It's very picturesque. The marina and clear water stretch as far as the eye can see. As children, Leo and I would hike the large hillside up to the ruins of the Venetian Fortress above the city."

Their main dishes arrived. The waiter rolled the cart over and carefully placed the steaming hot dishes on the table. "Do you know much about Cape Sunio? I was considering a half-day trip there too."

He drank from his water glass. "Cape Sunio is worth a visit if you have a boat take you down the stretch of the Athenian Rivera. The Temple of Poseidon isn't what you will want to see; it's the landscape."

Olive placed her napkin on her lap. "And that's closed due to the strike?"

Alex nodded. "Unfortunately."

She pouted.

"Are you in Greece for more than a week? You can find flights to the outlying islands such as Mykonos or Santorini. I'd stay overnight if you are going out that far. Those are my sister's favorite locations, though a bit too touristy for my taste. I'd recommend exploring the Peloponnese and Meteora."

"I'm here for five more days." They began to eat. "I'll have to make a decision tomorrow. If I go to Santorini though, I might spend more time scuba diving than exploring the city."

"Is that one of your hobbies?" He worked on cutting his steak into smaller pieces.

Olive nodded. "My home island is famous for its manta rays, sea turtles, humpback whales, and coral reefs. I had to find a way to explore life under the sea. It's so quiet and relaxing." She took a bite of her burger. "Who knows, maybe I'll be the one to discover the lost city of Atlantis."

Alex grinned. "Ancient lore *does* speak of Santorini as the basis for the legend of Atlantis."

Olive was growing used to Alex's teasing nature. Just as she was beginning to appreciate his dancing eyes as one of his defining features every time he smiled. She asked several follow-up questions about Santorini, Mykonos, and the Greek islands and learned that his grandparents were originally from the island of Crete. He spoke of them in hushed, soft tones.

He must have a close relationship with them.

After splitting a traditional dessert of baklava with coffee, Olive was ready to conquer Areopagus Hill.

CHAPTER 5

No Margin for Error

"Areopagus was used as the seat of the Athenian High Court and Council of Elders. The apostle Paul spoke here to the Athenians. There is so much history in this one place. These stairs alone have been here since 500 BC," Alex said.

The entire hill was cut from stones of varying shapes and sizes. A freezing wind blew from the west. The sun had begun to set. It would be dark in half an hour. If they hurried, they could watch the sunset from the summit of Areopagus Hill.

It won't take that long, maybe ten minutes to climb.

She stared at the set of uneven, marble stone steps. Some were eroded and missing chunks in places. There was no handrail.

We had enough problems earlier on the Acropolis summit, and those steps were better maintained than these.

"Is it safe to take these?" Olive rubbed her clammy hands against her jeans.

"No," he admitted. "Even in full daylight, the rocky steps are tricky to navigate." Alex unconsciously rubbed his knee. "There's another set of steps around this way."

She followed him and let out a relieved breath. The modern steps were made from metal and had handrails.

"Is there something wrong? You *were* walking a little gingerly after the stumbles earlier."

Alex straightened. "It's nothing." His voice was tight. "Go. I'll meet you up top."

Olive's stomach clenched. Something in his tone triggered concern. Was he purposely evading answering her question? "Alex?"

"You are about to miss the sunset." She pursed her lips and tapped her foot. He cleared his throat and scratched his head. "If you must know, one of the muscles in my leg tightened up during lunch. It is not anything that hasn't happened before. Go. I'll be right behind you." He all but pushed her up the first step.

Olive's eyes raked over Alex. *He's hiding just how much it must hurt right now. I'll give him some privacy. It's what I would want.*

"I'll meet you at the top." Without being told a third time, she left him behind and started up the steps. The metal echoed and vibrated with each step. She picked up her pace. The temples atop the Acropolis grew larger and closer. Slightly out of breath, she double-timed it to the summit.

There was a mixture of dark imposing storm clouds over patches of purple, orange, pink, and navy-blue hues of clear sky. As one of only four people at the top, it was like having her own personal oasis. Of all the places she had seen in Greece so far, Areopagus Hill was by far one of the most special.

Her head whipped in every which direction, looking out over the glimmering modern city. Perfectly placed spotlights highlighted the white marble of the temples and rocks on the outcrop of the hill. She clicked away on the digital camera, attempting to capture the beauty that surrounded her. Alex's little compact camera performed brilliantly at nighttime photography.

All the amazing photos I've taken today are thanks to him. This puts my own camera to shame.

Where was Alex? He had said he was going to be right behind her. Olive mentally gave him ten more minutes to join her. The sun was almost completely gone.

I've been up here for at least a half an hour.

The view no longer held quite the same appeal. Instead, all she could think about was the man who brought her here.

She paced to and fro as the last sliver of light disappeared. A few stray droplets of rain fell against her forehead. She shivered. She was now completely alone. There was still no sign of Alex. Her instincts told her something was wrong. She scrambled back over to the steps, squinting out into the darkness. With no ambient lighting up on the hill, it was difficult to even make out anything below.

"Alex?" she called out.

He heart beat faster. She listened intently for his reply. Nothing.

She held her hands up to her mouth. Louder, she yelled, "Alex?"

A weak voice replied, "Down here."

Olive swallowed hard. Her breathing intensified. A light mist began to fall from the sky. Putting her hand on the cold, damp metal rail, she descended as quickly as she dared down the steps broken into eight sets of five steps to the bottom. Suddenly, her foot slid out from under her. She let out a cry and grabbed the rail with both hands, trembling.

"Be careful. It's dangerous when wet," Alex called out. Adrenaline shot through her body. She still couldn't see him. She had to get to the bottom of the stairs.

"What happened? I'm nearly there."

"Slipped. My leg buckled," he growled.

Finally, she caught a glimpse of him sitting against the backing of the staircase. One leg was straight, the other bent. His head rested on the bent knee.

"How bad did you hurt yourself?" She crouched down onto her hands and knees, catching her breath. Alex's curls were unruly and disheveled from the rain. She resisted the urge to touch them.

"My knee was pretty done in after the earlier climb. Even after a year of recovery and all of the hard work in physical therapy, my body continues to fail me." Alex looked up at her, his eyes glossy. "I've ruined the evening."

"As I told you earlier, you haven't ruined anything." She pressed her lips together and gestured to the top of the stairs. "I slipped earlier too. Wet steps aren't favorable to anyone."

Alex dryly said, "That is an understatement."

His sense of humor is still intact. That is one positive. Her breathing slowed.

"I get you are a proud, stubborn man, but I need an honest answer from you if I am going to help you. What *exactly* hurts? Is anything broken?"

"No broken bones, but I likely sprained my knee when I fell. I can't put much weight on it. Hence why I'm down here." He let out a sarcastic laugh. "The irony is that I was just cleared as fully fit by both my surgeon and physio to resume full physical activities."

Olive sucked in a breath. She splayed a hand on her chest. Memories from her own knee injury began to resurface. *Focus. Alex needs your help right now.*

"I have experience with knees." She ran her hands over his injured limb. His jeans were heavy and damp. He sucked in air when her hand touched the area around the base of the kneecap. "I can feel a lot of swelling, but nothing displaced."

She could piece together what had happened—Alex was overzealous. Knees and body parts, however, weren't machines. Muscle, strength, and control had to be regained over time. All of the warning signs had been there earlier.

"Happy to hear it," he said.

The rain was picking up. "We have to get you to the bottom of the stairs." She rubbed her hands together. "I can offer you a piggyback ride to the bottom, or you can use me as a crutch." Olive's brain couldn't come up with any other options.

Alex snorted. "I am a six-foot-two man to your four-foot-something frame. I am heavy and will break you if you carry me."

"I am five feet tall exactly, and would you care to make a wager? Guaranteed, I am among the strongest women you will ever meet." She put a hand on his shoulder. "You are going to have to trust me. I can do this."

In a soft tone, he said, "I can't promise I won't be forced to put a tremendous amount of strain on your shoulders. But I'd appreciate the help."

Alex scooted himself into a more upright sitting position. Olive slipped his arm over her shoulder. "If there is one single advantage to being a foot or more shorter than you, it is that I *can* be a crutch." His body was like a heater, warming her against the freezing air.

She braced herself. "Normally I would never say this, but you are going to have to walk on your injured knee as normally as you can. We can't risk you hopping down the steps."

"We have to take this slow." Alex grunted as he pushed off the better knee to a standing position. They both breathed sharply.

"Slow is fine. Slow is safe." Olive kept her voice neutral. Internally, however, she *wasn't* prepared for Alex to be as heavy as he was. It was taking all of her mental strength and fortitude to stay upright. She was absolutely terrified if she slipped up, they would both fall. Then what would happen?

Think positive. There is no margin for error.

"On my count." Olive counted out each and every step all the way to the bottom of the staircase. "Three. Two. One. Step. Three. Two. One. Step."

Glacially, Alex and Olive inched their way along. The constant rhythm of keeping count proved to be enough of a distraction to see them safely through to the bottom. On the flat ground again, Olive breathed a sigh of relief.

Alex pinched the bridge of his nose. "I don't trust myself enough to drive the Vespa in the state I am in."

Olive staggered. "What about a taxi?"

"This is a pedestrian walkway. No taxis."

The rain came down in sheets. The moon and stars were fully obscured by clouds. "Okay." Olive searched for cover. Her gaze turned to the nearby grove of trees. Some cover was better than nothing. They stumbled over together, Olive bearing the brunt of Alex's body weight.

Sharp pine needles rubbed against her face. They sank down against the scratchy, rough bark of the tree's trunk, exhausted. Dried pine needles and leaf matter provided some protection from the mud. She pulled her knees toward her stomach. She momentarily rested her head against the trunk.

From his pocket, Alex pulled out a mobile phone with a shaking hand. He shoved it at her. The display screen was nearly shattered. "The pass code is 0814. I couldn't get it to turn back on, but maybe you'll have better luck than me. I think the battery is dead."

She held it in her hand, then groaned. "I've had my phone in my pocket this entire time. I could've used it earlier to phone for help!" She pulled it from her pocket and tapped the screen. It glowed in the darkness to display the time at five-thirty in the evening. She handed him back his phone.

"We were both a little frantic earlier. It happens," Alex

tightly replied. He sat with his legs out straight and eyes closed.

"Who can I call that can help us?" Olive unlocked her phone and opened the keypad.

Without hesitation, Alex said, "Leo."

"And his number is…" Her hand hovered above the dial pad.

"Let me think—I haven't had to memorize any mobile numbers in a long time." Alex frowned. "The country code is going to be +30. The phone number is—" He rattled off a number she hoped was correct.

Olive cradled the phone close to her ear. It rang several times before a grumpy male voice picked up. "Hello?"

The man on the receiving end didn't sound like the barista from the day before. Her stomach clenched. "Hi. Is this Leo? This is Olive Nakamura, the, um, coffee girl."

"Speaking." The voice was curt.

Alex tapped her shoulder. "Better I get on with being yelled at by my cousin." Alex huffed. "If you could put it on speaker, please."

She touched the volume icon on the screen and held her phone between the two of them.

"Leo. It's Alex. I fell down a flight of stairs, injured my knee, and am sitting outside in the rain under a pine tree with Olive, not far from the Acropolis. Can you please come and pick us up?"

That's one way of summing up what happened.

With the phone's backlight, she could see the emergence of a five o'clock shadow on Alex's face. His eyes were red-rimmed and bloodshot. His clothing wet and clinging to his body. Their coats, back at the Vespa.

I'm probably just as messy looking.

"Alexander!" Leo exclaimed. He ranted in Greek to Alex,

who inclined his head. The only word Olive could discern out of the entire exchange was Vespa.

Leo switched back to English. "Olive, is it? I never did learn your name yesterday. I am on my way to you two right now. Do not move from your spot. I'll ring if I can't find you."

"I can do you one better. I'll share my location with you." Olive tapped the screen again and went into her settings.

"Much appreciated," Leo said. She disconnected the call and slid her phone into her pocket.

Alex scooted closer to Olive. He rubbed his hand on her arms. "You're shaking like a leaf. All I can offer you is my sopping wet jumper."

Olive laughed. "I can't forever be borrowing your clothing. But I appreciate the sentiment." Her body was stiff and sore all over. She could not wait to change and be warm again.

"Thank you for your help back there." Alex cleared his throat. "I *am* stubborn and don't accept help easily."

"Anyone would have done the same." Olive rubbed her hands together and blew on them. "If you don't mind me asking, what surgery did you have done? ACL? Meniscus? PCL?"

"You're very knowledgeable." He stared out into the darkness. "It was my ACL."

"I went through the same injury during my gymnastics tenure. My ACL and meniscal tears set me back almost two years. It was exceptionally trying to be patient *and* have to listen to others who reassured me I was ahead of my recovery timeline."

Alex let out a throaty laugh. "It is nice to know the rush of emotions and frustrations are universal. Did you ever feel normal again?"

"After my second surgery, yes."

His breath hitched. "A second surgery?"

"Lucky me was in the ten percent of people forced to have

a second surgery. Instead of making the knee stable, my first ACL graft just disintegrated." She sighed. "It's all in the past now."

Alex took hold of Olive's hand and squeezed it for reassurance. It was double the size of hers. The metal of a signet ring on his pinkie finger brushed against her fingers. He rubbed circles with his thumb on the web of her hand. Goosebumps popped up on her arms.

Alex was so close to her. Electricity pulsed through the air around them. Their gazes locked. She took in the intense molten chocolate and the warmth they radiated. She still smelled the faint notes of bergamot mixed with the pine from the surrounding trees.

He whispered into her ear, "You really are one of the strongest women I know." His breath was hot upon her skin. He placed a soft, short kiss on the nape of her neck. His stubble rubbed against the tender, exposed skin. Her pulse raced as if she were running toward the vault for a Yurchenko double twist. She melted into his chest.

Suddenly, his body stiffened. He dropped his arms and scooted back, hissing in pain. "I'm sorry. I shouldn't have done that."

She froze and blinked in rapid succession, tongue-tied. *Alex just kissed me! I have never in my life let anyone get this close to me so soon after meeting them. Why did he have to pull back like that?*

Her neck still tingled. She wanted to grasp him by the collar of his shirt and kiss him smack on the mouth when, suddenly, the heavy fall of footsteps approached them. An unexpectedly bright beam of light illuminated their forms. Olive was forced to close her eyes until the light was lowered.

"Alex! Olive! Thank goodness." Leo, clothed in a heavy yellow jacket and black jeans, carried an oversized umbrella and an industrial-sized flashlight. He lowered his hood. His work boots squished through the mud. "You two are all red. I hope you're not feverish."

Leo knelt down and from his black and gray camo-print, military-style backpack, he removed two gray woolen blankets and two flasks. "Wrap yourselves in these. Drink all the hot chocolate. Alex, can you walk at all?"

"Not without assistance."

Olive nestled herself within the wool. The heavy fabric of the blanket, though slightly musty, successfully blocked out the chill of the night. She greedily drank the richly flavored hot chocolate. Its sweet vanilla and hazelnut notes were a welcome boon to her icy insides.

Leo's countenance darkened. "You know what that means."

Alex mumbled, "Unfortunately, I do." He pulled his own blanket around himself and sank lower down the tree trunk.

Leo pulled the straps of his backpack tighter. "Olive, are you well enough to walk? I have my SUV pulled up to the edge of the footpath."

"Yes."

Leo handed Olive the umbrella and flashlight. "If you could please take charge of these while I carry Alexander to the car? It'll take too long otherwise. I'll take you two back to my flat and treat you there."

CHAPTER 6

A Cousin to the Rescue

"You are inherently lucky my flat is on the ground floor and is so close to the Acropolis," Leo said. Olive walked ahead of the cousins to the army-green front door with frosted glass. "The entry door should be open." She turned the brass knob.

The door opened to reveal a loft-style flat with reclaimed red brick walls and mahogany hardwood floors. The white cabinets, black appliances, and slate-gray counter tops of the kitchen took up the entire length of the largest wall. The living room area contained a rustic wooden coffee table atop a bamboo carpet, a navy-blue couch, and two black bookcases.

A large canvas photo of the whitewashed houses with blue roofs and the azure sea of the island of Santorini adorned the wall behind the couch. Light enclosed in glass globes hung from the ceiling. Black stairs led to the second floor.

Leo's shoes squished against the floors. Alex heavily leaned on Leo. He hopped into the apartment and onto the couch. Olive closed the door behind them.

Leo gestured to two mugs on the coffee table with yet more hot chocolate. "Drink these. We have to warm you up slowly." Olive nodded but could not help but stare at the muddy footprints leading from the door to the living room. Her fingers itched to clean them up.

"When you're done, leave the cups on the coffee table." Leo adjusted the thermostat. The heat kicked on with a bang and brought a dusty scent with it. "Here are some towels for you both and changes of clothing. You need to get dried off quickly."

Leo removed his yellow raincoat, revealing a long, black, fitted turtleneck. *He certainly owns a monochrome wardrobe.*

"Thank you. I really appreciate it." The damp was seeping into her skin. She finished her cup and stood.

"My wife is larger and taller than you, but her clothing will have to make due. I wish she wasn't away at a bachelorette party right now; I could really use her help." Leo glanced in Alex's direction. "Don't tell her I said that." Leo washed his hands in the kitchen sink and rolled up his shirtsleeves to reveal a tattoo of a firefighter's helmet crossed with two axes on his forearm. "The bathroom is up the stairs and to the right. Alex, you can change down here."

Gratefully, she picked up the dry clothing and climbed the stairs to the second floor. The top of the landing revealed the flat's main sleeping area, a full-sized bed covered with blue sheets and white comforter, and a black side table topped with a succulent plant. Across from the bed were a rustic working desk, floating shelves, and framed photos.

Olive could hear Leo and Alex chatting below in hushed tones. "Of all the dumb things you could have done, why did you think it was appropriate to climb Areopagus?" She could hear him rummaging through a kitchen drawer. "You of all people should *know* your limitations."

Guilt took hold. Alex had only been trying to be a dutiful tour guide and to show her the city. He had put his own health and welfare at risk for her. Sean had never been so considerate. He had only cared about number one—himself. She found the bathroom, entered, and shut the door behind her. She stared at herself in the mirror and clutched the edges of the sink.

Her skin was pale and clammy. Her long locks were tangled. It was going to take her hours to comb out the mess. She washed her face with warm water.

Funny, my last time out on a date-date, Sean insisted I "dress to impress." Nothing I wore was ever "appropriate" for him. Why did I ever buy those skin-tight dresses? Unless it's a leotard, I hate being constricted. I'm a leggings and T-shirt kind of gal. If he saw me now, Sean would only have insults to hurl my way. I won't let that happen ever again. The new Olive stands up for herself.

She changed into a pair of black yoga pants, a white long-sleeve shirt, and fluffy, pink cashmere socks. The V-neck cut of the shirt revealed a reddish-green bruise between her collarbone and shoulder from where Alex had leaned on her. She gingerly touched it. The area was sensitive to pressure.

It's a small price to pay. Until the end of the day, Olive had thoroughly enjoyed herself. She arranged her hair to cover the mark. It had been fun to lose herself in the tour of the city and to have a say in what activities they did and the places they saw. *Even if it ended with Alex getting hurt, today has been a good day.*

Satisfied, she unbolted the door, gathered her wet clothing, and rejoined the men. Leo stood over the stove, warming hot soup and a sizzling meat dish. "The lemon chicken soup should be ready in a few minutes. While we're waiting, it's your turn, Olive."

"My turn? Whatever for?" Olive paused on the last step.

"My firefighter cousin intends to give you a quick wellness exam." Alex sat on the couch in a black hoodie with a blanket draped over his legs.

"I was getting to that." Leo glared at Alex. "I thought you were a barista?" Olive's eyes darted back and forth between Alex and Leo.

"That's my primary job. I'm also a volunteer paramedic with the Hellenic Fire Service."

"Oh." Olive's respect and admiration for Leo grew.

Leo put on a pair of clean latex gloves. "It will only take a moment. We can step into the back of the kitchen, away from Mr. Know-It-All, for added privacy."

She stepped down the last step. "There isn't really a way out of it, is there?"

"As much as we like to joke and kid around with one another, Leo always has our best interests at heart." Alex turned serious. "He knows what he's doing."

Yesterday, Leo had been so invested in her health after the coffee incident. A gut instinct told her to trust him. "Okay, then."

Leo pointed to a plastic freezer bag where she could leave her wet clothing. He led her to the bar area in the back of the kitchen, far away from Alex. They both sat down.

"Where did you receive your medical training?" Olive asked.

Leo had her follow a penlight with her eyes. "From the army." He also checked her pulse and temperature.

"The army?" Olive raised an eyebrow.

"It's compulsory for all men over eighteen to serve in the armed forces. I enjoyed it and stayed in long enough to become a medic. I keep my skills sharp through my volunteer work." The thermometer beeped. "Pulse is steady. Your temperature is still lower than I'd like but within normal range."

Olive sat back in her chair. "That's always good to hear."

"I don't see any surface scrapes or abrasions. Do you have any questions?" He stood and began putting away his medical kit.

She blinked slowly. Wordlessly, she moved the hair from her left shoulder and pulled at the collar of her shirt. "It didn't begin to throb until we arrived here."

"That's nasty." Leo sucked in air. "For the swelling, I have some ibuprofen. It's going to darken over the next few days. We'll heat it tonight. Tomorrow, and for the next few days, please use ice. Use your arm as normally as you can tolerate. It'll assist with the blood circulation."

Softly she added, "Please don't tell Alex."

"Patient confidentiality. I won't." Leo cleared his throat. "My cousin doesn't know just how lucky he was tonight. I wish he would stop taking so many chances." He sighed. "You did a tremendous service for him. If there is anything you ever need. Just ask."

~

Olive enjoyed Leo's delicious Greek hospitality and was returned to her hotel close to ten. Many thoughts ran through her head after a long, hot soak in the tub. Sitting cross-legged on her bed, Olive picked up her phone and called Amanda.

"If it isn't the wayward traveler. How was your day today?" Amanda appeared on the screen, sitting at a vanity. Her face was slathered with a clay face mask and her hair wrapped up tight in a towel.

Olive adjusted the pop socket on the back of her phone and balanced it on the side table next to her bed. She reclined on her side. "Tiring and exhilarating until the end."

"Care to share? I have ten more minutes before I have to wash all this stuff off."

"I took a tour of the city with this guy I met yesterday. It was my first time seeing some of the city up close." Olive braced herself.

Amanda's eyes bulged. "Pause. Rewind. You met a guy yesterday? And you went out with him today? On a date?"

Olive's cheeks burned with heat. "No. Nothing like that. This is so embarrassing." She face-palmed. "I spilled coffee all over myself yesterday, and one of the men sitting next to me came to the rescue by lending me his shirt to cover the stain."

Amanda's lips curved up in approval. "Go on."

"I only intended to return the shirt this morning, but he was waiting for me in the lobby. He offered me a tour of the city on a motorbike, and I said yes." Olive picked up her phone.

"And you went along with him? Just like that?" Amanda's face inched closer to the camera.

"I *did* share my location with you."

"A motorbike?" Amanda gasped. "Am I speaking to the same Olive Nakamura that less than six months ago was considering not even coming to Clara's wedding? The same woman who told me she would never ever open herself to the possibility of dating ever again?"

"I'm the same person I have always been. Today, I wanted to challenge myself and see if I could spend the day with a man and have fun." Olive sat back on the bed and leaned onto her stomach. "It worked. I think I'm ready to open myself up and take the next step."

"This is such an exciting development! You *are* learning how to fly again. When you find the right person for you, it can be so magical." Amanda's eyes sparkled.

When Alex kissed me, I was alive. I was wanted. It's never been that way before. She rubbed the nape of her neck. Remembering how soft and gentle his lips had caressed the very spot. "What do you feel when you're with Eddie?"

"The best way I can describe it is like a magnetic pull. We

have this intimate connection where nothing exists in the world except me and my other half."

Clara said something similar. She compared being with David to Cinderella's perfect fit with a glass slipper. Come to think of it, they had a similar experience when they first met. Is coffee the universal way to meet a prince charming?

Both of her friends had men in their lives who they wholeheartedly, deeply loved. Every time they spoke, there was a lightness and spark in their voices. She wanted to be loved. *I just hope when it's my turn, I get to experience one iota of what they have.*

Olive lowered her voice. "I might be open to a date or two in London."

"Oh! I can already think of a few people you could go out with. That is if today's man of mystery doesn't work out." Amanda's timer went off. She promptly ignored it. "Is there any possibility of a 'date'?"

"A date? Doubtful. We probably won't even see one another again." She ran a hand through her hair.

"Never say never." Amanda winked. "What's he like? Is he cute?"

"His name is Alex. He's fit and has wavy brown locks and the most intense brown eyes." She wracked her brain. She knew next to nothing else about him. What was his last name? Where was he from? What did he do for a living?

"And?"

"He has a cousin named Leo and a sister. His grandparents are from Crete. If I had to guess by his accent where he's from, he sounds British. He speaks English very differently from his cousin."

Amanda's timer went off a second time. "What are you not telling me?"

"That is for me to know and you to find out," she said defiantly.

Amanda squealed. "I can't wait to hear how the rest of this unfolds." Amanda stood. "I'll draw up a list of guys Clara and I think will suit you. Are you open to…"

Eddie's voice interrupted their conversation. "Collins, I need your help. I think I broke the dishwasher. They are supposed to be done, but all the dishes are still dirty." Olive was saved from having to answer the question.

"Five pounds says that he forgot to put soap in it or forgot to rinse the dishes beforehand." Amanda sniggered. "Sorry to dash off, but Princey can only fend for himself for so long. I'm so happy to hear Greece is agreeing with you."

Amanda and Olive promised to chat again in a few days' time. She placed the phone down. Locating the television remote, she clicked on the device and flipped through a few of the channels. The only one in English was BBC. She lowered the volume and let it play in the background. She turned the lights off, slipped under the covers, and closed her eyes.

She hummed a tune Leo had played on the acoustic guitar after dinner. *If I do cross paths with Leo or Alex again, it will be by fate's intervention.* She lay awake, reliving the day in her mind. Sleep evaded her.

At one in the morning, she clicked the lights on. She sat up in bed. *My tote bag is still inside the bin of Leo's Vespa. I have more clothes to return too. It looks like I'll be seeing Alex and Leo again after all.*

She opened the doors to the balcony and walked outside. The rain had stopped. The moon shined overhead, adding its own glow to the Parthenon. She heard the stray car passing on the street below. A cat meowed. An owl hooted. Leaning against the railing, her shoulder twinged. She would just have to wait and see what the very young day held in store for her.

CHAPTER 7

Stepping Out From the Shadows

Olive passed under the intensely pink branch of an overgrown bougainvillea plant clashing with the yellow and orange buildings around her. Insects buzzed in her ear. This area of the city was full of vibrant souvenir window displays. Already, she had stopped several times to look over the selection of scarves, magnets, and jewelry. Businesses wouldn't open until later in the morning.

I planned to drop the clothes off at the hotel, but having Leo direct me to bring it by his place gives me the perfect excuse to see Alex again!

Checking the map app on her phone, Olive turned left and toward the steps of a narrow cobblestone side street leading up toward the Acropolis. She paused outside two identical white buildings with green doors. Bringing up the contacts list on her phone, Olive tapped the number she'd dialed in the woods the night before. Leo answered after one ring.

"Kalimera, Leo. I'm at the bottom of the hill. When I sent you a text this morning, you mentioned your front door was green, but I see two green doors. Which home is yours?"

"Good morning to you too. My building is the first one on the right." A door clicked open behind Olive. She turned to see Leo in his familiar black uniform, waving at her.

Leo led Olive inside and directed her to the kitchen. The bar area of the kitchen overflowed with a colorful selection of fruits, pastries, bread, and yogurt. Alex sat on the sofa with a heaping plate of bread slathered in fresh honey with a side of fruit. He appeared fully recovered.

"Have you eaten breakfast yet? As you can see, I have plenty of food to go around." Leo handed Alex a steaming hot coffee mug. "Alexander is a black hole. He will devour everything in sight."

"Breakfast?" she stammered. "I only intended to pass through. I don't want to bother you a second, or rather, third day in a row."

"She's forever forgetting to eat breakfast," Alex said.

She grew warm and fuzzy. *After all that went on yesterday, I can't believe he remembers that.* "Blame it on the jet lag. My body is still out of whack."

Leo offered her an enigmatic smile. "You could never be a bother. We Greeks are social creatures who can sit and chat for hours. Hospitality is important to us."

Olive half smiled. "The same is true at home. We call it ho'okipa, the spirit of welcoming everyone with aloha and open arms."

"Then I can tempt you to join us?" Leo gestured to the round table they had eaten dinner at the night before. There were two empty place settings.

Alex glanced up from his plate. "Leo brought all the best pastries from the hotel kitchen."

Leo put a finger to his lips. "You weren't to mention that bit. Olive is supposed to think I am a brilliant cook."

"Stefani is the brilliant cook. But you make up for any shortcomings with your skills as a barista," Alex said.

"Stefani is my better half." Leo pulled out a chair. "And speaking of my barista know-how"—he studied Olive—"how about a mocha for the morning?"

Olive gaped. "That's my normal order." Leo first pumped the air.

Alex's mouth twisted. "Lucky guess."

"A mocha sounds divine." Olive sat at the table. She took hold of the serving spoon and helped herself to some fruit and yogurt. "How are you feeling this morning, Alex?"

"I've been better. The knee is swollen and stiff, but manageable. I should be able to finally return to light work again in two weeks, depending on the MRI scans." He placed his plate on the coffee table with the utensils on top. "And yourself?"

"A hot bath set me right." Leo offered her a steaming hot mug. She inhaled the scents of hazelnut and dark chocolate. "Have you had to be off work for a long time?"

Alex blew out his cheeks. "Nearly eight months. The next step is going to be getting to the gym to rebuild all my weakened muscles. I want to be fully back to pre-injury form within the next five months. I can't wait to run again."

"It will go quickly. You just have to be mindful not to overdo it," Leo added.

"With my sister and Drew sharing my London flat, both of them will keep an eagle eye on me until I am fully fit." Alex put his hands behind his head.

"And a good thing too." The coffee machine let out a spitting noise and a puff of steam. Leo spotlessly cleaned the nozzles.

Olive pictured the sandy-haired man from the day before when he mentioned Drew. "What do you do for a living?" She sipped the coffee and tasted a hint of vanilla to balance out the chocolate. "This is another perfect drink."

"Always happy to have a satisfied customer." Leo joined her at the table with a full plate of food. "Alex works in the sports industry."

She looked back at Alex. "Ah. That explains the mutual interest in the Panathenaic Stadium. Do you have the opportunity to travel often?" Olive asked.

Alex stroked his goatee. "I do. I have been incredibly lucky until now."

"It's rare he's here in Greece for more than a few weeks at a time." Leo tucked into his food. "You *could* consider moving here."

Alex scooted forward and stood. Unsteadily, he picked up his plate. "Greece agrees with me. But London is still my home."

Leo paused mid-bite and shot Alex a look of warning with narrowed eyes and tightened lips. Alex sighed and returned the plate to the coffee table. Leo nodded. "After we finish breakfast, I can drive us over to the Acropolis car park. We can retrieve my Vespa and your tote bag."

As much as she wished to spend more time with Alex, there was so much more she could explore and see on foot. "I wouldn't mind a walk. You are so close to the Acropolis. It seems a shame to drive."

"Under normal circumstances, we would walk. But I am returning Alex to his hotel and picking up Stefani from the airport." Leo shook his head. "Neither Stefani nor Penny is going to be too happy to see you injured again."

Alex winced. "Maybe I should consider returning to London today."

"Not an option. Remember, Yiayia and Pappou are coming all the way down from Thessaloniki to see you." Leo drank from his coffee.

"I know." Alex rubbed the nape of his neck.

Olive tilted her head to the side. She had finished her breakfast and was nearly done with her coffee.

"Those are our grandparents." Leo leaned back in his chair. "Thessaloniki is in the north and a magnificent city surrounded by the bay. So close to Macedonia, and worth a trip if you can spare the time."

"I hope Yiayia brings fresh tomatoes and oregano from her garden." Alex blew a chef's kiss. "She has a green thumb."

Leo patted his stomach and sat upright. Olive stood. "May I do the dishes for you?" she inquired.

Leo waved his hand. "These are going directly into the dishwasher. All I have to do is refrigerate the leftovers. Would you like some to take with you?"

"No thank you. I'm heading out to the Port of Piraeus at nine." Olive snapped her fingers. "Let me return the clothing you lent me and your camera to you before I grow any more sidetracked. That's the entire reason I came over after all."

Leo stood. "I'll leave Alex to sort out the details. We'll leave in five minutes." He collected the dishes and set to work cleaning up.

Olive walked over to her backpack and retrieved a plastic bag with the clothes. "I had the hotel wash them, so they're clean." She gave the package to Alex. Their hands briefly touched. The rough tips of his fingers brushed over her knuckles. She shivered and breathed shallowly. Warmth ran through her body.

She cleared her throat. "As for the camera, I was wondering if I may pay you for the SD card. It has so many irreplaceable photos from yesterday. I wasn't able to upload anything."

Alex blinked several times. "Keep the SD card. I have several." He locked eyes with Olive. "And better yet, keep the camera."

Olive's cheeks flushed. "I can't do that. It's an expensive camera."

Alex stroked his chin. "What about this as a compromise." He let out a deep breath. "Hold on to the camera and use it throughout your trip here. You can return it to me before you leave."

"But I'm only in Greece for a few more days. I'm going to Venice, Salzburg, and then on to London. I don't know when I'll be able to get it back to you," Olive sputtered.

He snapped his fingers. "You can return it in London. Perhaps I can even provide you with another tour." Alex winked.

Thousands of butterflies pushed against her stomach, attempting to escape. *He wants to see me again.* Every reason why she shouldn't encourage him ran through her head. *I hardly know him. What if I grow too attached. Am I ready for another relationship? I never want to be as heartbroken as I was with Sean, ever again.* There was an air of mystery that drew her to him. Their paths continually crossed.

Olive looked up through her lashes. "I'll leave it up to destiny."

"Destiny has already brought us together once. This time, I am intervening. Do you have your mobile? Mine is still on the fritz." Olive nodded and handed him the requested item. "This is my number. Just in case you want to make your own destiny."

Leo cleared his throat. He jingled the keys and stood with his hands behind his back, pretending to glance away.

"We're ready," Alex said.

Leo laughed. "Whatever you say." He strode to the couch and leaned over to assist Alex.

"Just like Stefani and me," Olive heard Leo say under his breath.

She zipped up her backpack and followed the two men out to the carport.

All of my friends have been lucky in love except for me. I've always felt so inadequate despite their encouragement. Alex doesn't tell me what he thinks I want to hear. He speaks to me as an individual. He sees me as a woman and not as an Olympic athlete. I've always been defined by my past, but this is the first time I've been able to truly step out from the shadows.

~

The boat slowed its motor and drifted the remainder of the way to the pier into Hydra. The collection of white nineteenth-century-styled buildings with red-roofs rose up into the cliffs of the island. Clear blue water underneath the boat revealed schools of fish skimming over pristine yellow-white sand. The captain lowered the ramp. Tourists clamored down the pier toward the waiting line of mules and donkeys, the island's version of a taxi service.

Olive shifted her tote bag from her left shoulder to her right. The afternoon sun beamed down. Skipping the donkey service, she turned right and walked past the many outdoor cafes to a side street off the harbor. A salty scent lingered in the air. Her hand skimmed over the stones of the sea wall, and she watched the fishing boats sway gently in the sea's waves.

Her feet carried her down a cozy coastal lane nestled a stone's throw away from the main thoroughfare. Her destination was a cheerful red building. She glanced at the jewelry displays, still searching for an owl pendant. To the window's left, a cork board displayed activities for tourists. A glossy flyer for the Athens Masters 1000 tennis tournament caught her eye.

The main text read: *For one week only, treat yourself to matches played by some of the world's top rising stars at the season opener of the professional men's tennis circuit.* She skimmed over some of the names—Alexander Georgiou, Andrew Russo, Marco Paganini, Henry Lee, and Sean McPherson.

She staggered backward. Sean was playing in this tournament? The air was sucked out of her body. She grew lightheaded. She ran her finger under the dates of the and swallowed hard. The event was due to begin in three days!

Even halfway around the world on the small quaint island of Hydra, I see his name. Yesterday went so well, but now he's in the same city I am. Her muscles clenched.

A female worker from inside the jewelry shop stepped out and said, "You're as white as a sheet. Too much sun. Even in winter. Come inside." Having a moment to process the shock, the blood returned to her face. The worker handed her a glass of water. "Are you a tennis fan? I see you are intrigued by the poster."

"My mother is a fanatic. I, um… just saw a name I recognized, and it surprised me." She forced a smile onto her face.

The worker made a clicking noise. "Shame that tickets are sold out. The headliner this year was to be Alexander Georgiou. I waited too long to buy my tickets. They sold out weeks ago."

"What a shame," Olive sympathized with the worker.

"Indeed, but it worked out for the best. Alexander was the only reason I was considering attending. It was on the news this morning that he's still not back from injury as of yet and won't be able to play in the tournament this year."

Olive finished her glass of water. "Thank you so much. I appreciate it." Her eyes traveled to the jewelry cases of gold pendants. She cleared her throat. "Do you have any Athenian owls?"

The worker came to. "We have modern variations of the

iconic owl, and more traditional." She pulled out a few necklaces for Olive to examine.

Olive's mind spun. She was still focused on the tournament. Could she escape Athens without encountering Sean? What were the odds they would meet in a city of over three million people?

CHAPTER 8

A Lesson In Greek Philosophy

Three days passed. On the last day of her stay in Athens, the Ministry of Culture's strike was over. Olive had a full schedule to keep. The lobby of Aphrodite's Garden, the hotel where Leo worked, was a hive of activity. Banners with the logo for the Athens Masters tournament had sprung up since her last visit. The mandolin music playing aloud was recognizably from the popular *Zorba the Greek* film.

She shifted her weight from foot to foot, dancing in place. In her arms, she held a tournament T-shirt, hat, and program. Fans with credentials around their necks lingered close to the elevators. There was a nervous and excited tension in the air.

Olive stepped up to the register. "How will you be paying today?" the cashier asked. The noise level of the fans rose exponentially. A security team encircled two men stepping out of the elevator.

She was forced to speak louder than normal and leaned in toward the table. "With a card." Olive tapped her leg, wishing the cashier would work quicker. She raised her head to the ceiling. Of all the times for the players to cross the lobby on their way to the awaiting cars, it had to be now.

It's my own fault. I wanted to buy Mom some souvenirs, and this is the result.

"No signature required. Here are your card and your items. Enjoy your day." Olive shoved her credit card and receipt into her purse.

From the elevators, there was a clear view of the merchandise table. She looked for the quickest exit. She clutched the bag close to her body. *I'm almost home free.* The circle of fans was heading for the hotel entrance.

The elevator bell rang out again. A second wave of fans rushed forward to the next set of athletes. They waved phones, cameras, hats, giant tennis balls, programs, and other items to be signed. She turned in the opposite direction and power walked toward the café, making herself smaller, staying close to the wall.

Just as she thought herself to be clear of the chaos, a raspy female voice sharply said, "The standards are so low here, the hotel will let just about any riff-raff into the lobby these days. Are you so desperate that you've taken up following Sean play on the road?"

The hairs on the back of Olive's neck prickled. A vein in her eyes twitched. She let out a deep breath. "Tessa, unpleasant as always." Olive spun around to confront the five-foot-nine, strawberry blonde woman in a figure-hugging, plunging-neckline, navy blue jumpsuit. Tessa McPherson, Sean's new wife, and a professional tennis player on the women's tennis tour.

"By now, I would have thought you might do *something* with your hair or at least wear makeup. Some of us take pride in looking our best." Tessa's lip snarled. "Then again, you don't exactly have much to work with. If I come across as a child—"

Tessa struck a nerve. Olive attempted to keep her tone cool

despite anger radiating through her body. "As much as I would *love* to stay and continue to listen to you insult me, I have things to do and places to be."

"Always running away." Tessa let out a low, mocking laugh. "Oh, *honey,* I knew you wouldn't have the guts to attend our wedding. Not that either of us wanted you there."

Olive's fists clenched. "Too bad. I never received an invitation. It must have been tossed away somewhere." She bit back the retort she *wanted* to say in favor of taking the high ground.

"Pity, even an emotionally stunted person as yourself might have at least found somebody who actually wants you." Tessa snorted. "But then again, I don't know anyone that desperate." Tessa flipped her hair over her shoulder. "Ta ta, shorty." Her stiletto heels clicked against the ground.

Olive buried her face in her hands. *Why do I always feel the need to engage with Tessa? Every. Single. Time.* Olive had been so concerned about the potential of coming face-to-face with Sean that she had completely forgotten about Tessa, who could be equally as nasty.

The steam from a hot cup of coffee tickled her nose. Leo's imposing form presented her with a white espresso cup and biscotti. He glared in Tessa's direction. "Drink this."

She bowed her head. "Did you overhear the entire exchange?"

"Enough of it. She wasn't exactly quiet."

Olive accepted the coffee. "For Tessa, that was tame. If she has one gift, it's coming up with insults quickly." She sniffed her drink. It was the same strong, bold roast she'd had when first meeting Leo.

He untied the apron from around his neck and left it on a hook behind the counter. "Care to talk about it?"

"No, but I'm sure you are curious." Olive let the bitter liquid run down her throat.

"As a human, curiosity is in our nature. Have you heard the story of Pandora and her box?" Leo walked with her outside into the garden terrace of the hotel relatively devoid of people.

"Parts of it." Olive bit into the crunchy biscotti. "I remember hearing the gist of the myth. Pandora couldn't resist her curiosity and opened a box, releasing a series of horrible calamities into the world."

Leo nodded. He raised his tone, and asked, "Do you know why she couldn't resist opening the box of horrors?"

They approached the fountain of Aphrodite. The Greek goddess of beauty and love stood in a clamshell rising from the ocean. It was draped with pink and red flowers. Birds chirped out.

Olive shook her head.

They sat down on the bench overlooking the fountain. "Her fatal flaw, as created by the gods, was curiosity. You could go so far as to say it was *predetermined* that she would be unable to overcome it."

"And the point of the story?" Olive finished the coffee and placed it down on the saucer next to her.

"Impatient aren't we."

"You can consider that my American flaw," Olive deadpanned.

Leo slapped his thigh. "The point is that in Pandora's box, hope remained behind. Even when all was seemingly lost, there was always hope."

Olive massaged her temples. "You sound like a Greek philosopher who is challenging me to decipher a deep or hidden meaning."

"We Greeks *invented* philosophy," Leo challenged.

He had a point there. Her forehead pulsed with an aching

throb. The encounter with Tessa opened her own Pandora's box of memories she had attempted to bury deep within.

Leo sighed. "I had only hoped to distract you long enough for you to let your mind move away from the unpleasantness of that woman from earlier. Have I succeeded?"

"Marginally." Olive observed the Mediterranean garden in front of her.

There was a white backdrop enclosing the space surrounded by potted lavenders, succulents, citrus trees, and other drought-tolerant plants. Trellises of orange, red, and pink bougainvillea added colored accents to the space. The lemons overpowered the rest of the scents in the Mediterranean garden.

"Excellent. Don't let one person ruin your day." Leo stood and collected her coffee cup.

"I'll try not to let her, but there is always a lingering rancid aftertaste." Olive grimaced.

"Well, in spite of her, I hope you've still enjoyed your time in Greece. I'm sad your stay is so short. Will you promise to stay in touch with me?"

Olive ran a hand through her hair. "I will. I've really enjoyed being able to get to know you over the last few days. I appreciate you calling me to check in to see how I was doing."

"You are already a friend of my family. Stefani and Penny already love you for keeping Alex safe, and they have yet to officially meet you. That speaks a lot to your character. You are one special lady. I'm only a phone call away." Leo pointed to the far side of the garden. "There is another person who wanted to say goodbye to you too. You might say your meeting was *predetermined*."

Olive's head shot up. "Alex," she breathed.

His hair was shorter, no longer down to his ears. He had shaved, revealing chiseled cheekbones. He wore dark-washed jeans, a blue cashmere crew neck sweater, and a black jacket.

Oversized aviators covered his eyes. She almost didn't recognize him.

She hugged Leo tightly. He chuckled. "Save that for my wayward Georgiou cousin." He pushed her forward. "He's been waiting for you."

Olive halted and sputtered, "Georgiou?"

Leo's brow furrowed. "That's our last name. Georgiou."

"As in Alexander Georgiou, the professional tennis player?" Olive splayed her hand on her chest. "I should've made the connection earlier." Her cheeks grew warm.

"You didn't know?" Leo pinched the bridge of his nose. "By now he should have said something. This one is on him." He muttered in Greek. "Communication is not Alexander's forte. You know where to find me if need be." They hugged once more. He returned to the café.

Internally, she was flustered and angry at herself. In Hydra, she'd read his name on the poster for the tournament. It had even boasted the player's photos. Yet, with the discovery of Sean in Athens, she had failed to take note of Alex. That's where she knew him from!

He "works in sports" is the understatement of the year. Mom is going to flip out when I relay the story to her. She would have recognized Alex on the spot. Her favorite tennis player, right in front of my face. Who was the man with Alex when we first met? Drew? That must be Andrew Russo. These days, I seem to have an affinity for attracting tennis players. It's both a blessing and a curse.

Alex crossed the garden and lowered his aviator sunglasses. "Here we are again," he started.

Olive licked her lips. Her mouth was dry. "So, you play professional tennis?"

Alex wrung his hands. "Guilty as charged."

"Why didn't you just straight up tell me?" Olive clenched her jaw.

He flinched. "It was so refreshing to have you treat me as a normal bloke when we first met. I almost never have the ability to go about incognito." He kicked at the dirt. "Take today as an example. I saw you earlier in the lobby when I was walking out of the lift. I wanted to stop and speak to you, but security kept us moving. Too many fans present." He chuckled. "I was forced to sneak out of the car and had to text Leo to see if he could catch you before you left."

"I can empathize with wanting to be treated as a 'normal person.'" She kept her words vague.

"I'm careful with my identity because I have to be. Being financially well off and in the limelight paints a target on my back. But people don't understand that being a professional athlete is not all about victory and roses." Alex's mood darkened. "Nothing is ever a guarantee in sports."

Olive's heart thumped. She spoke softly. "The outside world only sees the end product—the wins and the gold medals. Few ever understand just how isolating and lonely the journey to reach that goal is. There are numerous sacrifices that have to be made."

"Exactly." He stared into space. "There are so many times over the last year I questioned if the surgery, rehabilitation, and grind to return to play was even worth it. I've never doubted myself more than I do now."

Olive reflected back to the self-assured man she had first met five days ago in the lobby of the hotel. The one who had talked her into sneaking into the Temple of Olympian Zeus and had driven her on a motorbike around the city.

The man in front of me now is different. He lacks the same confidence. He's more reserved. He's trusted me with a part of himself. It's time I return the favor.

"I have never shared this with anyone, even my own friends and family. They'd never understand. After my injury, I found myself crashing into a proverbial wall. It was one of the most trying periods of my life. I didn't want to get out of bed. All I could do was feel sorry for myself and ask why this was happening to me," Olive said.

A tear leaked down her cheek. She felt raw and vulnerable. "I didn't know what I would do if I couldn't continue to be the person I was before the injury. I saw myself as a failure."

Alex collapsed onto the closest bench. Olive slowly lowered herself next to him. He listened intently to her and held her hand, squeezing it for support. "Rehab was slow and painful. My body never recovered as it should've. My knee kept giving out. That's when the medical team realized my first graft had failed, and I required the second surgery."

Alex winced. His breathing slowed. He stroked her hand. "And how did you get through it?"

"My family pushed me to explore interests outside of gymnastics. They knew I was struggling, but they didn't know the extent." Her lips quivered. "I was grateful to find a wonderful sports psychologist. She taught me to see myself as a complete person not as just an athlete."

"That is the same process I am struggling with now." Alex let out a long breath and nodded slowly. "My sister, my cousins, and Drew have done so much for me, but the rest I have to do on my own. I can't disappoint any of them."

That's a lot of pressure for him to put himself under. But even if I told him that, as one athlete to another, we are a single-minded bunch. He's said before he doesn't accept assistance easily. I just hope he understands help is there for him when he hits his own wall and needs it.

Olive breathed deeply. "The best advice I have ever received is to only look forward and never backward. The past can never be changed, no matter how much we may wish it to. In my case, I had unfinished business to attend to. I did not want any 'what-ifs' hanging over my head. That drive is what ignited the fire in my belly." She stared out into the garden, then turned her focus back to Alex.

"You weren't just any gymnast. You were an Olympic-caliber athlete, weren't you?" Alex sputtered. He placed his hand on his forehead and shook his head.

"Once upon a time." Olive's lips twisted upward.

They sat in silence. He put a hand on her cheek. His eyes glimmered, and his Adam's apple bobbed up and down. "Thank you for sharing your story with me. I know I face a long, uphill journey over the next few months, and knowing what you were able to achieve sets my bar even higher."

Olive's early anger had simmered away. "If you need *any* friendly support, I'm here. There are no shortcuts to the top. The journey is going to include rough patches, but no matter what, every step will bring you closer to your end goal."

Alex appraised Olive. He met her half-grin. "I'd like that."

Pandora's fatal flaw was curiosity. Mine is fear. It's stopped me before. My instincts, in that instance, were spot on. This time, though, the fear is different. It's more of a fear of the unknown. Alex won't be like Sean. I can feel it deep within my bones.

Two female fans approached where they sat. Alex and Olive stood. From his pocket, Alex grabbed a black baseball hat, shoved it onto his head, and put his aviators back on his face.

She tilted her head. "You look more conspicuous with the sunglasses." Alex removed them. "Is there a reason you shaved and trimmed your hair?"

The women walked right past them and sat on the bench adjacent to where they stood.

"My Yiayia despises long hair and my goatee. If it were up to her, men would either keep a full beard or be clean-shaven, no in-betweens. I did this"—he pointed to his face—"to humor her."

Olive brushed Alex's cheek with her hand. His face was rough and bumpy. "It's a good look for you."

He chuckled.

They reentered the hotel lobby and were greeted by the warm air within. He moved a stray lock of hair from in front of her face to behind her shoulder. His voice grew hoarse. "I'm not good at saying goodbyes."

"Then don't." Through her lashes she stared up at him. "This doesn't have to be a goodbye. We have plans to see one another again in London."

"I know; it's just that's so far from now." Alex breathed in.

"It's only three weeks away." Olive licked her lips.

He took a step closer to her. She could feel the heat coming off of his body. "If I wasn't contractually obligated to make a media appearance at the Athens Masters opening ceremonies, I would spend the rest of the day with you."

The chocolate of his eyes almost melted her composure. "I wish you could too."

But for both of us, this might be a blessing in disguise; otherwise I might never be able to leave Greece.

She placed a hand on his chest. His heart was beating in time with hers. "Until we meet again then?"

Alex took hold of her hand and brought it to his lips, tickling the top of her skin like the butterfly drinking nectar from a flower. "Until we meet again." He slipped out of the lobby and into a waiting black unmarked car.

What are you doing to me Alex? I set rules for myself. I was never supposed to let myself grow close to another tennis player ever again. Now I'm on the verge of crossing that line.

CHAPTER 9

A Newfound Freedom

Olive kept her arms and small purse pinned to her sides. The aisles of the showroom were narrow. Shelves three-feet high displayed colorful glass jewelry, vases, and figurines for sale. The tour guide pointed to a display window and explained each step of the glass-making process. Olive pulled out her borrowed camera and filmed the ease with which the craftsman blew into a metal tube and shaped a lobe of iron red hot glass into an orb shape.

After shopping for a pair of earrings, she exited the glass shop. Rain splattered against the nylon fabric of her umbrella. She walked along the Grand Canal of Murano, an island twenty minutes by boat from Venice. The air smelled of salt and of fire. Bridges of varying shapes and heights connected the two sides of the waterway. She climbed the steps of the closest one and paused in the middle to snap a selfie.

Boats slowly motored past her. Buildings in this part of the island were painted shades of red, orange, or yellow. Each had its own private dock in front of the entryways. Couples walked nestled closely together under their own umbrellas. They laughed and were engrossed in one another. She pretended not to pay them any notice, yet it was almost impossible. Today was Valentine's Day.

If the encounter with Tessa five days ago has taught me anything, it's that I am not emotionally stunted. I do have feelings, and I'm tired of being alone. But just because I'm alone doesn't mean I have to settle. This time, I'm doing things the right way.

The rain grew heavier. A gust of wind caused her umbrella to flip upward. She climbed down the other side of the bridge and turned left, rushing under the awning of the closest shop. She wrestled with the fabric of the umbrella and struggled to close it. Droplets of water flew everywhere, soaking her. She wrinkled her nose. Part of its metal skeleton was exposed.

She caught a glimpse of her reflection in the window of the shop, a hair salon. She combed her hand through her limp locks. Valentine's Day wasn't just for those who were in a committed relationship. It was also a day for self-love.

Fear is not going to hold me back. Today is the day I follow through with actually cutting my hair. I've always second-guessed how it would make me look; having long hair was a safety blanket for me. It was a part of my identity being Hawaiian. Today, I'm finally ready to let loose. I'm doing this for new me and not because Tessa said anything.

She was in Italy, the fashion capital of the world. If she was going to change her hairstyle, this was the place to do so.

Olive shoved her broken umbrella into a plastic bag and entered the hair salon. A woman with jet-black hair cut in a chic A-line style greeted her at the receptionist desk. "Bonjorno senorina. May I help you?"

In broken Italian, Olive said, "Si. I'd like to have my hair cut, per favore."

The woman surveyed Olive's waist-length, tangled, wet hair. "A cut?"

Olive emphatically nodded. "Si." She pointed to her shoulders. "A cut. A big change. I want a new look for a new me."

"I will see what we can do. Uno memento, per favore." The receptionist disappeared into the room behind her.

The floors were made of hardwood. The walls a soft gray with two canvases depicting the famed Rialto Bridge at different times of the day. Black leather chairs and a tall indoor shrub filled the remainder of the waiting area space. Through the open door leading to the back, Olive could see matching black leather chairs in front of floor-length mirrors with gold frames. One client sat, chatting with a stylist.

Olive sunk into one of the chairs. She picked up an issue of *Vogue Italia* and combed through the pages, paying particular attention to the models in the high-fashion advertisements. Bubbles of excitement came through. *Maybe I should go really short. I could add highlights or do layers.* There were endless possibilities.

The clicking of stiletto heels against the wooden floors heralded the return of the receptionist. Olive hopped to her feet. A man with short-cropped, bleached-blond hair, wearing red trousers and a white dress shirt with three-quarter rolled-up sleeves, walked out. "Ciao. I am Tommaso." They shook hands. "Follow me, please."

Olive entered the back room and was seated in a soft, black chair. Tommaso draped a white cape over her clothing. "Giana said you wish for a 'big change'?" He spun Olive around, facing the mirror and set to work brushing and coming out her wet hair.

"Si. I've always had long hair. I've never had my hair professionally cut and styled. My ex-boyfriend tried to get me to cut my hair, but I backed out of cutting it shorter at the last minute. This time, I'm ready." *The old me would never have said anything to anyone.*

"You are already beautiful, but I will make you shine from

within. We will make your ex jealous." Tommaso worked slowly on a particularly difficult knot.

"Oh, we've been apart for three years and he's married now, but I appreciate the sentiment."

At the time Sean dumped me, I thought it was among the worst things to ever happen to me, but everything happens for a reason. I needed to discover who I was and to know that it's more than alright to be out on my own. I had to learn to fully love myself inside and out.

"Then we will style your hair so you can turn any man's head." His hands worked quickly. In less than twenty minutes he was ready to begin trimming. Olive wanted his skills with a brush and comb.

He parted her hair down the middle. "Your hair is long and thick. Split ends, but otherwise healthy. Do you have any special requests?" He placed his hands on his hips.

She spoke to the mirror. "Just make it shorter and add in some color. The rest I'll leave up to you. A blank canvas." After a moment, she added, "Well, maybe nothing too ostentatious, color wise. I'm going to a friend's wedding in a few weeks."

"I have an idea." Tommaso rubbed his hands together. He walked in a circle around the chair. "Andiamo. Which means, as we Italians say, let's go."

For two hours, Olive enjoyed chatting with Tommaso about what it had been like growing up in Rome and studying fashion in Milan. She learned that he created all of his own clothing. Hair styling came later as a means to complement his design skill set.

While her hair color set, he explained, "For your body shape, the goal is always to elongate the torso. Look for clothing that has a drop waist, vertical lines, and V-neck cuts. It is especially important your clothing fits you and isn't oversized."

"I suppose this T-shirt and jeans look isn't going to go with my new hair." Olive took notes on her phone.

"It most certainly can. All you have to do is make a few tweaks here and there to what you already own. So many people go out and buy entirely new wardrobes when there isn't a need for it. Accessories, like a belt, can make a bold statement." Tommaso led her over to the sink. He removed the foil with the hair dye and rinsed her hair.

"I'll never be able to get the hang of all this," she said.

Tommaso laughed. "At the end of the day, fashion is subjective. You wear the clothes; they never wear you. Being confident and feeling powerful in what you wear goes a long way. Make your own rules. It's what I do with my designs."

After drying her hair and trimming it to perfection over the course of another forty-five minutes, Tommaso lowered Olive's chair and removed her cape. "Bellisima." He winked to her. "You are all finished. Time for the big reveal." He turned her to face the mirror. "Uno, due, tre!"

Olive sucked in a breath. The woman who stared back at her had shoulder-length layers and wispy bangs. Her dark brown hair was chestnut color with blonde highlights. There were soft curls. Tommaso bent down to her level. "The color suits you. Brings out the brown in those hazel eyes."

"I look like an Italian model!" Olive whispered. She fingered a stray curl. "My hair *never* holds these."

Olive thanked him. She paid the bill and departed for the vaporetto stop to return to Venice. Bouncing with an extra spring in her step when she walked, she carried herself with a newfound freedom. She found herself transforming with each city she visited.

A transit driver shouted, "San Marco. This is the stop for the Piazza di San Marco."

The boat pulled into the dock. Seagulls cried out above her. The rain had stopped, though imposing dark clouds still lingered. She disembarked and meandered toward the row of gondolas rising and falling with the swell of the tide. The lighting was just perfect for a photo. She took a few moments to snap some selfies of herself rocking her new look.

Rows of gondoliers stood on the back of their sleek boats in striped shirts and wore straw hats. They awaited their turn to service the long queue of people waiting under a red and white striped wooden "gondole" sign to embark on a romantic ride through the city's canals.

Olive grimaced at the sign displaying the higher-than-normal prices for the day—one hundred Euros for thirty minutes before sunset and one hundred and sixty Euros after sunset.

I suppose everything is relative. That just seems extortionary. I do remember reading on a blog post that you can negotiate prices in some of the quieter areas off the Grand Canal.

"Isn't there any way you can pay to bypass all of these plebeians?" the shrill voice of Tessa McPherson complained. "I didn't come all the way to Venice to freeze my bum off and waste time waiting in line."

Olive's posture stiffened. She looked at the end of the queue toward the voice. It was the last couple on Earth she wanted to see. She was tempted to sadistically laugh. Was this a cosmic joke? Sean and Tessa were ten feet from her. She let out an exasperated sigh and stood behind a sign advertising a day cruise to the neighboring islands of Murano, Burano, and Torcello. She could see them, but they couldn't see her.

On Hydra, she had been in full-on shock at first encountering Sean's name. Today, their presence was more of a prickly thorn in her side. She counted to ten and exhaled. The muscles in her neck corded with tension. Her chest tightened.

The twenty-five-year-old, five-foot-ten Sean McPherson had a square jawline, brown hair, and brown eyes. His hair was styled in an undercut. He and Tessa spoke loudly.

"You *wanted* to squeeze in Venice to the itinerary. *I* offered you Paris," he sharply retorted. "I'm not paying extra for this dumb tourist trap. This trip is already costing enough. We flew here in first class and have a penthouse suite. If you want to bypass the queue, you can pay for it."

"Some honeymoon this is turning out to be. All we've done is wait, wait, wait." Tessa rolled her eyes. "I understand you're still angry, but you don't have to take out your humiliating first-round loss in Athens on me."

"The referees are biased against me. Besides, I had to listen to *you* complain over your loss in the second round of the tournament to an *unranked* player for the duration of our stay in Santorini." He grunted.

"You're wrong. You lost because you are fixated on the return of Georgiou. I am sick and tired of hearing your bellyaching. Move on. What did you expect from a player who is half-Greek and half-English? The crowd was going to love him either way." Tessa and Sean moved up two spots in line.

Tessa crossed her arms. "You have the winning record against him. He hasn't even played on the circuit in over a year. He'll never be as good as he was."

Sean's forehead creased. "He defeated me in the third round at the Australian Open in Melbourne. Then he had the gall to withdraw from play in the next round. It was my best shot at winning a major title." He clenched his fists. "If he had any class, he should've withdrawn before he played me and let me advance."

"That's your soddy excuse?" Tessa rolled her eyes. "You have a history of choking under pressure. You had the opportunity to win a Grand Slam title when you were up two sets to Georgiou in New York at the US Open. Yet here you stand, the first and only player to lose the final three sets of the Grand Slam final. You'll never win until you learn to conquer your own mental game."

"My mental game is fine!" Sean grumbled. "At least I've come close to a major title, unlike you."

"I make up for my lack of titles with endorsements. Shall I remind you who I have in my portfolio and in my network?" Tessa counted on her fingers. "Let's start with the companies that begin with the letter A—"

Olive had heard enough. How could a couple survive if they were constantly trying to one-up each other? A small part of her was happy they were struggling as a couple. Yet, the other half of her hated to see newlyweds, even if she wasn't on good terms with them, have a row with one another. She scratched the back of her neck and sauntered from her hiding spot past the queue in full sight of both Sean and Tessa. Neither one of them batted an eye in her direction.

So, Sean and Alex had a history of playing against one another. Were they rivals? Sean was only starting out on the pro circuit when he dumped her for Tessa. How long had Alex been a pro player? Her mother would be in the know, but for her sake, Mom rarely mentioned tennis in her presence.

Olive's footsteps carried her inside the Piazza di San Marco and past the towering red-bricked Campanile and Basilica di San Marco. She stopped and appraised the intricate carvings on the church's façade and gold mosaic paintings. She stared up at the copy of the four horses atop the roof brought to the city after the fall of Constantinople. The ground was covered in puddles, but that did not stop the square from being filled with hundreds of cooing pigeons.

Passing through to the back side of the basilica, Olive

trudged along until she found a quieter lantern-lit ally off the Grand Canal. Signs with arrows at each intersection read "per Rialto" pointing her toward the most famous bridge in the city. The delectable aroma of hot Italian food seasoned with oregano and garlic wafted by each time she passed an open doorway.

There was less foot traffic in this area of the city. She heard the water lapping up against the cement walkway and the chatter of two gondoliers. She started to climb over the connecting bridge when a gondolier in a red-and-white striped shirt said, "Senorina, would you like to take a gondola ride with me? I can offer you the best price."

She stopped in her tracks and pivoted. Her hands fidgeted. "Quanto costa?"

The gondolier tipped his cap to her. "Ah, the bellissima senorina speaks Italian? For you, seventy-five Euro for one hour."

She wrapped one of the loose curls around her finger. "That is *much* less expensive than the gondoliers are charging in San Marco."

The gondolier shrugged. "I am new to the profession. With your help, I will pay back the cost of my boat and begin to earn some Euros."

The second gondolier added, "We both started last week. Gondoliers own their own boats and, sadly, we are not given much opportunity to find customers. All new gondoliers are stationed in the quieter canals and have to earn their way to being placed in the more populated areas."

She stepped down the bridge and inched closer to the glossy lacquered black boat. "In that case, I *will* join you."

She patted her pocket and found the ten Euro note she had received in change earlier in the day from Tommaso. "This isn't much, but consider this my small investment in your future." She handed the note to the second gondolier.

He removed his hat and held it to his chest. "The senorina is too kind."

"I only wish it was more."

"Molto grazie." The gondolier kissed her hand.

The gondolier in the red-and-white-striped shirt watched the interaction. "That was very kind of you." He helped her to settle into the red leather seat. "My name is Luca. This afternoon, the canals of Venice are yours."

Similar to a headboard on a bed, a wooden backing, upholstered in red-and-yellow jacquard fabric, took up the entirety of the back of the boat. A gold lion adorned the front bow. Luca took his place behind Olive and stood on a matching red woven carpet.

Luca untied his boat and pushed off from the pier, waving goodbye to his friend. "We will commence with a trip through the quieter areas of Venice."

Goosebumps grew on her arm. From inside the boat, the water was a dark aqua color. Larger moving vessels gave the gondolas plenty of room to maneuver around them, leaving white water in their wake. Anyone could walk through Venice; it was another experience to float through the city.

"The senorina is alone today? On Valentine's Day of all days?"

Olive leaned back into the squishy seat of the boat. It was wider than she expected. Luca pointed to a white cashmere blanket. She draped it over her legs. The air was colder on the water. "I have friends, but I'm traveling on my own."

From the water as a vantage point, the world of hotels, cafes, and homes were larger and packed much tighter together. Lanterns that lined the sides of the canal walls began to softly glow with the setting sun.

"The senorina should call a friend then. Share the city of Venice with them," Luca urged. He turned the boat down a quieter canal. "Too much traffic on the Grand Canal. Now you hear the sounds of the city."

Olive closed her eyes; she heard the clinking of glass from those dining in restaurants above them. The buzzing of insects coming out in the twilight hours and the constant stroking of Luca's paddle making contact against the water. Olive sighed and opened her eyes. Who could she call who would appreciate this as much as her?

It was five in the evening in Venice. In Hawaii, it would only be six in the morning. Her mom might be awake, but she would be readying herself for work. She weighed the pros and cons of phoning Amanda or Clara. London was an hour behind Italy. *Clara will be in rehearsal. Amanda is just beginning her new semester of school.*

Her thoughts turned to Greece and her adventure with Alex, exploring the Greek capital on the back of his motorbike. She bit her lip. *I've wanted to call him all week. The new me is all about taking risks.* From her purse, Olive located her phone, unlocked the screen, and tapped the number next to Alex's name. It rang three, four, then five times.

Alex answered in a groggy voice. "Hi, Olive. Funny you should ring me now." He yawned. "I'm just waking up from my power nap. How are your travels going?"

She rested her chin on her hand. "Hi, Alex. They're... er... good. I've been surrounding myself with culture."

Luca chose that moment to begin boisterously singing.

"Just where are you? The man in the background has an excellent tenor voice."

"I'm in Venice. On a gondola." Olive pulled the blanket up to her shoulders.

"In that case, let's do a video chat. No one should be on a gondola in Venice alone."

"How did you know I was alone?" Olive blinked slowly.

"You just confirmed it."

Olive tapped the camera button on her phone screen. Alex's face appeared a moment later. He looked as tired as he sounded. She took a moment to see stubble covering his face, and small purple bags and fine lines under his eyes. "Olive, your hair." Alex tripped over his words. "It was beautiful before, but now. Wow." He wolf-whistled.

She let her locks bounce in front of her and upturned her lips. "I'm glad you approve. I can't get over how light my head feels now compared to how it used to be."

"Is that the tenor singer?" Olive flipped the camera up to Luca who tipped his cap to him. "Welcome, signor, to Venice."

"Grazie," Alex responded. Olive pushed the button on the camera. "I have to say, I'm jealous. I've visited Italy before, but I've never really taken the time to explore and appreciate Venice." He cleared his throat. "Not that I don't enjoy seeing your lovely face, but may I see what you are seeing? That way it will be as if I am almost sitting beside you."

Her cheeks warmed. Olive flipped the video. "Of, course."

CHAPTER 10

That's Amore

Alex's face lit up like a child on Christmas Day. "This is brilliant. I wish I had my DSLR handy to capture the city." His soothing voice relaxed her. Her hands quivered. She hoped the shaking video could be passed off as a result of the watercraft's unsteadiness.

The boat floated down a narrow alley. The red-brick buildings were not as well maintained and colorful as on the Grand Canal. Paint and plaster chipped off the walls. Black shutters framed the windows. A stray tree branch extended over the water. Luca ducked his head. To Olive, it was strange to see the doorways at the level of the water. The stern of a lone, empty white boat tapped against the building, tied to a wooden pier.

"I can't believe you've never taken a gondola ride before. As a world traveler, I just assumed you'd take advantage of each and every unique opportunity." Her voice rose in surprise.

"There are many places I've passed through, but I've rarely ever stopped to enjoy my surroundings. Until I was hurt, I lived out of my suitcase and shuffled from hotel to hotel.

Travel was just a part of the profession. My sole focus was on practice and winning matches." The gondola passed under a bridge. Pedestrians stood above, waving at the passing boat. "Recently, I've come to question and reevaluate my priorities in life."

"Does this have anything to do with why you looked like a zombie when you first answered the phone?"

He let out a frustrated breath and ran a hand through his hair. "I've been having a rough go at it since coming home to London. I don't take kindly to having my gym workouts short and regimented. I have little enough control of my life already."

"And who did you vent your frustrations on?" Olive guessed.

Alex grumbled, "This time, it was my sister, Penny. To make it even worse, she's letting me get away with my soddy behavior. It's very out of character for her." She heard him moving items about the room. "We can talk about this later. I don't want to ruin your gondola experience."

The boat suddenly lurched. Olive dropped her phone and gripped the sides of the vessel Her breathing intensified.

"You two alright? I can hear you, but all I can make out is the white of your blanket."

"Fine." Olive splayed a hand on her chest. "Luca has everything under control."

Luca apologized and kicked off a cement wall with his foot to turn the watercraft around and out of a dead end. "Si. It won't happen again. I just forgot where we were for a moment." He put his arm muscles into stroking forward.

"It's fine, Luca." Olive slid back into her seat. She inhaled through her nose to slow her racing pulse. "Balancing on a moving boat *and* rowing takes a tremendous amount of skill. You make it look easy."

Luca blushed. "All practice." He kept his focus on the canal.

Olive picked up her phone. She explained to Alex that it was Luca's first few days as a gondolier. His frown lines disappeared. He reclined into his sofa. They settled back into a cozy rhythm. Luca's confidence seemingly returned as he chose to hum the melody of a Puccini operetta.

The canal widened. A red and black sign posted on the overhead bridge gave the height at two-point-two meters. The upper levels of the buildings here were painted in reds, yellows, oranges, and green. Window boxes held red flowering plants.

"Until the minor incident back there, how has your day been today?" Alex inquired.

"It was jam-packed. I took the vaporetto this morning to the glass island of Murano. I'd hoped to make my way to the other islands in Venice's lagoon—Burano and Torcello—today, too, but it started to rain." Olive hesitated. "When I was returning from Murano, I ran into a mutual acquaintance of ours."

Alex raised an eyebrow. "And just who might that be?"

Olive lowered her voice. "Sean McPherson."

He crinkled his nose. "There are many names I have for *that* man." Alex's voice tightened. "He isn't the type of person I would have ever pictured you associating with."

"I learned *that* lesson the hard way." Olive resisted the urge to face-palm.

Alex stood and paced. "McPherson is notorious for his foul language, angry outbursts, and general unsportsmanlike conduct. He's made quite a few enemies among the chair umpires in tennis." He shook his head. "Just this last week he was ejected and given an automatic loss from his first-round match in Athens after two code violations."

"He has a frail ego and always has to have the last word," Olive added.

Alex sat on the edge of his seat and rested his elbows on his knees. "Indeed. We've been rivals since our junior years. Just how do you know him?"

"Like me, he's from Hawaii. We share a complicated past." Olive wasn't yet ready to volunteer more than that. Being in a gondola with Alex was about enjoying the moment and not sullying her experience with memories of Sean. She was annoyed at herself for having mentioned his name in the first place.

The sky was a mixture of purple, blue, and orange as it had been the night they had hiked Areopagus Hill in Greece. Luca steered them onto one of the most famous expanses of the Grand Canal. The imposing white stone of the Rialto Bridge was sprawling with tourists each jockeying for an ideal spot on one of the twos railings of the bridge. They held out long selfie sticks and some even had large cameras looped around their necks.

Alex let out a long whistle. "Rialto Bridge."

Inside its noble archways, stalls sold souvenirs and snacks. High-cost restaurants capped the northern and southern edges of the bridge. Olive smelled fresh pizza. Vendors stood outside yelling in Italian and English over one another about their dinner specials.

Luca stopped rowing. "Would you care for your photo to be taken, senorina?"

Olive whipped out her camera and passed it along to Luca. "Please." On her phone, she changed the back-facing camera to the front-facing camera. "Alex, you have to be in this one too."

"On the count of three, say 'that's amore.'" Luca clasped the camera and relaxed his grip on the oar. Olive posed and held Alex's face on the camera to her side. "Perfecto. Uno. Due. Tre."

Warmth rushed to her cheeks. The turn of the phrase was

not lost on her. Did Luca think they were a couple? Her throat was dry. Butterflies fluttered to escape the confines of her stomach. She squeaked out, "That's amore." Alex's voice never wavered.

Luca handed the camera back to Olive. She kept it out to snap a few more photos. The gondola lingered under the bridge. The water here was a dark navy. A delivery boat laden with packages motored past.

"If you could text me a copy of the photo, I'd appreciate it. The perfect memento from our gondola ride."

Olive folded the white blanket. "Of course."

The gondola returned to where they had started their journey. Luca tossed the rope to his friend and jumped onto the pier to secure it. She set her phone down. "Luca. Thank you for an incredible ride through Venice. It was surreal." She stood and reached into her purse.

"The senorina does not pay tonight." He tucked the money back into her hands. "You and your friend have a special connection. I was honored to be a part of your Valentine's Day."

"Luca, I insist." She shoved a wad of bills into Luca's hand. "I want you to be able to pay off the cost of your boat."

He passed the roll back to her. "Luca," Olive's voice warned.

From the phone, Alex said, "Please, accept the payment. Olive will not walk away unless you agree to her terms."

Olive emphatically nodded. "What he said."

"Are you Americans always so persistent?" Luca tucked the money into his trouser pocket.

She picked up her phone and was assisted out of the gondola. "We do have that reputation for a reason."

Luca removed his hat. "Grazie." He kissed her hand. She was left breathless. At this rate, her face would be forever a rosy red, like the color of a rich, red wine.

Alex cleared his throat. Olive held the phone up to see Alex steepling his fingers against the countertop of an expansive white quartz kitchen island, his jaw tense. "Seeing as you invited me along for the gondola ride, I'd like to have dinner with you."

Olive's jaw dropped. "Din… din… dinner?"

Alex crossed his arms. "Unless you would prefer to have a Valentine's Day meal on your own."

Luca chuckled. "The senorina should nod."

Olive's gaze traveled from Luca and back to her phone screen. Her head bobbed up and down.

"Grazie, Luca." Alex grinned. "If I might trouble you to direct her to the restaurant called The Hidden Glen, I'm certain it's within walking distance of the Piazza San Marco."

Luca's eyes widened. "Ah, the Hidden Glen. Si. It is a five-minute walk from here. But it's tricky to get a reservation."

"It shouldn't be a problem." Alex blinked slowly. "My brother-in-law is the owner."

Luca laughed. "I will lead you there myself."

"Oh no. I couldn't ask that of you." Olive held up her hand. "I can find it."

"Let me return your kindness, senorina." Luca's large green eyes pleaded with her.

She let out a breath. Luca promised it was no trouble. He asked his friend to keep an eye on his gondola and led Olive and Alex through the lantern-lit maze of narrow turns to The Hidden Glen.

Olive climbed the last set of remaining stairs. Her leg muscles quaked from overexertion. She placed her hands behind her head, deeply moving air in and out of her lungs. "Next time, I take the elevator."

Alex's voice carried a hint of amusement. "I promise the view will be worth the reward. Many of the older buildings in Venice can't accommodate a modern-day lift. Drew never saw the need to add one to this building."

From the inside pocket of her purse, she pulled out her phone. "I would have been happy to eat a hot dog you know."

"A hot dog?" Alex grimaced. He puffed out his chest. "Italy has so many unique dining options to offer. If you are here to truly have a sampling of European culture, food is a vital part of the experience."

"I was only joking. Never a hot dog in Venice. Pizza, maybe." Olive let out a wheezing laugh. The dim enclosed stairway gave way to an open terrace. Strings of paper lantern lights flickered overhead. Potted red flowers and a smattering of small shrubs created a garden-like effect.

"Let the seating host know you are here with the Russo party. They will take it from there." Despite being confused by Alex's cryptic instructions, she walked up to the host and gave the last name Russo.

The seating host perked. "Please follow me. Your table is ready."

She passed the crowded dining room and was shown to a private, outdoor seating area in the back. "Wow." She spun around in a circle, soaking in the atmosphere.

Surrounding their repurposed wine barrel table, LED mood lights were entwined with hanging plants. Every ten seconds, they changed colors. In the center of the room, a water feature flowed into a small pond holding orange, white, and red koi fish. Olive's gaze, however, was taken by the view.

Below the restaurant, the entire city of Venice stood aglow with shimmering evening lights. The trees at the piazza below gave off the appearance of the city being in the midst of a forest. Boats floated along the inky canals like small fire-flies. Olive lowered herself into a wicker chair, placed her phone on the table, and balanced it upright with the pop-socket ring.

"The chef will prepare any items you desire. Please press the button on the table when you are ready with your order. Here is our wine list." The host offered Olive a maroon leather-bound compendium of choices. "Will there be anything else you require?"

"I will assist the senorina from here. Grazie," Alex's said.

The host nodded and left her alone.

"I've never been on a virtual dinner date before." Alex rubbed his hand behind his neck. "I hope you don't mind my taking charge of dinner. I didn't want to lose the opportunity."

"No, this is perfect. Although, this is the fanciest place I have ever dined," Olive admitted. "At home, dining is much more casual."

Alex wolfishly smirked through her phone. "Is this a fair compromise to your hot dog plans?"

"It is so much better," she gushed.

"I'd recommend the chef's special. It's always a local dish and has yet to disappoint me," Alex said.

"Seeing as there is no food and only wine on this menu, I'll just have to trust you." Olive pressed the call button. A waiter appeared within three minutes. She placed her order.

"This is actually our second meal together if you don't count dinner with Leo. I have to say, I like dinner more without his annoying chatter," Alex joked.

"*I* enjoyed his company." The waiter returned with a small basket of fresh bread. "Not to mention, he was pretty important in saving our skins." She helped herself to a piece. It was soft and crispy and melted in her mouth.

"Alright, I'll give Leo his due. As for the food, you can thank Drew, my sister Penny's husband, for that. He's the Italian-born foodie. If he didn't play tennis, he'd be a chef." He scratched his chin.

"Huh. Go figure." She took hold of her wine glass and swirled around the red Chianti wine.

"This place is Drew's baby. In the off-season, he devotes a good amount of his time planning menus, finding wines, and the like." A doorbell rang in the background. "One moment. My own dinner has arrived."

She drank deeply from her wine glass. *Tennis. Tennis. Tennis. I am a human magnet for the sport. As Amanda might say, it's a small world after all.*

Her main dish arrived. The waiter rolled up a cart and carefully placed the steaming hot entrée on the table. The cover was pulled off to reveal a pasta dish—bigoli in salsa. Alex padded back into the phone screen.

"And what are you enjoying tonight?" Olive asked.

He held open a white takeout container for her to see. "Grilled chicken, broccoli, and some other mixture of veggies." Placing the box on the kitchen island's counter, he rifled through the brown paper bag in search of cutlery. "Wish it was a nice juicy steak and chips. On Adala's orders, I am on a clean-eating meal plan."

Olive placed a napkin on her lap and pulled out her own utensils. "And who is Adala?"

Alex glanced up. "Adala is Adala Messer, the new coach my sister and I hired. She had me meet with her nutritionist earlier this week. It was eye-opening to find out just how many nutrients were missing from my diet. I've learned a lot about how it can impact how my body is able to recover after a session on the court or a workout at the gym."

Olive tilted her head to the side. "Clean eating. I remember it oh so well. Consider it a means to fuel your body. That's what I used to tell myself." She rolled some pasta onto her fork. "Messer. That name is on the tip of my tongue."

"She's the one-time world's number five player and two-time Australian Open champ. Played for Switzerland and retired a handful of years ago." Alex poured himself a glass of water. "I thought a female coach might help bring new insight into my game. Adala has an especially keen eye for tactics."

Olive snapped her finger. "I met her at the Paris Olympic Games eight years ago. Aggressive player but really friendly. My mom was over-the-moon excited to meet her. We went to her bronze medal match."

Alex rubbed the back of his neck. "I forget you are a highly-accomplished athlete in your own right."

Olive grinned. "I'm retired, remember. Though I still coach from time to time. I'm a self-employed consultant for college-bound athletes nowadays."

"Impressive. I wasn't aware there was an entrepreneur in our midst." Alex began cutting his chicken. "What led you down that career path?"

She took a bite of her pasta and chewed slowly, savoring the rich flavor. "When I was sixteen, I was tasked with the decision to either retain my amateur status so I could compete in college gymnastics or turn professional. There were numerous lucrative offers out there, but my dream had always been to compete on a college team."

"Which pathway did you choose?" Alex asked.

"My parents and I decided I should stay amateur. The value of the scholarship outweighed any endorsements." She swallowed hard. "It ended up being the right call. I didn't make the Olympic team on my first try, and later that summer I hurt my knee. All the pre-Olympic business offers dried up. Nobody wanted a broken alternate."

She drank deeply from her wine. "I was grateful that the University of Washington was the sole school that continually checked in on my recovery progress. They never withdrew their scholarship offer."

"I will never understand why gymnasts can't have it both ways." Alex frowned.

"It's one of the major reasons I started my business. I wanted to offer others the help and assistance I never had to decide what might be in their best interests. Be it turning pro or finding scholarship programs out there for those who want it," Olive said.

Her time in college had been so special and important in shaping who she was. *Without my time in Seattle, I would have struggled even more to learn how to transition from athlete life to a normal life. Nor would I have met Clara or Amanda.*

Alex shook his head. "I cannot think of a more perfect profession for you." He smiled. A true smile that reached his eyes and brought a warm, fuzzy, tingling sensation to her chest. "I should hire you as my next manager. My sister is my manager now, but after this season, she will be settling down with my new niece or nephew on the way."

Olive held up her glass to toast him. "Congratulations are in order, then."

Alex raised his water glass to her. He drank from it and placed it back on the counter next to his now-empty takeout container. "You'll meet Penny when you arrive in London."

"Looking forward to it."

She cleared her own plate and removed her napkin from her lap. "That was one delicious meal."

"Wait until you see the dessert menu," Alex teased. They sat in silence for a moment. He moved about the kitchen and rifled through the cabinets in search of his tea kettle. He filled it with water and placed it on the stove top to boil. Retaking his seat, he cleared his throat. "So, why is an amazing woman like yourself alone on Valentine's Day?"

Heat rushed to her cheeks. *He thinks I'm amazing?* She played with one of the loose curls that was nearly straight. She crossed her legs.

"Olive?" Alex lowered his voice. "Forget I asked. Too personal."

I opened the proverbial Pandora's box earlier.

"No. It's fine. My closest friends already know the entire story." She closed her eyes and took a deep breath. "I count you as a friend now too." She sat taller and examined the concerned form of Alex, his hands folded on the kitchen island. "My last relationship was with Sean McPherson, and it was a walking disaster."

"McPherson?" The tea kettle whistled in the background. Alex's jaw clenched, and the vein in his neck bulged. "You and McPherson?" he repeated.

The volume of the kettle rose. Alex continued to stare in shock. "Are you going to get that before it burns your apartment down?" Olive said.

Alex yelped and rushed over to the stove to turn down the temperature on the stainless-steel range. He poured the hot water into a pot and shoved a tea ball of tea leaves into the teapot. She could hear him mutter under his breath. She couldn't fathom why Alex was reacting so, just from hearing Sean's name. *Is there more going on in their rivalry than meets the eye?*

Alex poured himself a cuppa and sat, grasping the cup firmly. "I won't press you for the details, but he emotionally hurt you?" His voice growled.

Olive nodded. "He did."

"When I next face him on the tennis court, victory is going to be oh so sweet." Alex gritted his teeth. He placed his cup down, picked up the phone, and stared directly into the camera. "If McPherson ever bothers you again, you let me know. But more than that, I—"

As the words left his mouth, the screen faded to black. The mobile device was hot in her hands. *Of all times for the battery to die, of course it has to be now. What had Alex been about to say?* She pushed the now useless device aside and stood.

Her stomach muscles clenched. She rubbed her eyes. Did he feel the same pull toward her that she did toward him? It was as if a magnetic field was pulling two opposite entities together. She wanted to call Alex back immediately, but having time and space to process all of the information was equally important to her. She was forever looking ahead to the future. Where did Alex fit in? Her heart was in a dangerous place. She was starting to fall for him.

CHAPTER 11

Mr. Gorgeous

"Senorina, the meal is taken care of as instructed by Mr. Russo. Please enjoy the rest of the evening." The waiter thanked Olive for her patronage. She slid her card holder back into her purse and readjusted the black, camera-sized handbag. She exited the Hidden Glen and descended the six flights of stairs down to the bottom of the building.

She rubbed her arms against the chill of the evening. The nylon fabric of her jacket made a swooshing sound. The bells of the campanile rang out nine times. She advanced past a queue of patrons waiting to enjoy a late-evening dining experience. The scene was repeated at the numerous restaurants she passed. Dinner in Italy oftentimes did not even commence until eight in the evening.

She wandered through the tangle of back lanes of the ancient city, not yet ready to return to her hotel. Crossing bridges, she observed gondolas silently gliding underfoot. Without the hordes of daytime tourists, Venice was an incredibly intimate place. The peeling plaster from the buildings was illuminated by the moonlight. There were no cars or other ambient noises, only the silent lapping of water, the distant mummer of people, and Olive's footsteps echoing against the stone walkways.

In a deserted piazza, the sounds of a violin and cello caught her attention. She walked under a white marble archway into a building and through a set of open wooden doors. An audience of thirty people listened intently to a string quartet. She took her seat on a wooden bench covered in merlot-colored fabric in one of the back rows.

Gold-gilded glass chandeliers flickered overhead. The green walls were adorned with fresco paintings. The floors, constructed of white marble, matched the building's exterior. A roaring fire behind the musicians heated the room and brought out a welcoming vibe. Snacks and wines sat atop a grand piano to her left. She recognized the notes of Vivaldi's *Spring* and tapped her hand on her knee in time with the music.

Her mind ran wild with thoughts of Alex sitting next to her in a gondola in the flesh. She could smell the bergamot and wooden scents of his cologne and see him dressed in a pale-green dress shirt, burgundy jumper, and jeans. His arm would wrap around her to protect her from the cold. His leg would subtly brush up against hers under the white cashmere blanket.

She would rest her head on his shoulder and listen to him marvel at their otherworldly surroundings. Luca's voice would draw them into one another. After gazing longingly into one another's eyes, they'd share their first *real* kiss. The music evoked lightness and joy, mirroring her mood.

She leaned back in her seat and returned to the present. How would tonight have ended if Alex had been physically present at dinner? Would he have given her a greedy, passionate kiss? Or more of a soft and tender one? She rubbed the nape of her neck where Alex had kissed her the second night they met. She had been so uncertain and wary of letting a complete and utter stranger get close to her. But within two weeks, everything had changed. He filled her waking thoughts and appeared in her dreams.

He had taken so much time out of his busy schedule, going well out of his way to spend time with her. Watching his interactions with Leo had endeared her to him. It was how she might have imagined siblings might treat one another if she had had one. What would his sister be like? The music ended. The audience clapped appreciatively in muted tones and conversed among one another, making a beeline for the refreshments.

At that moment, a wave of energy pulsated through her body. She couldn't wait any longer. She rushed back outside and into the night, somehow navigating her way to her hotel by way of two vaporetto to the Giudecca neighborhood of Venice. Tapping her key card against the lock, she all but sprinted into the room and hastened to the closet. From her luggage, she extracted her phone charger and plugged it into the wall.

Throwing herself back onto her bed, she lay on her back, staring at the wooden beams in the ceiling, willing her phone to return to life. Her pulse raced. Ten minutes passed. The screen of her phone lit up and asked for her pass code. She punched in the numbers and swiped to the phone icon. A voicemail notification, however, caught her attention. She tapped play.

"Good morning, Olive, or is it evening? Your dad and I hope you're having fun today. We look forward to reading your daily email recap later. I'm sorry to bother you, but we have some big news for you! Call us when you receive this message. There are so many details to discuss."

Her mom never called her unless it was *really* important.

She sat up. With shaking hands, she returned the call and waited for the familiar voice to answer. "Mom?"

"Hi, baby! I didn't think you would call us back so soon." Her mom spoke with a thick, Hawaiian pidgin accent.

"It's almost ten-thirty here, and pretty much everything closes in Venice by eleven." Olive shrugged. "What's the big news you have for me?" Her breathing intensified and her pulse quickened. She walked to the window and stared out at the black, inky water and floating wooden pier that belonged to the hotel.

"We have received an offer on the Kona condo from a seller and have decided to accept it." Her mom hesitated. "The only caveat is that as a part of the terms of the sale, the buyer wishes to move in as soon as possible. Your father and I have agreed to be fully moved out in three weeks' time."

Olive nearly dropped the phone. The initial shock of the words was only just beginning to take hold. Turning from the window, she shuddered. "You've already sold the condo? But I thought it just went on the market last week."

Her mother's voice softened. "It did. The market is hot right now. Our agent hosted an open house this past weekend. You wouldn't believe how many people attended. We received multiple offers, and all of them are well above what your dad and I expected."

Olive gulped. She was breathless. Words died in her throat. She shook her head, trying to make sense of it all. She paced the length of the room.

Her mom filled the silence. "I understand it's a shock, but it really is an unexpected windfall. An opportunity like this doesn't come around often. With the extra money, we'll be able to have so many more options on Maui, and maybe even a house."

Mom and Dad always found a way to let Olive do gymnastics even when times were tough. They invested so much into her. Gymnastics was an expensive sport. Even when Coach Paul offered Olive a scholarship to help offset training costs, there were leotards, travel, and so many other expenses. Owning a house would mean the world to them.

Her voice cracked. "I get it. I'm just having trouble knowing that I'll never see the condo again."

She had assumed the entire process of selling her parents' condo would be slow and buy her a few months. The Nakamura family had lived in Kona, Hawaii since she'd been born. With the exception of college, she'd never known another home. It was difficult to come to terms with moving on.

Her mother seemed to read her very thoughts despite being thousands of miles away. "A house is just four empty walls. A home is where the people you love live. The condo has been wonderful for the last thirty years." Her mother let out a deep breath. "It's difficult for us to say goodbye to it too, but your dad has been offered his dream job. You and I would be selfish to stand in his way. Besides, you'll always have a home with us, no matter what."

She sniffled and sank onto the bed. She knew what her mom was saying was true; the condo didn't truly mean anything without her parents. "I guess this means I'll be moving to Honolulu sooner than I thought."

Her eyes misted over. Her chest constricted. She was going to be moving out on her own for the first time in her life. When she'd finished her college gymnastics career, all she could picture was being close to home again. It was the single lifeline she still had to something that was so familiar. *If I wasn't a gymnast, who was I? I was just Olive.* Now, the lifeline had been cut.

"Don't worry about moving your things, baby. They can stay with us as long as you like, permanently even. There is no hurry for you to leave," her mother emphasized.

Olive rubbed the back of her neck. "I can talk to Clara and

Amanda about pulling out of the wedding; they would understand, given how fast you're having to move. I can be on-hand to help pack up or see to any last-minute tasks."

Her mother clicked her tongue. "No! I want you to enjoy your vacation and Clara's wedding. You are a bridesmaid. Remember, weddings are stressful. It is going to be your job to help calm Clara's nerves. So long as you don't mind me packing up your room and the office, you should stay in Europe as originally planned."

"Are you sure, Mom?" Olive asked.

"Positive." She heard her dad's muted voice in the background. "Your dad wanted me to remind you that should you have the chance to send any wines home, he'll pay for the shipping."

The words brought a ghost of a smile to her face. Her dad, a viticulturist, specialized in pineapple wines and sparkling wines, but nevertheless still appreciated wines from other regions of the world. He had a large collection of wine labels and was always seeking to add more to it.

"Tell him I will be sending a Merlot his direction. The one I had tonight with Alex had all these amazing flavors he'd appreciate," Olive said.

Both she and her mom collectively sucked in air. "Olive... who is Alex?"

She face-palmed. Her ears burned. "A friend I made in Greece."

"A male friend?" Her mom's voice insinuated.

Why was she being so shy? Her mom was a person she could normally tell anything to. Her best and oldest friend. She had already mentioned him to Amanda. Why was this time any different? Was it because she was afraid of what her mom's reaction might be?

She clenched her jaw. "Yes."

Olive could picture her mom's pouting expression from

holding herself back from saying anything more. "Just be careful. You know your own heart and mind, but as your mother, it's my prerogative to worry."

Alex's image sprang to the forefront of her mind. It calmed her nerves. "He's a person you may have heard of actually. His full name is Alexander Georgiou."

I want Mom's approval on this. It may be silly, but after her vehement disapproval of Sean, I want to start things off on the right foot.

Her mom gasped like a teenage girl. "Mr. Gorgeous?"

Olive sat up ramrod straight. "Alex is your Mr. Gorgeous?" Had she a moment to glance in the mirror, her entire body would be beet red.

Her mom had pet nicknames for many of her favorite tennis players. Over the years, Olive had lost track of them all. There was one player, however, who had a special place of honor reserved in her mom's heart, and that was Mr. Gorgeous.

Dad is never going to let me hear the end of this once he finds out.

"He most certainly is! And if he is around, don't waste your time speaking to me. Go on and spend time with him. If I were twenty years younger—"

"Gah. I don't want to hear that!" Olive momentarily pulled the phone away from her ear. She heard her dad laughing in the background.

"We're all allowed to have our own celebrity crushes," her mom gushed.

"Mom, be serious." She stood again and sighed. "My phone died at the end of our virtual dinner together. I *was* going to call him back, but then I needed time to think."

"What is there to think about? Call him back now."

Olive snorted. "Who is being the adult here?"

"Touché, mon cheri." Her mom laughed. Olive pinched

the bridge of her nose. "Do you know why Mr. Gorgeous is my favorite player?"

She'd never thought to ask.

"Alexander was one of the players I was assigned to look after when I volunteered on the Honolulu Open Hospitality Committee four years ago. Do you recall the player who sent me an autographed program, chocolates, and a big bouquet of flowers as a thank-you? That was him! The man is a stand up gentleman."

I was blinded by how fast my relationship with Sean was spiraling out of control. By that point, all we did was fight. How did I ever last with him two full years?

"Mom, who did Alex play in the finals that year?" There was a prickling sensation on the back of her neck. She gripped her phone tighter and paced the room.

Her mom's tone sobered. "Alex played Sean in the final. Sean lost in straight sets."

A light bulb went off in Olive's mind. That was her watershed moment. *This was the match that Sean erupted over. He was supposed to meet my parents and instead was abysmally rude and scary angry.* She closed her eyes. *I have Alex to thank for my being able to begin to question why I was even in a relationship with Sean.*

Olive shared a watered-down version of how she met Alex and her adventures with him to the present. She sat on the floor and leaned against the bed. "Do you think that our friendship might develop into something stronger?" Her stomach fluttered with butterflies.

"Olive, you've always been a woman who has been certain of what she wanted. You never let anything stand in your way, regardless of what life throws at you. It's that drive and determination that have made you so successful in any task you try your hand at. From everything you've told me, it's clear that Alex is a person you already hold in high esteem. Whatever I say won't make a difference. In the end, it's what you think."

Olive held her breath. "That's not what I asked you."

"You always have my blessing. So long as you're happy, that is all that matters to your dad and me." Her mom chuckled. "With Sean, you lost your spark and the light inside that made you, you."

Olive wanted to hug her mom tightly. Those were the exact words she needed to hear. "I love you, Mom."

"I love you too." Her mom disconnected the call.

Olive wasted no time and immediately dialed Alex's number. It rang and rang, and finally went to voicemail.

"Hi, Alex. It's Olive. Sorry about earlier. My phone died at dinner. Meanwhile, I had to return a call to my mom. Tomorrow, I leave for Salzburg. My intent was to stay at the Hotel Elefant for five days, but I think London is calling me. I can't wait an entire week to see you. Tell me, should I come to London early?" Her hands shook. "My phone is on and charging if you want to talk. Um... otherwise, have a good night."

She quickly touched the red icon, jumped onto the bed, and set the phone next to her. She slid under the covers and pulled them over her head, still fully dressed. A giddy teenager all over again. The deed was done. The ball was now in Alex's court.

CHAPTER 12

A Few of My Favorite Things

The steady click-clack of the train's wheels making contact with the trackway hypnotized Olive. Her hazel eyes gazed out the window. A fresh white blanket of snow coated the majestic, dark hunter-green pine trees of the forest. In late February, the weather in the Alps could be unpredictable. Inside the cozy train compartment, every square inch of space was occupied by ski enthusiasts. They chatted softly amongst themselves in German.

Thank goodness I made a seat reservation when I booked the ticket to Salzburg.

The train began to decelerate. The conductor announced the imminent arrival at Salzburg Hauptbahnhof, the main train station of Austria's fourth-largest city. Few passengers made any movements from their present locations for the doors. Slipping on her gray puffer jacket, Olive reached for the teal backpack beneath her seat and tapped her seatmate on the shoulder. A boy of perhaps ten years old wearing a Munich football jersey pulled out an earbud and shifted his attention away from his tablet.

Olive pointed to herself and said, "Salzburg." The boy

stared blankly at her. His head inclined to the woman watching the exchange from the aisleway. She chuckled and explained to the boy, "Sie steigt aus dem zug." Olive assumed this translated to *she is getting off the train.*

The boy lifted the tray table, held onto his tablet, and pulled his legs up onto the seat for Olive to pass by. "Danke." Olive thanked him. The woman gratefully slid into the vacated seat.

A few minutes later, she breathed a deep sigh of relief. She had *just* made it onto the platform as the train's doors beeped, closed, and subsequently departed the station. Small flecks of snow fell from the sky. She still was not used to the novelty of shorter hair. She was becoming more adept with a curling iron. Her curls, still intact from this morning, bounced as she walked with care to avoid slipping on one of several patches of ice that lingered on the pathway. Around her, passengers rushed about.

Entering the station, she rubbed her hands together and glanced around the bright and modern station. Large screens displayed arriving and departing trains, times, and platforms. She spied several restaurants and shops offering magazines and souvenirs for sale. From inside the outer pocket of her backpack, she checked her phone. There was still no message from Alex.

The clock in the station chimed six times. Olive pulled herself out of her musings. She picked up her luggage and strolled outside to the station's taxi stand. The snow had subsided and revealed a royal blue sky. The first stars of the evening twinkled overhead above the snow-dusted Slate Alps. There was a lingering scent of salt and mud in the air. She pulled her coat tighter around her body.

Forget dinner. What she really wanted, now that she was in Austria, was a fresh, hot apple strudel. She pictured her reward for a long, ten-hour day of travel and salivated, envisioning the sweet glaze on the pastry melting into its crispy edges. She could taste the pieces of warm apple and the semi-sweetness of the dessert on her lips.

Spotting a line of bright yellow taxis, Olive strolled over to the closest one. "Gutan Abend. I am trying to get to the Old Town to this hotel." Olive showed the driver the address on her phone.

"Ja. I know it. It is a ten-minute journey. May I take your luggage?"

Olive slid her backpack off her shoulder and placed it atop her rolling bag. "Danke." Handing her luggage over to the driver, Olive slid into the car. The short jaunt from the train station to the historic city center of Salzburg gave her the impression that she had stepped back in time.

The taxi left the modern streets behind and entered the historic quarter of the city. She spied cobblestone streets, sprawling steeple towers, and a fortress rising above the seven-hundred-plus-years-old hotels and museums. The bells of the Salzburg Cathedral rang out.

"This is as far as I can take you, miss." Her driver stepped out of the car and retrieved her belongings from the trunk. They were just outside the gates to the Old Town. "The rest of the streets are solely for pedestrians. But your hotel is just one lane over there."

"Danke," she said and passed the driver a ten Euro note. "Keep the change." He thanked her and drove away.

Olive's luggage noisily rolled along the cobblestones. She passed under the medieval gate and straightaway found herself gazing up at the yellow façade of Mozart's birthplace. She continued down the alley the driver had pointed out to her. The soft glimmer of red lanterns illuminated her pathway. She spotted the black and gold wrought iron sign of the Hotel Elefant. Laughter and the clinking of glasses rang out from the pub on the ground floor. She ascended the three steps into the lobby.

A woman with chestnut-colored hair pulled into a low ponytail was checking in at the front desk. "I just don't understand. I have the hotel reservation here." She frantically spread out a series of papers from a plastic sheet protector onto the front desk. "See. I have the confirmation number and the receipt for the credit card charge."

The front desk agent, a woman in her mid-twenties with shoulder-length auburn hair and tortoise shell glasses, cleared her throat. "I'm sorry. I can see the reservation was made three days ago, but the problem is not on our end. It was canceled by the third-party site you booked through. You'll have to call their customer service line to sort out everything. In the meantime, unfortunately, we have no more rooms remaining. But I'd be happy to recommend another location for you."

The woman with chestnut hair placed both hands on the desk and leaned forward. Her voice was full of desperation. "I don't have enough money to book another room. My only extra money is allocated to my meals and tour tickets! I lost my job before I left home to backpack through Europe."

Olive's heart lurched. She couldn't watch the scene play out any longer. "Maybe I can help. The lady can have my room. I can find another location."

The front desk agent and the frantic woman both stared open-mouthed at Olive.

Olive approached the desk and set her luggage down. She handed over her passport to the woman at the front desk. "The reservation is under Nakamura."

Upon closer inspection, the woman with chestnut hair was also in her early twenties. She had on a black wool beanie, black belted puffer coat, jeans, and knee-high boots. She stood five-foot, six-inches tall and had gray-green eyes with gold flecks. The woman wrapped her arms around Olive and squeezed tightly, smelling of fresh pears.

"Thank you so much. You have no idea how much this means to me. I have every single penny accounted for until June." Olive tapped the woman's arms. She immediately released Olive and blushed. "Sometimes I forget my own strength. Sorry." She spoke with a Texan drawl.

"I'm Olive Nakamura. Are you from Dallas?"

They shook hands. "Sabrina Hill, and close, I'm originally from Waco."

The front desk agent passed back Olive's passport. "Miss Nakamura, we have you booked in one of our suites. I processed the upgrade this morning, myself."

Olive sputtered. "Upgrade? I thought my reservation was for a single room."

The front desk agent opened a desk drawer. "This card was left for you. I believe it should explain everything."

Olive grasped hold of the ivory white envelope. Her name was written on the front in swirly calligraphy. Turning it over, she broke the gold sticker seal and slid open the card. The thick cardstock held a handwritten message.

Dear Olive,

Surprise. Your room has been upgraded to the best room the Hotel Elefant boasts. Ring me when you check-in. Just as with Venice, I've never really explored Salzburg. As tempting as it is for you to fly to London early, I don't want you to cut your Austrian adventure short. If you are amenable to it, I'd love to spend a day seeing all of Salzburg's sights with you this week. You tell me the day, and I'll be on the first flight out to meet with you. Your friendship with me is special. Let's talk.

Cheers, Alex

Olive grew dizzy. "Oh, Alex," she whispered and clutched

the letter to her chest. Her attention turned to Sabrina. She selfishly wished she could take back her earlier offer.

Alex will understand. I can't just toss somebody out in their moment of need. It's an unexpected surprise anyway.

"You still wish to give away your room to this woman?" The front desk agent furrowed her brow.

"I will."

"Ya'll just hold on one moment." Sabrina held up her hands. "Did your boyfriend change your room to a suite to surprise you?"

Olive's cheeks flushed. "He's just a friend—"

Sabrina cut her off. "Either way, I am not about to spoil your surprise. You were very kind to offer, and I'm so incredibly grateful." She picked up her purse. "I was just trying to avoid calling my mom or older sister to ask for more money, but this gal knows when it's time to tuck her tail between her legs and ask for help." Sabrina gathered her belongings and started for the door.

"No, Sabrina. Don't go. The suite has more than enough room for us to share it."

"Why are you being so kind to me? Aren't you worried you might not be able to trust me?"

"I'm all about paying it forward and a big believer in karma. What goes around comes around. I've been gifted a suite update. My gut instinct tells me to share it." Olive placed her hands on her hips. "Besides, where I'm from, hospitality and the spirit of aloha are so incredibly important. It's what we Hawaiians are known for."

Sabrina splayed her hand on her chest. "I'll never be able to thank you enough. You're a real lifesaver."

Olive finalized the details. The two women made their way up the wooden stairs to the top floor.

〜

Entering the suite, Olive walked to the windows and drew the burgundy drapes. Sabrina flicked on the light switch and tested out the hunter-green sectional sofa in the main living room area. Two side tables displaying cuts of fresh flowers sat on either side of the sectional sofa. "This is the perfect bed for the evening. Just throw me a blanket, and I'll be nice and cozy here," Sabrina said.

A gift basket containing snacks and a vase of pale pink roses sat atop a round glass coffee table. A large-screen television adorned the pale-yellow wall across from the sofa. Portraits of elephants decorated the other walls of the living room. A pair of French doors revealed a master bedroom with a king-sized bed, an ebony black fireplace, a matching dresser and side table, and a charcoal-gray wingback chair.

"Alex, you've really spoiled me this time," she whispered to the empty room. She quickly took out her phone and sent a text message to Alex.

Olive: *Just arrived in Salzburg. Talk about being surprised! You are the best. Thank you. Can I call you now?*

Three dots blinked on the screen.

Alex: *It was so hard to hold back from sending you any messages. Happy to hear you enjoyed it. I'm tied up now. Call me tomorrow, unless you want me to be there in the morning. For you, I can make it happen.*

Olive: *As much as I would love that, what would your new coach say?*

Alex: *Spoiling all my fun. Once an athlete, always an athlete. I have a rest day off in two days.*

Olive: *Duly noted. Let's plan to make it a date!*

Alex: *:)*

Returning to the living room, Olive found Sabrina sitting cross-legged on the couch. "You really did me a huge favor today. I'm only here for one night, and I wanted to make the most of my time. It's been a rotten last few weeks. Salzburg is one of the small treats I've allowed myself."

Olive sat down next to Sabrina. "Sometimes speaking about it with a friend helps. I've had my own share of rough patches. What happened?"

Sabrina took a strand of her hair and wrapped it around her finger. "Until recently, I was an admin assistant. The pay was decent, but the hours—" Sabrina shuddered. "It wasn't uncommon for me to work a twelve-hour day six days a week. My work consumed me."

Sabrina pulled her knees into her chest. "I had planned to take my first vacation in five years this June. It has been a lifelong ambition of mine to attend the annual Jane Austen Festival in Bath. When the tickets went on sale last month, I was so focused on making sure I added the right events to my shopping cart that I may have ignored all my incoming phone calls. Somehow, they were accidentally forwarded to my boss."

"You were let go because of Jane Austen?" Olive raised an eyebrow.

"When you put it like that, I suppose so." The two women giggled.

Olive rested her head on her hand. "We're all human. Mistakes can happen."

Sabrina shook her head. "Not when it comes to being an assistant to Mr. Graves. One mistake and that's it." She snapped her fingers. "You're done."

"It sounds like you're better off without working for this Mr. Graves." Olive opened the gift basket. "Maybe the takeaway from all of this is that you're meant to actually *enjoy* the work you do." Sabrina reached for the box of chocolates, untied the outer red ribbon, and carefully unwrapped the gold foil. "We better enjoy this box of truffles. Chocolate makes everything better."

"That's *exactly* how I feel. But my family hasn't quite

come around to the same idea." Sabrina reached for a square chocolate with a white stripe from the corner of the box.

Olive tilted her head to the side. "How so?"

"My mom and my sister were horrified when I said I was going to take off an indefinite amount of time to do something I've always wanted to do—attend the JA Festival and travel through Europe. I'm supposed to 'get my priorities straight.' My mom and I had a horrible fight. But I'm here now, and there isn't anything either of them can do to stop me."

"Good for you." Olive stood and reached for the bottle of champagne and two flutes. "Your family will come around in time. They love you and just want what's best." The cork made a satisfying pop and a thin layer of white foam formed at the top of the bottle.

Sabrina sighed. "That's what makes it all the more painful. This is the longest I've gone without speaking to my mom. But at the same time, I'm happier than I've ever been. For too long, I was trapped. Now that I've broken the vicious cycle, I feel so free."

"This deserves a toast." Olive poured out two glasses. "Self-care and mental health are so important. I'm on my own journey of self-discovery. So far, I've found that Europe could not be a better place to do so." Her eyes sparkled. Sabrina wondered just what had happened to Olive throughout her own travels.

Sabrina accepted the champagne flute from Olive. They raised their glasses to one another and clinked them together. Sabrina took a drink.

"If I can help it, I am never going back to Waco. I've decided to try my hand as a digital nomad. That way, I'll be able to travel and work from anywhere in the world. All I need is my laptop computer."

Olive sipped from her flute and considered Sabrina's

words. The bubbles floated from the bottom to the top of the glass and made a satisfying fizzing noise. "Digital nomad. Huh. That is something *I* should look into." She rejoined Sabrina on the sofa.

I've been struggling to figure out where I'm going to live and work. I've never considered working remotely. Sabrina is onto something.

Sabrina nodded. "I can show you the blog I've been reading that's really inspired me, if you'd like. It explains in detail everything you need to know about life on the road."

"I'd love to see it," Olive started. "If you don't mind me asking, what line of work are you planning on going into?"

Sabrina placed her glass down on the table. She walked over to her backpack and unzipped the largest compartment. "Mostly virtual assistant gigs for now. In the long run, I have only wanted to work for myself." She removed her space-gray, brick-like computer from the bag.

"Everyone has to start somewhere." Olive nodded. Sabrina sat on the floor, placed her laptop on the coffee table, and turned it on. "If anyone can do it, you can. All you need is the belief, the drive, and stubborn determination." Olive helped herself to another truffle.

Where did Alex find these? I've never had such rich flavors melt in my mouth. Chocolate, champagne. The man knows the way to my heart.

Sabrina typed in her password. "What do you do for work, Olive?"

"I own a small consulting business. I work with high school-aged kids who aspire to become college athletes." Olive's cheeks colored.

Sabrina's eyes widened. "That sounds amazing."

"It's very rewarding and has been going well the last year or so, but as I said earlier, getting started was tough. I made so many mistakes in the early stages of my business that, at times,

I wasn't certain it would ever get off the ground. But I stuck it out, and I'm grateful to have learned from those mistakes."

It has made me resilient. I can handle anything thrown my way.

Olive and Sabrina finished the box of chocolates and polished off the bottle of champagne.

"Have you been able to advertise and post your skills on any job boards?" Olive asked.

"Actually, I have." Sabrina grinned. "Now I just have to wait for some clients." Sabrina launched her internet browser and opened her bookmarks. "Speaking of which… here's the blog if you want to skim it."

Olive exchanged places with Sabrina. Half-heartedly, she scrolled through the information. Her eyes glazed over. "Do you mind if I email the link to myself? It's been a long day, and my brain is a little fuzzy, though it could also be the champagne."

"Go right ahead." Sabrina reached for her glass and finished her champagne.

"At this rate, I'll never be able to wake up early enough for my tour." Olive covered her mouth with her hand and yawned.

"Oh, you have a tour booked for tomorrow?" Sabrina hid her own yawn. "Which one?"

"Don't laugh," Olive started, "but I'm here for the *Sound of Music* tour." She finished composing herself an email message and stood.

"I would never laugh. *I* am here for the same thing." She belted out an off-key rendition of "A Few of My Favorite Things." Olive joined in.

Soon, it was eleven at night. Olive yawned again and rubbed her eyes. "I'm off to bed. If you need anything, just knock on the door."

Sabrina, however, was already asleep. Olive took a

comforter from the closet and covered her newfound friend. Silently, she entered the master bedroom and closed the door behind her.

If I'm able, I want to scale my business so that I can work from anywhere. Karma is a real thing. Give a little, get a little.

~

After a rich breakfast of fresh meats, a side of fruits, yogurt, a croissant, and a bold, rich Illy coffee, Olive and Sabrina stepped into the brisk morning air of the Old Town area, refreshed and ready to explore. Many shops in the surrounding area were packed tightly together with wrought iron signs hanging outside their businesses.

Large glass windows boasted fun, colorful displays of handmade cuckoo clocks in all manner of shapes and sizes, chocolate made in the likeness of Mozart, and traditional Austrian folk clothing. The streets were wide to accommodate for horse-drawn carriages. Fresh piles of snow crunched under Olive's boots.

Outside a Christmas ornament shop, Olive even spied an artist through the glass, hard at work hand-painting eggshells with rabbits and other themes for Easter. Each twist and turn of the back alleys of Old Town brought out new and exciting discoveries to uncover.

They passed their morning visiting two places not included in her tour booked for the afternoon—Mozart's Birthplace and the Mozart Residence. Olive had always found it sad that the musical prodigy had died at the young age of thirty-five. To that point in his life, he had composed over six-hundred compositions.

At noon, the duo made a beeline for the square just outside the Salzburg Cathedral where they parted ways. Sabrina was booked on the more economical bus tour. She promised to keep Olive updated as to how her adventures unfolded.

Olive set off for the small line of horse drawn carriages. The corners of her mouth turned upward at seeing the horses covered in blankets and hats. Some of the equines stood patiently; others stomped their hooves against the gravel in boredom, waiting for passengers.

In the lead carriage, she spied the person she was seeking—a gentleman waving a larger-than-life sign of Julie Andrews's face. She rubbed her hands together in excitement.

"Hello, I am here for the *Sound of Music* tour that departs at twelve-thirty. The surname is Nakamura." She adjusted the backpack on her shoulder.

"Perfect timing, Miss Nakamura." The tour representative tapped her tablet screen and checked her in. "We are just waiting on the arrival of one more person. Go ahead and sit anywhere you would like."

"Is it a small group today?" The carriage, not overly large, had four benches that could comfortably seat eight people.

"We have a total of four people confirmed for the semi-private tour. Most of our clients opt for the bus option," the representative stated.

"Great. I'll just have a seat." Olive climbed the three steps on the side of the carriage and selected the middle bench. A neatly folded red-and-black plaid blanket welcomed her. The heavy wool would protect her from the chill. She rubbed her hand over the rough fabric, and draped it over her legs.

On the bench directly behind the driver, a mother and daughter chatted animatedly in Japanese. They took turns snapping away photos of one another, reminding her of her own mom. They'd always talked about traveling to Salzburg as a family, but they never could seem to align their schedules.

Olive pulled out her camera and rubbed her hands over the plush fabric of the case. She had numerous photos and video clips she couldn't wait to share with Alex. Her SD memory card was nearly full. She thought about how much he'd love to photograph the architecture and Salzburg's residents.

The carriage suddenly shook from side to side. She reached for the edges of the bench in front of her. A lanky man of six feet, two inches with dark, honey skin and curly, cropped brown hair sat next to her. He wore a camel-toned overcoat, navy scarf, and jeans.

"Sorry. I'm not overly coordinated these days," he said in a low tone only Olive could hear.

"Alex," she exclaimed. She smiled brightly. The familiarity of his voice sent pleasant chills down her spine. She breathed deeply, her pulse racing furiously. She loosened her grip on the side of the carriage. "I missed you," she whispered into his ear and embraced him tightly.

"Should I even ask how you found me?" Olive held his hand and placed it in her lap, resting her head on his shoulder.

"Your location, via your mobile, is still being shared with Leo," Alex said moving the blanket to extend over his own legs.

Olive chuckled. Heat radiated off his body close to hers.

"And a good thing too. I was prepared to hire a private detective to track you down. I just missed you at the hotel this morning." Alex's neck colored.

I have to pinch myself. As if the hotel room wasn't an amazing enough surprise, Alex has given me a surprise that's beyond all expectations—himself. He could be at home recovering and getting back into the practice groove. Instead, here he is, sitting beside me. This tour is going to be all the more special being able to share it with him.

The tour guide clapped his hands together. "Now that we have all the members of the group present and accounted for, it is time we departed. I see you have all found the blankets kindly provided to you by our carriage driver. Excellent. There will be hot chocolate available at our first stop." The guide reached into his jacket pocket and unveiled a small Bluetooth speaker.

"*Getting to know you ... getting to know all about you ...*"

"Wha... sugoi!" The Japanese mother and daughter clapped in delight. Their joy proved to be infectious. Everyone in the carriage began to sing in time with Julie Andrews's voice. Olive and Alex swayed side to side, bellowing the lyrics aloud.

On a microphone, the guide announced, "For the next four hours, we shall be visiting many of the locations utilized for the classic film, *The Sound of Music*. Additionally, we shall learn about the real-life von Trapp family and some of the brief history of Austria. Our first stop will be Schloss Mirabell and its picturesque gardens."

CHAPTER 13

The Laendler

The carriage began to move. The horses' hooves click-clocked along the pavement. They approached the Salzach River. The sun reflected brightly off the bridge above the muddy, snowy, rushing water. Olive squinted. Upon closer inspection, she viewed thousands of padlocks of varying shapes, sizes, and colors. Just how many couples had etched their names on a lock and chained them to the bridge, leaving a small piece of themselves behind?

Olive heard the telltale click of a camera shutter. She pulled out the loaned compact camera and snapped away a few photos of her own. Alex checked the image on the back of his large DSLR camera. The lens was almost as long as her arm.

"New toy. But for what it costs, it isn't performing as well as I'd expected." Alex adjusted the settings on the lens.

"Too bad you'll have to wait until London to have this little beauty returned to you." She gestured to the mini camera.

"Some things are worth waiting for." He winked. "I play the long game."

At the first stop, Mirabell Gardens, snow covered large

patches of the grounds. There was little plant life to behold. The tour guide led them to a covered walkway. The archway of shrubs created a tunnel for Olive to run under while Alex diligently filmed her singing "Do-Re-Me," recreating the famed scene from *The Sound of Music*. They neared the statue of Pegasus and the lion's head gate.

With a gleam in her eye, Olive snuck over the roped-off barrier and signaled for Alex to capture her jumping off the side of the fountain. She thought it a shame the rim of the fountain was too icy to march around. She counted aloud to three and jumped into the air, letting out a ringing sound of laughter. Alex gave her a thumbs-up.

Heavy footsteps pounded out over the pavement. "Halt!" A member of the gardens' security staff sprinted over to Olive. He shouted at her again, gesturing wildly with his hands. "Was machen, Sie? What do you think you are doing?"

She held her shoulders rigid. Her eyes widened at being caught in the act. Their tour guide rushed to her aid. She pretended to play the part of an innocent American tourist. Folding her hands together, she batted her eyelashes. "I'm so sorry. It was my mistake. I can assure you it will never happen again."

Alex clutched his ribs whilst shaking with silent laughter.

The security guard crossed his arms. The tour guide translated, "Miss Nakamura, the security guard would like you to hold up your hand and promise not to climb over any more barriers."

She held up the appendage. "I promise." The security guard narrowed his eyes at Olive until she had climbed back over to the correct side of the barrier. The tour guide clapped his hands together. "Wunderbar. Now for the hot chocolate." He guided the group over to an outdoor café.

Alex trailed behind Olive. "That was some display you put

on. I wonder where you might have learned such bad habits." He scratched his chin.

"I have absolutely no idea." They locked eyes with one another and burst out laughing.

More than halfway into the tour, the group stopped at its fourth destination—the mansion of Schloss Leopoldskron. Trees along the pathway opened up to reveal a stately white home situated upon a mirrored lake with the ghostly Alps in the background. Birds chirped loudly, busily scrounging for food to feed their newly hatched babies.

The tour guide recited from his script. "You might remember the von Trapp children rowing a canoe and subsequently falling into the lake in the film, or perhaps the gazebo utilized for the film sequence featuring the song 'Sixteen Going on Seventeen.' Schloss Leopoldskron served as a backdrop in more than ten exterior scenes in the film. We will be stopping here for the next hour. You will find signs on the grounds directing you to a few points of interest. Please return to the carriage promptly at three."

The carriage halted, and its driver lowered a set of steps for its occupants. The Japanese mother and daughter immediately set out for the lake. Alex stepped down right behind her. She resisted the urge to wander off aimlessly in one of ten different directions. This was the site she had most been looking forward to seeing. She heard the shutter of his camera clicking.

"Where shall we start our adventure?" Olive looped a hand through his arm. "Will it be the lake or Schloss Leopold-skron?" She fingered the heavy fabric of his coat. He let the camera hang lax around his neck. She was growing more comfortable teasing him the more time they spent together.

"Walking around the lake is more than I can handle." She watched his Adam's apple bobble up and down. "My sprained knee is mostly recovered, but my muscles are sore from yesterday. Adala had me play a game against her, and she's also just begun reintroducing simple footwork drills to my workouts."

She took in how Alex was still clean-shaven. His face free of facial hair made him appear much softer and more youthful. She could make out the clear definition in his cheekbones. The fine lines and purple rings were gone. He was more relaxed and at ease.

"Then maybe just a quick peek at the lake." Even at a slower pace, Olive still had to take two steps for every one of Alex's. "It's great you're able to pick up a racquet again. Does your coach have a timetable for your return to the men's touring circuit?"

"Adala's ambitious. She wants me ready for the start of the grass-court season and Wimbledon." Alex stared straight ahead.

"That gives you four and a half months? That's awfully fast." The gravel crunched beneath their feet. The bare trees were covered in snow, and as the wind blew, it created creaking sounds.

"Less than that if I play in a qualifier warm-up tournament. I had hoped to just be back on tour in five months"— Alex pinched his lips—"but we'll see. I'm setting my sights on the US Open in September."

They reached the closest edge of the mirrored lake. Ducks swam across the lake, creating ripples in the image of the house. Olive slid her hand out from his arm. They ventured apart to capture a few shots of the scenery on their cameras.

Alex was staying tight-lipped. Did that mean his practice session had gone worse than he was letting on? She was unable to read his body language. Just as she thought she had Alex figured out, he still proved to be an enigma.

～

Alex and Olive passed through the opening of a black cast-iron gate topped with horse statues. Three steps led up to the entryway of the stately mansion capped on either side by lanterns. Olive glanced over her shoulder. Short green hedges twisted as if they were a part of a maze. The lake from this side was frozen over. A thin layer of frosted glass-like ice crackled and floated precariously on its surface.

Snow-covered canoes sat frozen and stuck to the wooden pier. The facade of the home was designed in the grandeur of the Rococo style. Twelve sash windows cut across each of the four levels. During a heavy storm, the white cream color of the building could easily blend in with the snowfall. In the very far distance, the Hohensalzburg Fortress, the highest point of Salzburg, peaked above the building.

The wooden entry doors were propped open. Behind them, a set of modern glass doors was pulled open by a door attendant in uniform. The lobby was light and airy with white walls and gold-gilded mirrors and finishes. Classical Baroque music played in the background.

A woman in a matching uniform to the door attendant glanced up hopefully from behind an antique mahogany wooden desk. "You are checking into the hotel?"

"No... er... my friend and I were told this was a home open to tour as a part of the *Sound of Music* tour," Alex said.

The woman adjusted her glasses and looked down her nose at the pair. In a bored tone she said, "The library and dining rooms of the schloss are opened to members of the general public." She gestured to a brochure rack. "Our guest rooms and conference area may be seen through photos in the hotel's brochure."

Olive stepped forward and picked up two brochures. "Danke."

Alex clenched his fists. Olive steered Alex out of the earshot of the woman. "There is no need for her rudeness. It's one of my pet peeves," Alex mumbled. "My soddy excuse of a father used to treat my sister and me as if we were beneath him."

That's the first I've heard Alex speak of his father. What happened in your past, Alex? Our relationship may be growing, but it's not nearly strong enough for me to help with that. You have helped me already in so many ways. Will I be able to return the favor?

The long hallway opened into what the hotel considered to be their dining rooms. Her mouth opened wide. This was more of a ballroom. The highly-polished, marble, brown-and-white checked floor glistened. The main feature wall was dominated by a larger-than-life painting of a woman sitting on a throne above a peach, and a rose-gold toned fireplace.

Circular tables contained place settings and utensils for ten people. Olive stared up at the crystal chandeliers dangling from the ceiling. She spun in a circle, studying the detailed carvings and yet another intricate painting of the home's former occupants. It reminded her of Versailles. She closed her eyes and, in her head, she recreated the film's familiar scene with Julie Andrews dancing with the von Trapp child actors on the patio outside the main ballroom.

She imagined guests of the ball—women in long sweeping gowns and men clad in form-fitting black tuxedos—dancing in the background as the children imitated the adults. Captain von Trapp, played by actor Christopher Plummer, would spy his young children and proceed to cut in and dance with Julie Andrews. She swayed and moved her feet side to side, marking the counts—one, two, three, one, two, three.

Alex touched her shoulder. Her movements ceased. She opened her eyes and was taken aback to see him standing right beside her and offering his hand. "Would you care to dance?"

Olive's heart leaped. She nodded, unable to voice any words. Her throat grew dry. How did he know this was exactly what she had been dreaming of? Alex removed his camera from his neck and placed it on a nearby table. She set her daypack next to it.

He pulled out his phone. "We require some music." His nose wrinkled. He scrolled through a selection of songs on his phone. "*Sound of Music... Sound of Music...* how about this little bugger?" A string rendition of the Austrian folk tune "The Laendler" played aloud. He placed the phone next to his camera. His massive hand dwarfed hers, rough with callouses.

He escorted her over to an open area in the room, clear of any dining tables. She curtsied and kept her gaze on Alex. He bent over at the waist. "Shall we?"

Her breathing quickened. Her body remained rooted to its spot, frozen. Alex, with a gentle grip, pulled her along. Olive's body moved of its own accord. Her mind went blank, unable to fathom that this was unfolding in real life. She stared at her feet, awkwardly shuffling along.

Alex placed his hand under her chin. "I'll go slow. Follow my lead. I learned this particular dance for my sister's debutante ball many moons ago. Have you ever danced it before?" Alex inquired.

"Once," she squeaked. "My dad and I used to make up our own version of it when I was little as one of our holiday traditions. We always watch *The Sound of Music* on Christmas."

"That's brilliant," Alex whispered into her ear. "Breathe and picture that moment."

Olive exhaled. An army of a thousand and one butterflies fluttered in her stomach. She stood taller. Alex, true to his word, expertly moved her through the dance. Every time their hands touched, electric energy passed from Alex to Olive. She shivered despite the warmth radiating through her body. Their dance created a spell where everyone else around them ceased to exist. She visualized herself in a long, elegant, light green, sweeping ballgown, long white gloves, and heels, with Alex in a tailed, black-and-white tuxedo.

He stepped lightly on the balls of his feet with practiced ease and an erect posture. She stumbled, but there was Alex, ready to steady her. He placed his hands on her waist. They swayed side to side, intimately inching closer and closer to one another. And then it was over. The music ended.

Her hands twitched as Alex released her. Neither one moved, locked in the moment. Defined abdominal muscles poked out through the thin fabric of his shirt with every breath. Olive could not tear her eyes away from the devilishly handsome man before her. They inched closer and closer to one another until their bodies were touching.

"You're so beautiful," Alex whispered.

In his dark chocolate-brown eyes was a look of unmistakable desire. He gently parted the ends of her hair away from her face. He brushed her lips with his thumb. They kissed in a long and passionate embrace. His breath was hot. Inside, she was ready to burst in delight, lost in the moment of being near the man that was constantly on her mind.

She committed the scent of his cologne—cedar and musk —to memory. The stubble on his chin grazed the softness of her skin. She shivered and buried her face into his chest. His grip never wavered. "Alex, I was hoping you would feel the same way as me."

They kissed a second time. Greedily, yet equally full of passion. It was as if she had arrived at a desert oasis and was able to quench her thirst after a long hike. Olive had waited so long for Alex to kiss her. His body was like a furnace warming her through the fabric of his now unbuttoned coat.

A smattering of applause broke out around them and abruptly broke the spell. Both of them immediately backed away. A group of two men and one woman grinned; one even wolf-whistled. Olive put a hand on her face, hoping to cool the burning red. She could feel her lips swollen from his kiss.

In that moment, Olive had been so alive and drawn to him. Being in his arms evoked an array of emotions previously slumbering within her. She stared at her hand again, now positive she wanted nothing more than to call Alex hers. She shivered in delight.

Alex snapped up the camera and his phone. Both fled the dining room. They walked until they found the empty library. Floor-to-ceiling built-in bookcases were packed full of books. There were two square wooden tables with four chairs each and red sofas on either side of the tables. The room was darker than the dining room.

Amanda would consider this room paradise. It is just like in Beauty and the Beast.

Alex double-checked to make sure they were alone. His shoulders hunched. "Olive... what happened back there... it can't happen again."

Olive breathed in sharply. "But the way you kissed me a few moments ago—" She grasped his hands. "I've *never* been kissed so fiercely and urgently. We clearly both want the same thing."

He stepped back and pulled his hands out of her grasp. "I can't control myself near you." Alex pinched the bridge of his nose. "Do you see how my body responds to you every time we are close? You are a temptation I can't afford to have right now."

Air moved out of her chest at a faster rate. Her mind whirled. "What do you mean by that?"

He placed his hands on top of his head. "I have to focus on my tennis. I can't afford even a single distraction. In the past, I might have been able to get away with being in a relationship but now"—his eyes bored intently into hers—"the game has changed. In the year I've been out of the playing circuit, so many new, younger, and fitter blokes have come along. I have to work twice as hard as I once did to even have the possibility to make it back to the top. It's what everyone wants and expects from me."

"I understand better than anyone. You know my story." She splayed a hand on her collarbone. "You will never be the same player you were."

The fight left his body. He melted into one of the sofas. "Of that, I'm painfully aware."

Her brow furrowed. "So this is it? You are going to give up on us just like that? You won't even give us a chance?" Anger simmered beneath her surface.

"There never was an us. You're just a friend I met in Athens." He gazed at the floor, unable to meet her eyes.

It was as if she had taken a sucker punch to the gut. "A friend indeed—" Her cheeks grew warm. "This isn't you talking; it's your fear of failure." She needed air. Deep down, shadows of her insecurities began to surface. "You're a terrible liar. Both of us know that you wouldn't be here in Salzburg or wouldn't have had dinner and a gondola ride with me in Venice unless you saw me as more than *just* a friend."

Alex winced. "I'm sorry it has to be this way."

Her eyes grew moist. "Not as sorry as I am. I thought I was ready to open my heart again, but it's just as painful the second time as it was the first."

She left Alex alone. Walking, then jogging out into the cold winter air, more hurt and confused than ever before.

CHAPTER 14

Atlas

"Urg! Men!" Olive kicked at the gravel on the pathway. "Too stubborn and proud for their own good."

She tapped her pockets for her phone and her earbuds. They were stored away in the side pocket of her purse. In her haste to leave the library, she'd left her handbag behind. All she had on her person was her wallet and passport, which never left her body. She shoved her hands into her pockets.

"I'm not wasting my time here." She set off at a punishing pace around the grounds.

The bitterness of the wind brought color to her cheeks. She welcomed the pins-and-needles sensation in her toes and fingers. The reeds near the lake thinned out. The water was shallow enough for her to take a good look at fish swimming beneath the thin layer of ice. The mansion, still in her view, was blanketed by a dense layer of trees.

When we earned the silver medal in Paris and failed to meet everyone's high expectations of our team, it was a bitter pill to swallow. The media was relentless in saying we had succumbed to the Olympic pressure and "lost the gold." We didn't lose anything. We won the silver. They never knew how beat-up our bodies were after weeks of punishing training. There were the Classics, then Nationals, and the Olympic Trials. By the time the Olympics were here, we had already peaked.

Did I lament that I was only able to contribute to the team on uneven bars? No, because I was just happy to be there and in the moment. Alex has to learn to count his blessings. You have to ignore what everyone else wants. You can only be the best version of yourself. The reality of him being a completely different player post-injury is going to hurt him more than any physical recovery. He has to learn to play smarter and not train harder.

Olive recognized Alex wanted to dedicate himself fully to his sport. Training was one of the tiny facets of their career that an athlete could have some semblance of control over. But being given a minuscule glimpse into what their relationship could have been like caused her deep pain and bitter regret. She'd allowed herself to hope. More than she cared to admit, she had wanted Alex to be the one.

She heard children laughing. A rustic wooden fence across from her separated the pathway from a playground. Two mothers pushed their heavily bundled children on a swing set. One of them waved at her. She returned the gesture but kept moving.

Maybe we wouldn't have worked out as a couple in the first place. It would've required both of us to commit to being in a long-distance relationship. Even if I do become a digital nomad, eventually, I'd return home. That's another thing I'll have to figure out. Where is home going to be? With my parents? Or somewhere else? Where do I belong? I'm not the same person I was a few weeks ago.

For now, the pressing issue was what to do about Alex. She would have to pick up her purse and finish the tour with him. Afterward, they could go their separate ways. Small snowflakes drifted down from the sky. She released her anger. What purpose would it serve her? There was nothing she could do about a man who had his mind made up. All she wanted to do was move on.

She spotted a rotting wooden canoe lingering in the reeds. She was half tempted to take the shortcut across the lake. She hadn't realized just how far she'd walked. How much time had elapsed since their row? She picked up her speed and jogged. Her side twinged from the exertion. Schloss Leopoldskron grew larger in her field of vision.

The gravel turned to smooth, paved cement. She slowed and bent over to pant, hands on her knees, fittingly next to a statue of Atlas holding up the weight of the world. She righted herself and walked to the entryway of the building. Alex leaned against the front of the wooden doors, arms crossed and forehead creased, her camel tan purse slung over his shoulder.

He spotted her and glacially descended the stairs to greet her. "You left this behind." He checked his wristwatch. "The tour guide checked in with me at two when I couldn't find you. I told him to depart without us."

"You did?" Olive accepted her purse and unzipped the main compartment to double-check its contents. The faux croc embossed leather was rough against her fingers.

"It's now three-fifteen. You were gone for over an hour on your own. It didn't seem fair to the Japanese ladies to delay on our behalf. I assured the tour guide we'd find our own way back." Alex's tone was clipped and to the point.

Olive zipped her bag closed. "I'll ask the concierge about a taxi. You'll likely want to get to the airport."

Alex puffed out his cheeks. "I have an open return ticket. I can fly back to London at any time." He blew out air and cleared his throat. "Before I go, I think I owe you an apology and an explanation for my earlier behavior. I was short with you for no good reason."

"Apology accepted." Olive rubbed her hands together. She was ready to be done with all this. "Let's get a taxi back to the city center. As much as I love the scenery here, I'm freezing."

They climbed the steps and spoke to the doorman. The taxi would be there in ten minutes. Olive and Alex huddled close to a portable heater near the valet parking attendant's booth. She held her hands over the device, welcoming the warmth it provided.

Alex shoved his hands into his pockets. He stared out in the distance. She could see the tight lines around his eyes. Instinctually, she knew he was mentally beating himself up. Clearly, he was just as miserable as she. Her mood slightly softened.

In the span of two hours, I've gone from being elated to feeling hurt and dejected. As angry as I am, I can't stand for us to part on bad terms. Deep down, I know he feels as I do. He's only fooling himself, thinking that pushing me away is going to help his cause.

Now, we're both miserable. But no matter what, even if I'm relegated to the role of a friend, I have to make him understand I care for him and that it will be worse if he holds his emotions within himself. I want nothing more than to see him succeed.

"Alex?" He raised his head. His eyes were dull and devoid of their usual warmth. "Look, I'm still cross with you, but for both of our sakes, we have to discuss what happened back there."

Alex sputtered. "Of course."

A yellow cab appeared at the end of the hotel's drive. Its windshield wipers waved from side to side, deflecting the falling snow from its windshield. Olive switched her purse over to her shoulder. "We'll have the taxi drop us at the Museum of Natural History and go from there. Will that work for you?"

He nodded.

"Alright then."

The taxi pulled to a stop. The duo slid into the car and returned to the area just outside the Old Town.

The lighting inside the Natural History Museum of Salzburg was dim. Pink and yellow anemones danced with the water currents inside of the fish tank. Orange and brown starfish clung to the rocks at the bottom. A school of electric-blue fish with yellow stripes swam past, followed closely by a small shark.

Olive read the placard of information posted on the wall. "Being near water always helps calm my nerves. Usually, I take a trip to the beach, but this is the next best thing," she said.

Alex silently trailed beside her. He had been quiet for most of the taxi ride, seemingly lost in his own thoughts. His line of sight followed the apex predator of the tank. The water was hazy from the salt within.

He started, "It's difficult for me to trust anyone other than myself." Olive gave her full attention to him. "Growing up, my parents often left my sister and me with my English maternal grandparents—Nan and Granda. While I love them dearly, they were not at all suited to raise us. They're of an entirely different generation and class. Their children had a live-in nanny."

They moved to the next tank displaying a set of cave-like features and a tightly curled up octopus, camouflaged to perfectly match its surroundings. Alex walked with his hands clasped behind his back. "My sister and I had to depend on one another until we were sent off to boarding school."

Olive tilted her head to the side. "What is the age difference between you and your sister?"

"Five years." The suction cups of the octopus were

attached solidly to the glass. Alex traced the outline of the arm with his hand. "There were moments I've acted more as a father figure to her than as a brother."

Olive sucked in air. Five years could very well be ten or more years to a child or teenager. Alex must have had to grow up and mature quickly.

The end of the aquarium exhibit opened to a touch pool and area for interaction. Alex and Olive washed their hands and joined the queue behind a young family of four. "And what happened when your tennis turned from a hobby to a career choice?"

"My Nan and Granda were thrilled. They could see how much joy it brought me. My father and I, however, had a huge row. He thought it a disgrace to the family name for me to put all of my eggs into one proverbial basket instead of following him into his financial brokerage. He cut off all my financial support. We haven't spoken in several years."

She saw sea stars, seaweed, urchins, and a few sea cucumbers. The seaweed's scent smelled of dry wood. Olive ran her hands over the spiky ends of the urchin, careful not to remove the creature from the water. "And your mother?"

Alex picked up a sea star. He turned it over and ran his finger over the thousands of tiny moving grippers. "She was long out of the picture. She remarried as soon as she could divorce my father. Her current husband isn't aware that my sister or I exist." Alex carefully placed the sea star back onto a rock and touched the sharp, pointed ends of the deep purple sea urchin.

She felt deep pangs of sadness. Hearing more about the circumstances of his childhood made her more empathetic to Alex. Family was so important to her. Her parents were always her biggest advocates and cheerleaders. "You have been alone for so long."

Alex shrugged. "I have Penny and both my maternal and

paternal grandparents. My Greek side of the family was keen to ensure I always knew they were there if need be. Family is a huge part of their culture. Leo's been a brother to me. Greece is just so far away from London."

They entered the reptile exhibition hall. The first few cases contained colorful yet poisonous frogs from South America. Their viewing glasses were covered with moisture, causing the glass to fog up. It added a layer of difficulty in finding them inside their exhibits. Amphibians were masters at hiding.

In the crocodile tank, a three-foot-long juvenile stood immobile on its makeshift island, basking under the warmth of an orange heating lamp. Its eyes were yellow with thin black slits. It stared back at Alex and Olive, a living, breathing dinosaur.

Alex leaned forward against the rail protecting the viewing glass. "When you called me out earlier as being fearful, you were exactly right. There is no denying that I am petrified of not being able to play tennis well enough again to be a world's top-ten player. It's the only skill set I've always been able to depend on. I'm nobody without it."

Olive was having a difficult time keeping her waterworks at bay. The raw emotion Alex was sharing with her broke her both in body and spirit. She was forming a new picture of him. The outside world saw the tennis player persona, the jokester, and the gentleman. She was unearthing the man behind the athlete.

She put a hand on his shoulder. His muscles tensed. "That's not true. You are a brother. A cousin. A grandson. A photographer. And my friend."

He inclined his head. "In spite of everything I said to you earlier, you still want to be around a man like me?"

She put a hand under his chin. She raised his head so he was looking directly at her face. "Alexander Georgiou, it is going to take a lot more than that to get rid of me."

She knew her parents would immediately adopt him as their own when they met. She rose up onto her toes. Alex leaned over and met her halfway. Her eyelids fluttered. She offered him a sweet kiss. They both tasted her vanilla-flavored lip gloss.

"I'll stand aside if you want me to so you can focus on tennis, but you *have* to have a support system in place. I can't emphasize enough how important mental health and well-being are. Embrace the man you've become. Don't mourn for the man you were. Making a comeback is terrifying. It's a journey into uncharted waters. Trust me when I say that you *will* sabotage yourself by trying to go it alone. I've been there. I know."

Alex's eyes glistened with unshed tears. His voice was crackly. "I don't deserve your friendship. I don't deserve you."

The heaviness of the conversation sapped and drained away her energy reserves. She pursed her lips. "It bothers me when you say that. Yes, you do deserve me. You deserve all that you have."

The crocodile opened his mouth, revealing two rows of exceedingly sharp teeth—a deadly smile. "Even the croc agrees with me."

"So he does." He looked up to the croc. "I can tell when I am outnumbered two to one."

Alex wrapped his arm around Olive. "I'll ring a sports psychologist first thing once I'm home." Her body tingled. They passed through the room of snakes, stopping to appreciate the ancient lizard cousins of the croc perched under their own heat lamps atop a brown log. "If I am going to go about having a relationship with you, we can't just be friends. If you're open to it, I want to date you."

"Date me?" Olive blushed.

"I was foolish to try and ignore our natural chemistry. I

care about you so much. This is my third chance. I won't let it slip by me again," Alex said.

The museum played an announcement on its overhead speaker. "Ladies and gentlemen, thank you for sharing your day with us. The museum is now closed. Please proceed to the front exit and enjoy your evening."

Alex and Olive walked in tandem to the museum lobby. "There will be times during my stay in London that I'm going to be at the mercy of my friends' schedules. The wedding I'm here for is a big deal. It's going to consume my life."

Alex nodded. "If my sister's wedding was anything to go by, I will gladly stand in the background. Drew's enormous Italian family has me right terrified of weddings. Besides, I will have my own training schedule to work around. But no matter what, nothing is going to stop me from dating you right and proper from the beginning. Just wait until you're in my hometown, Olive Nakamura! Will I have plans for you."

They walked out into the dark, snowy night. After the roller coaster of emotions she had experienced throughout the course of the day, Olive could say with certainty she had finally obtained a state of pure bliss.

She walked with a slight bounce in her step, warm and floating on air. She and Alex fit together. Neither one of them was perfect, yet she couldn't imagine being able to better connect with another person. Was this the magnetic pull Amanda had described? Olive certainly hoped it was. *The answer awaits me in London.*

CHAPTER 15

Roommates Reunited

In the arrival's hall of London Heathrow airport four days later, Olive flinched. Was it too late to find her own transportation to central London? She was tempted to duck into one of the duty-free shops, but that would only delay the inevitable.

A red-headed woman obnoxiously danced and waved a large sign that read: *Who is excited Olive is here? This gal!* At the bottom the woman stuck her head through a square cut hole. She pulled out her phone and tapped the screen. The tune of "Back in Black" by AC/DC played aloud. A small crowd around her watched in amusement. Others distanced themselves from her and watched from out of the corner of their eyes.

Amanda played a mean air guitar during the solo section. Before she could hide, Amanda gleefully shouted, "Olive!"

Olive's cheeks flushed. *Same old Amanda. She never does anything by halves. At least she didn't dress as a stormtrooper with a sign that said Vader. That would have been even more humiliating.*

Amanda loved to find fun ways to greet her friends at the

airport whenever possible. Olive's personal favorite had been the summer of her junior year when she arrived at the Seattle-Tacoma International airport to find Amanda dressed as a giant inflatable T-Rex.

She brushed a stray hair behind her ear and marched over to the redhead. Amanda squealed and dropped the sign. "The party can officially begin now that you are here!" Amanda hugged her tightly. "Your hair is so short and cute." Olive twirled. "It's going to take a long time for me to adjust to the new hair."

"You're telling me." Olive laughed. "I'm surprised Eddie isn't with you."

Amanda placed her arm around Olive's shoulder. "He wanted to be here to surprise you, but there are some pre-planned engagements he can't skip out on. Lunch with his dad is one of them. I'm glad I don't have to share you yet." Amanda sang and clapped to the tune of the song *Celebration*. Together they walked toward the exit. Two men in suits trailed behind them.

It took Olive several moments to acclimate and not constantly peek over her should to see if the men in suits were still there.

"You'll grow used to them. They are awesomely awesome at blending in and at evasive driving. I mean they have trained with the real-life James Bond MI-5 agency and special forces."

"Evasive driving? Special forces?" Olive asked uncertainly.

"Yup. It's one of Princey's favorite stories. I'm sure he'll be happy to recount the entire story over dinner. You don't mind dining at Kensington Palace tonight, do you? It'll be easier than going out and having to sort out all the security details," Amanda said.

Her stomach clenched. The reality of being a bridesmaid in *the* wedding of the year was finally beginning to sink in. Her friends were literally connected to royalty. Some days she couldn't wrap her head around the paths the lives of her two former roommates had taken.

Olive rolled her small hand luggage behind her. "No, that's perfect. I only have one evening dress with me though. I was planning to save it for the rehearsal dinner." Different scenarios ran through her mind. Could she have enough time to go shopping for another outfit?

"Formal dress?" Amanda laughed. "You have this all wrong. C and I haven't changed that much. We still dress for comfort. I'll be wearing yoga pants and a fleece jumper. Clara will probably wear something along the same lines."

Olive's shoulders sagged in relief. Her cheeks flushed. "Oh."

Amanda raised an eyebrow at the size of Olive's suitcase. "Is that *all* you brought for your entire trip?"

Olive clicked her tongue. "Don't you worry. I have two bags inside the bag that can be filled with more items and expanded. I shipped some of my souvenirs home. There is no way I would have fit my cuckoo clock in here." Olive patted her backpack. "Your supply of chocolates and coffee from home takes up so much space. I'll be happy to have the lot taken off my hands."

Amanda fist-bumped Olive. "The trick is going to be hiding it from the guys. David is like your dad with being able to pick out individual wine flavors."

Olive snorted. "So, part bloodhound?"

Amanda smirked. "Indeed."

Outside, the sky was clear and blue. Planes roared overhead, approaching the airport. The men in suits directed the women to an unmarked black Range Rover and opened the door for them.

Inside, the driver greeted Amanda. "Welcome back, Miss Collins. I see you have found your friend, Miss Nakamura. It's nice to make your acquaintance. I'll likely be the driver for the duration of your stay. My name is Michael."

"Nice to meet you. I am thrilled to hear we'll see each other a few more times. Having a friendly face in a new city is always a huge plus," Olive said.

Pleasantries exchanged, Amanda directed Michael to take them over to Olive's hotel in Mayfair. From the backseat, Olive stared out the window at the passing roundabouts. The car entered the A4 motorway.

"It's forty-five minutes to central London with no sight-seeing, but Michael *could* take the scenic route." Amanda looked to her for an answer.

She folded her hands on her lap. This *was* her very first trip to London. Why not start it with a bang? "Would it be too much to ask?"

The driver glanced into the rearview mirror at the women in the backseat. "Not at all, Miss Nakamura. It brings me great enjoyment to see you young ladies react with such excitement at places I've seen time and time again."

"That settles it. London is an amazing place. Who knows, maybe I can even convince you to end up moving here." Olive blanched. Amanda bumped her shoulder. "Only joking. I don't think you'll ever leave Hawaii. Not that I blame you. It's a literal island paradise."

Amanda is unusually perceptive, even if she's joking.

The city of Kona had a population of fifteen thousand residents and London nearly nine million. How would it compare to the time she'd spent living in Seattle during her college years? Could she see herself making a home base here? What if Alex weren't in the picture? Any decisions she made would first and foremost be for herself and *not* just because of her burgeoning relationship, though it was an important consideration.

Amanda grinned. "Michael, cue the Olive soundtrack to track two please."

"Yes, Miss Collins."

They laughed, lip-synced, and danced to the Spice Girls in their respective seats. Amanda channeled Scary Spice and Olive Sporty Spice.

Michael drove them over the iconic Tower Bridge and past Westminster Abbey. Olive stared out the window wide-eyed at the imposing citadel of the Tower of London and the colossal, modern, sleek, contemporary glass building known as the Shard. Compared to the other European cities Olive had visited, the architecture of London was vastly different. There were so many old historic buildings to balance out the new, more abstract designs.

She wondered where Alex resided within the metropolitan area. Did he have a swanky flat in the happening SoHo area? Or did he choose to live within the quieter outskirts? She pictured a cozy loft-style apartment similar to Leo's. She saw herself curled up on the couch in Alex's arms with a red-and-black plaid blanket draped over them. They'd chat over hot chocolate and freshly baked snickerdoodle cookies still hot from the oven. She could taste the cinnamon and vanilla sugar on the tip of her tongue.

Amanda waved a hand in front of Olive's face. "Earth to Olive." Olive jerked and fluttered her eyelashes. Amanda's green eyes gleamed. "You're thinking about Alex, aren't you? You have it bad, girl. Do you think he'd care to join the five of us tonight?"

Olive sputtered. "Alex? Dinner at the palace?"

Amanda blinked slowly. "You're right. Too much too fast. Maybe next week, then? I assume you two are going to be meeting up relatively soon. He's a Londoner, isn't he?"

"Yes, I think." Olive licked her lips. "We haven't really discussed the details."

Alex doesn't have a clue as to who Amanda and Clara are. Can I trust that he'll react cool as a cucumber if I tell him whose wedding I'm here for? What if he doesn't want to associate himself with them? I have kept my royal connections a secret from the world because of situations like this. I don't know who I can trust outside my tiny bubble.

The car pulled up to the rounded driveway of the Edwardian Arms Hotel on Park Lane, one of London's most exclusive hotels. Behind the imposing water feature and perfectly manicured flower beds, she saw the greenery of Hyde Park.

"I'm staying here?" Olive gaped.

Michael opened the car door for the women, and the hotel valet rolled out a gold luggage cart to collect Olive's baggage.

"Surprise." Amanda hugged her. "Only the best for you. You're welcome to stay with Princey and me, or Clara and David, but C and I thought you might enjoy having a bit more privacy and the freedom to come and go as you please. We're on the other side of the park from you. Actually, Princey lives at the Knightsbridge barracks most of the week."

Olive was truly stunned and at a loss for words. She'd never expected to be staying here! "I don't know what to say."

They walked up a plush, red carpet and entered the lobby dominated by white, red, and gold tones. Elegant was the only word she could use to describe its interior. She took in the gold columns, black-and-white polka dot marble floors, and bright natural light. Employees stood with perfect posture, clad in immaculate hunter-green, white, and gold-trimmed uniforms.

A middle-aged, balding man with gray hair and glasses approached Olive and Amanda. He wore white gloves and stood about five-foot-seven. "Miss Collins, Miss Nakamura, my name is Harrison. I am to be your personal butler for the duration of your stay. If you would please follow me."

"Don't we need to check in first?" Olive glanced at the

dark cherry wood desks adorned with turn-of-the-century art deco Tiffany-styled lamps.

Harrison chuckled. "I assure you, the Office of the Duke of Leeds has seen to all your needs." Amanda straightened her shoulders. "The private lift will be right this way."

They passed a series of floral arrangements taller than Olive's five-foot frame. The pink, blue, yellow, and red hues added to the inviting atmosphere. It was *Downton Abbey* meets *The Great Gatsby*. Everything was so refined, and the attention to detail mind-blowing.

The lift took them to the penthouses located on the top floor. Entry into the main sitting room revealed emerald-green velvet curtains, an off-white sofa sectional matching the off-white marble fireplace, and two blue wing back chairs in the sitting room. A sliding door onto a terrace opened to her private rooftop garden overlooking Hyde Park.

Olive had a difficult time breathing while Harrison pointed out the dressing room, pantry, formal dining room, conservatory, bedroom, and finally the spa bath. "I may never leave this room again."

Amanda laughed. "That's too bad. Clara and I hoped you might enjoy afternoon tea in the salon downstairs. She's meeting us at one."

Olive's head snapped up. "High tea?" Olive splayed a hand on her chest.

"Surprise number two," Amanda said. "You can only have a first impression of London once."

They thanked Harrison and dismissed him.

Amanda and Olive entered the dressing room. A single black silk garment bag with white stitching hung from the rail inside the wardrobe. "There isn't an official dress code for tea, but a majority of patrons tend to dress up. Clara had a special frock designed for you by her go-to designer, Clarissa Lee.

Don't feel obliged to wear it now, but I wanted to make sure you knew it was there for you."

Olive reached for the garment bag and ran her hand over the fabric, testing its weight in her hands. Holding her breath, she unzipped it to reveal a flash of tea-rose pink fabric. It was smooth and buttery soft, a type of mulberry silk. She removed the dress from the bag and held it up for a closer inspection.

The top was a scoop neck design with puffy three-quarter length chiffon sleeves and three pearl buttons. The tea-length skirt flared out asymmetrically. A black belt cinched in the waist to complete the look. The edges of the skirt shimmered in the light.

"Va va voom! This is more like an evening dress," Olive exclaimed. Her hand brushed over the detailing of the buttons. Olive shook her head. "This is all too much, A. What did I do to deserve all this special treatment?"

"Seeing as you never do anything for yourself, C and I finally have an excuse to spoil you. It's just a small way for us to give back to you for being the one who has always been there for us. In Seattle, you were always the one who would get up and drive Clara to rehearsal in the snow. The one who made sure I always had clean clothing if I was rushing out to flight attendant training."

Amanda placed her hands on her shoulders. "Even after I moved to California and you were in Hawaii, whenever I needed a shoulder to cry on or someone to vent my frustrations to, no matter where I was in the world or what time it was, you *always* picked up."

Amanda wiped a stray tear from the corner of her eye. "When that wanker Sean cheated on you, it hurt me so much to see you so lost and depressed. Clara and I had planned for your trip here to signify new beginnings. But you've managed to do just fine without any help from us."

Salty tears escaped her eyes. Her lips quivered and her

hands shook. These were her friends. True friends. She could live another lifetime and never be so lucky as to meet women like Amanda and Clara again. She hugged Amanda again. She caught a whiff of her friend's pumpkin spice lotion.

Olive carefully laid the dress down on the top of the dresser. "I'll wear this to tea. Mind helping me get changed?"

"Only if you help me. My dress is in my tote bag," Amanda said.

Olive's eyes widened. "Aren't you afraid it's going to wrinkle?"

"There's a steamer in the back corner. Or, if worse comes to worse, we can put Harrison through the paces. I'm sure it's not the first time he's been asked to iron or press a dress with little notice."

On her second afternoon in London, Olive found herself inside Clara and David's kitchen. Amanda hummed to herself while scooping up a fresh batch of white chocolate macadamia nut cookies onto a cooling rack. The semi-sweet and nutty aroma filled the air.

The tails of two white English springer spaniels wagged against the hardwood floors of the kitchen as they observed the occupants and waited for any stray food crumbs to come their direction. Olive sent off a quick text message to Alex.

Olive: *Hi, Alex! Made it to London yesterday. From what I've seen from the car, it is just as beautiful as I've pictured it. My friend was waiting with one of those over-the-top airport signs in the baggage hall for me. I was both amused and embarrassed at the same time. Hope your practice is going well today.*

She hit the send button and turned her phone face down.

Clara, a petite, five-foot-five ballerina with dark, honey brown hair and hazel green eyes, stood next to Amanda. She poured freshly ground coffee beans into a high-tech Nespresso machine. She scratched her head in bewilderment while glancing at the instruction manual. "This machine is supposed to make life easier, not more difficult. I understand that this machine can perform fifty different functions, but all I want to do is make a pot of regular coffee."

"Do you want me to take a look at it? It's like the fancy one my parents own. Once you can navigate one machine, all others are all relatively the same." Olive grinned.

"No. You relax. You are the guest." Clara flipped wildly through the back of the book. She turned it sideways attempting to decipher the illustration. Amanda placed her spatula down and bent over to study the machine.

Olive's phone vibrated with a new message. She raised an eyebrow. A response already?

Alex: *Hello, Olive. Happy to hear you are on my side of the pond. Do you have any photos of the airport sign? I gather Amanda has an outgoing personality. Is she the one getting married? My first practice was the same as last week. Discouraging. My day would be much brighter if I knew I could see you later tonight. Do you have any plans?*

"Don't quote me on this, but I think all you have to do is dump the beans inside this slot and press the green button." Amanda pointed to the opening at the top of the machine. "Or as Yzma from *The Emperor's New Groove* might say, 'Pull the lever!'"

With her friends occupied, Olive twiddled her thumbs and shot off a quick reply.

Olive: *No photos of the sign. I was too embarrassed to take one. The wedding I am here for is for my other friend, Clara. I wish you'd asked earlier. We've already made dinner reservations. What about tomorrow?*

"*The Emperor's New Groove* has to be the most under-rated Disney movie," Olive mused.

"I agree! It's made me want to take a trip to Machu Pichu just to explore the spectacular Mayan ruins." The oven timer went off. "Time for the last batch of cookies to come out."

"Got it! We'll have a fresh pot of coffee in three minutes." Clara beamed. She busied herself with finding three coffee mugs and waltzed from side to side. "This smells divine."

Olive peeked at her phone. Three dots blinked. Alex was still typing a message to her.

Alex: *I have morning practice, a physio appointment, and afternoon practice. Any free time I have after that is yours to command.*

Olive: *Can I come and watch one of your practice sessions? We can catch dinner together after.*

Alex: *I don't know...*

Olive: *What if I volunteer to be your practice partner?*

The dots blinked.

Alex: *I'll have to clear it with Adala. No promises.*

Olive: *All I ask is that you try. Text you later.*

Amanda untied her apron. "Cookies are done. How long do you think we have until the cavalry arrives?" Amanda glanced to the doorway. The dogs barked and padded over to the foot of the stairs. Their nails scratched against the floor.

"About two minutes," Olive deadpanned.

Clara raised an eyebrow. "You think that long?"

Amanda opened her mouth to comment just as Clara's fiancé, David, the Duke of Leeds, entered the kitchen. He sniffed the air. "What is that delectable aroma I smell?" He reached for the still brewing pot of coffee.

Clara gently slapped his hand away. "Sorry, this one is only for us girls."

Olive shoved her phone into her pocket.

"What about the cookies?" a hopeful voice asked behind David. Amanda's boyfriend, Eddie, the Prince of Wales, leaned against the door frame. He patted the two dogs on the head.

"The same rules apply." Amanda crossed her arms and stood in front of the cookies. Both men exchanged glances and sighed. Eddie noticed Olive for the first time.

"Nakamura!" Eddie grinned. "Sorry we missed you yesterday."

"Welcome to our flat, Olive. It's better than my cousin's flat, isn't it? Clara always speaks highly of you." The larger of the two dogs pawed his pant leg. "No, Atticus."

Olive's cheeks colored. She stood and managed a half bow and half curtsy that caused her to flail and fall over onto her hands and knees. Her body couldn't decide what it wanted to do. She brushed her jeans off. David and Eddie assisted her to her feet.

They exchanged hugs. Both men stood over six feet tall and had the same sandy blond hair and blue eyes. David wore thick glasses and was formally attired in a three-piece, gray pinstriped suit. Eddie, lankier than his cousin, was dressed casually in black joggers and a fitted, plain white T-shirt. His hair was cropped short, reflecting his status as a member of the British Army.

"That was certainly a memorable introduction." Eddie winked.

"Brownie points for the Leeds-man. See, Princey, *that* is how you treat a lady."

Eddie raised an eyebrow. "Nakamura isn't a lady. She's a friend."

The two spaniels gave up on the humans and made their way over to their waiting bowls of kibbles.

"No comment. Both your apartment and Eddie and Amanda's are equally gorgeous," Olive said.

Eddie sniffed the air again. He glanced hopefully at the cookies a second time with wide eyes. "Are you certain you won't even share *one* cookie with a humble soldier? I *am* on foot duty later today. I'll have to stand stark still for two entire hours in an insanely heavy full Life Guard kit."

Eddie's disappointment reminded Olive of a sad puppy.

"Oh, go on Amanda. There are plenty of cookies. Share the wealth."

He rubbed his hands together in delight.

"And the coffee?" David's hand twitched near the pot.

"And the coffee," Olive affirmed.

"You give in too easily." Amanda retrieved six plates from the upper left-hand cabinet and placed a cookie on each one. "At this rate we'll be out of cookies and coffee in two days instead of two weeks."

David and Eddie high-fived one another. Without waiting for Amanda's spatula to retrieve a cookie from the cooling rack, Eddie picked one up and greedily bit into it. "Hot." He yelped and dropped the cookie onto the plate.

"You won't garner any sympathy from me." Amanda crossed her arms.

Clara poured herself and David cups of coffee. "This is a special reserve blend of dark roast from Olive's hometown."

"Kona is famous for its coffee. The volcanic soil is supposed to add and enhance its flavor." She sat down at the table. "You guys enjoy it. I have enough of it year-round. I would, however, love some vanilla almond milk if you have any."

"Second shelf on the right-hand side." Clara pointed to the fridge.

Olive opened the refrigerator door and retrieved the milk.

"Before I forget, there is a slight change of plans for tonight." David shifted uncomfortably. "Uncle Reg has asked for all of us to join him up in Windsor and, um—"

"Just come out and say it, mate." Eddie rolled his eyes. "David is trying to avoid saying Olive wasn't included in the original invitation, but if she agrees to it, I'll ring Father's office and say she will be joining us."

"I'm sorry." David shot a glance of sympathy in her direction. "Uncle Reg wasn't aware of our plans tonight. It's diffi-cult to say no to the king."

Amanda clapped her hands together. "Well, Olive, what do you say? Do you want to meet King Reginald?"

She nearly dropped the milk and clutched it to her chest. Few women would ever be offered the opportunity to have dinner with the King of England, but her mind was focused on another man entirely. Sheepishly she said, "Would it be horrible if I declined in favor of dinner with Alex?"

Amanda whooped. "Get it, girl. You'll be having a *much* better time than us. The king is awesome, but if I were in your shoes, I'd do exactly the same thing."

Just like that, Olive was suddenly free for dinner.

CHAPTER 16

An Unwelcome Encounter

Olive wore a high-necked, black-and-white polka dot dress that flared out at her knees, with red heels and a white belt. She tapped her knuckles against a white shiplap door. A moment later, a woman with curly auburn brown hair in a tan pea coat, with fierce gray eyes, answered the door. "Yes, can I help you?" She appraised Olive, looking her up and down.

Olive cleared her throat. She adjusted the strap of her red cross-body purse. "I hope I have the right address. I'm Olive. I'm having dinner with Alex tonight."

The woman pulled the door open a little wider. "You'd better come through then." The woman extended her hand. "I'm Penny. Alex's sister." They shook hands in a formal, stiff, business-like manner.

Alex's home was an open-concept, modern, three-bedroom flat with a spectacular view overlooking the River Thames. Boats floated across the muddy-brown water not far from Canary Wharf and the Isle of Dogs, a relatively clean and quiet business district area of London.

The walls of the sitting room were white. A framed print

of Arizona's Grand Canyon with its distinct red and earth tones was the focal point of the room. Floating shelves held knick-knacks and books playing off the crème-toned shades of the sectional sofa and circular glass coffee table.

In the kitchen, the cabinets were white with black handles, and had a cool gray tile backsplash. Penny led Olive to the kitchen island and gestured for her to take a seat at one of the three wooden bar stools. She carried herself with an air of authority.

"I just want a little tête-a-tête before I go and let Alex know you're here." Her voice grew lower. "Just so we are on the same page, I don't approve of you. The last thing my brother needs right now is a distraction." The temperature of the room dropped ten degrees.

Olive sucked in air sharply. Her stomach dropped. "And that's how you see me? As a distraction?" Alex's sister was certainly a straight to the point, no-nonsense person. Every move she made, down to her selected words, appeared carefully calculated.

"Precisely," Penny said.

In the past, Olive had all too often placed high values on what others had thought about her. At thirteen, she'd made the mistake of reading what strangers had written and said about her gymnastics on the internet. Internet trolls were still the worst sort of people out there, hiding behind the screen of a computer to hurt others. With Sean, she'd made the same type of mistake.

I thought he was the only person who might ever date me. I was so socially awkward. I had no clue how I should behave around men. In college, guys only wanted to have an Olympic medalist as their date to brag. Nobody wanted me for me. Sean was different. He was the first person who stuck around longer than one date.

But it had come at a cost. She'd attempted to cater all of

her interests to him. She'd changed how she dressed, and even dumbed down her conversations to keep and maintain his interest in her. In both of these instances, the hard lesson learned was one she instilled in others today—don't be anyone other than yourself.

"Your opinion doesn't bother me in the least." Olive shrugged. "All I care about is making your brother happy, keeping him healthy, and seeing where the chemistry we have together goes."

Penny raised an eyebrow. "And the fact my brother is a high-profile, wealthy tennis star doesn't contribute to your attraction for him?"

"Truthfully, his being a tennis player initially repulsed me. He's not the first tennis player I've dated." Olive weighed her words. "I am a self-made female entrepreneur. I have worked hard and busted my bum to become the success story I am today. I don't care about wealth or status. I'm more interested in finding a person with a stellar personality. I want a boyfriend who brings a smile to my face and understands how to treat and respect a woman. I won't settle for anything less."

"Impressive." Penny drummed her fingers against the kitchen island.

Alex lingered in the doorway for a moment. Olive heard him breathe shallowly. He pulled at his collar. "Penny—" His tone tightened. "Are you interrogating Olive?"

"Certainly. I would be remiss in my job as your manager if I didn't." She stood and pushed the bar chair into the island.

His neck reddened. "Penny—"

"Alex, calm down," Olive said. "Frankly, the fact your sister speaks her mind is refreshing. She doesn't have to like me. Not everyone will."

Penny cleared her throat. "I never said I didn't *like* you. I said I didn't *approve* of you. There *is* a difference."

Alex pinched the bridge of his nose. "Penny."

"Touché." Olive nervously laughed. She stood.

Alex held his coat and a bouquet of pink peonies. He practically shoved the flowers into Olive's hands.

Her eyelids fluttered. "They are gorgeous." She held the flowers up to her nose and sniffed them. Bits of pollen tickled her nose. They had a semi-sweet and almost spicy aroma. "Would you mind if I leave them here though? They might be a lot to carry."

Alex left the peonies on the kitchen island, then shepherded Olive out the door. "We're off to dinner. Bye, Pen." He quickly closed the door behind him and all but jogged to the lift. "I'm sorry to rush you out, but if I hadn't, we'd never escape."

He clicked the button. They waited in silence for a moment. "Your sister is interesting," Olive started.

He sucked in his cheeks. "I've lived with the woman for more than fifteen years. You can say it out loud; she's an acquired taste," Alex said.

With a ding, the lift doors popped open. They stepped in, and Alex pressed the button for the lobby level.

"I wouldn't say that. I'd use the word intense. One of my gymnastics teammates had similar mannerisms. I bet your sister would have made an excellent lawyer."

The movement of the elevator gave off a buzzing sound. Olive ran her fingers up the sleeve of Alex's navy jumper. The cashmere fabric was soft and warm to the touch. His light gray trousers were tailored to his taut legs and perfectly sculpted bum.

"Penny considered a career as a barrister but enjoyed her accounting course instead." Alex shook his head. "She's scary detailed and organized."

Not surprising.

"Do you two still live together now?" Olive asked.

"For the time being, it's Penny, me, and her husband

Drew. London is incredibly expensive. The three of us agreed it would make the most sense financially to purchase one shared flat." Alex wrapped his arm around Olive's frame. "Until last year, our schedules never aligned where all three of us were home for more than a few days at a time."

She shimmied closer to his body and noted how it was always running at a warmer temperature than hers. Today he smelled of rosewood and grass. She wondered if the grass scent came from his tennis practice.

"Since I've been home, it's more apparent than ever—a grown man needs space from his sister." Alex shivered. "I'm actively hunting for a new flat as we speak. It's time I invested in a piece of London property."

The lift doors glided open. Alex extended his arm to her. "Shall we?"

They made their way to the London Underground.

They stopped for dinner at a trendy sushi restaurant nestled inside London's Chinatown district. Sitting in a front booth, Olive expertly ordered several different rolls for them to enjoy. Most patrons were at the counter near the center of the restaurant, watching the four chefs create the sushi dishes as they were ordered. Japanese woodblock prints and rice paper scrolls with Japanese kanji characters adorned the walls.

"Sushi is a staple in the Nakamura homestead. Growing up, we pretty much only ate Asian food. Every meal to this day has nori, which is seaweed, rice, and some type of meat. When you live on an island, seafood is in your blood."

They opted to split a chicken teriyaki bento box.

"And are you able to prepare sushi rolls on a whim?" Alex asked. He helped himself to their shared appetizer, a bowl of edamame peas sitting in the center of the table.

Olive winced. "That's a point of contention between my mom and me. I never picked up any advanced cooking skills. I didn't have the time when I was training, and in Seattle, Amanda was the chef." She peeled the skin off the edamame. "When I moved home again, I took to eating dinner with my parents every night. In the rare event I have to fend for myself, I order take-out."

"From the way your eyes sparkle when you speak about your parents, it is incredibly obvious that you are close to them. I wish I could say the same."

She stayed silent, well aware Alex was not on the best of terms with his own parents.

Alex took hold of Olive's hand and drew circles on it. "I was thinking that after dinner we could—" Alex was interrupted by a shrill voice.

"Alexander! You're a sight for sore eyes."

Olive dropped her chopsticks. Her stomach clenched.

"You're here with shortie?" Tessa placed a hand over her mouth in disbelief. She wore a tweed, black-and-white houndstooth suit and was shown by a seating host to the booth across from them.

Alex's face drained of color. "Tessa," he murmured.

Resentment simmered below Olive's surface. *This is the last time Tessa is going to ruin my night.*

Tessa ignored Olive and spoke directly to Alex. "So, this is the best you can do? At least she's finally gotten a handle on how to dress like an adult, though she'll never be able to afford any *stylish* designer clothing." Tessa held her hand so the large diamond ring on her finger sparkled and was blatantly on display to the entire restaurant.

"Tessa," Alex warned.

"The same insults grow old after you've heard them several hundred times," Olive interjected. She clenched Alex's hand for support.

Tessa's eyes narrowed. "At least my *husband* has career prospects ahead of him. He's not relegated to low-brow tournaments."

"Alex and I have something you'll never have." Olive laughed to herself. "Manners and class."

"Those won't buy you a Ferrari or an estate." Tessa rolled her eyes. "You two both have your sights too low. Always settling."

Sean sauntered in and slid into the booth next to Tessa. He possessively wrapped his arm around her. "Georgiou." He curtly nodded.

"And look who else is here." Tessa gestured to Olive.

Sean's eyes narrowed. "Well, well, well. For a woman who said they'd never change themselves, you're a walking contradiction. The hair. The clothing." He smirked at Tessa. "Honestly, she used to remind me of the bride of Frankenstein with her shoddy attempts at doing her makeup."

She could feel Alex's hands shaking under hers, holding back his anger. She shook her head when he attempted to rise. She sent him a silent message. *I've got this.*

"What a pair you two make," Olive muttered.

She chose to ignore them both, more annoyed than insulted. In the past, she would have cowered and taken the insults personally, but as she delved deeper into her journey of self-discovery, Olive realized that Sean was rude and horrible to just about everyone, Tessa included.

Sean is a miserable person. I almost pity him, but that doesn't stop me from wanting to throw a banana cream pie in both their faces. She pictured Tessa screaming and pulling out a compact mirror, fretting over her hair, and Sean just sitting there with a wide-open mouth.

Watch the deadly aim and accuracy this bride of Frankenstein could have with said pie.

"Olive shines from the inside out. She could be dressed in

a rubbish bin bag, and she'd still be the most attractive woman in whatever room she's in." Hearing Alex jump to her defense sent chills through her body.

Alex signaled for Olive to gather up her purse and her jacket. His jaw clenched. He signaled to the nearest waiter for the check. "Olive and I were just about to leave."

"Indeed, what a shame." False sympathy oozed from Tessa's voice. "This brings back memories of the night you proposed and I dumped you, Alex."

What did she just say? Olive fought to keep her face neutral. She wouldn't give Tessa the satisfaction of a reaction.

"Oh. Did I say that aloud?" Tessa splayed a hand on her chest. "How clumsy of me." Alex threw down a wad of bills from his wallet onto the table. "Have fun with that one, honey. His career is over."

"Your loss is my gain. Have a fantastic dinner." Olive stood, straightened her skirt, and slid her coat over her dress. Her chest and shoulders were tight with tension. Tossing his napkin on the chair, she followed Alex as he strode out of the restaurant.

Her mind whirled. *Alex proposed to Tessa? I don't understand. Alex and Tessa are opposites.*

Her heels clicked against the cobblestones, putting some distance between her and the sushi restaurant. "Alex. Wait. I'm short. It takes me three strides to catch up with you," Olive called out slightly breathless.

Alex turned around and shoved his hands into his pocket. "Disgusting. Distasteful. Phony." His shoulders hunched.

She placed a hand on his forearm. The muscles corded with tension. "Take a deep breath."

"How can you be so calm about all of this?" He threw his hands up into the air. "They were both horrible to you."

She focused on her own breathing to slow her racing

pulse. "I'm definitely upset." She guided Alex's hand to her neck. He breathed sharply and ran a hand through his hair.

"Both Sean and Tessa have insulted me so many times over the years. Tonight was different. It struck me when we were inside that Sean has always been a person who seeks to belittle others to evoke a reaction from them. He treats everyone as if they were the dirt under his shoes. I've matured enough to know my own self-worth."

"I'm happy to hear that." Alex placed a gentle kiss atop her head. "If only Tessa could see she would be much better off without him. That wanker has ruined her. She is *not* the same woman I fell in love with."

Olive opened her mouth into an "O" shape. He had loved Tessa? She'd told Alex about Sean; why hadn't he done the same about his own past with her? His revelation unsettled her. The cloak of confidence she'd proudly worn earlier in the day was beginning to take on micro-tears in its fabric.

"Let's walk," Olive recommended. Alex grunted and followed her lead. They both needed air.

CHAPTER 17

The Lego Store

Olive had no idea where she was heading. Brightly-lit window displays and neon lights ultimately caught her attention when they reached the Shakespeare statue and fountain demarking the center of Leicester Square. This central London location was awash with tourists.

The businesses surrounding the square included fast-food restaurants, a casino, hotels, and a large movie theater—entertainment options for just about everyone. A Swiss glockenspiel chimed. They sat on a park bench in front of the movie theater. Olive welcomed the distraction of the area and searched for the bells and moving figures.

Alex spoke for the first time. "It is across from the M&M store, over there." He pointed to a red, white, and black painted clock. "Before they built that hotel, there used to be a Swiss tourism center next to it." His face was no longer flushed and red, but his sentences were still short and clipped, and his shoulders rigid with tension.

"What can you tell me about the movie theater?" She admired the popcorn lights, black granite, and art deco façade.

"The Odeon cinema hosts most of the major film premieres in the UK. The largest theater inside has eight hundred seats." Alex scratched his chin. "But the real gem of Leicester Square is the pub that's kitty-corner to the Paddington Bear statue. They serve the best pints and fish and chips in the area." He grimaced at the mention of food. "Some date this is turning out to be. We never actually had the chance to eat dinner."

"Dinner can wait a few more minutes." She squinted at a brightly lit, colorful, yellow and red shop. "Is that a Lego store? If it is, it's calling my name."

Alex nodded. "It's the London flagship shop. I haven't been inside in a long time."

"This is the largest one I've ever seen." Olive rubbed her hands together. "You don't mind indulging me, do you?"

"Not at all." Olive grabbed hold of Alex's hand and pulled him toward the shop. "The interior is brilliant. Off the top of my head, there is a double-decker bus, a traditional London red telephone booth, and even an Underground train car model."

"You're only making it more enticing." Olive picked up their pace.

"I wasn't aware you collected Legos."

"I have a few sets. Keeping my hands busy relaxes me. Legos are fancy puzzles, and I love the fact that you can liter-ally build and craft your own world." They crossed the square, passing a street dancer spinning atop his head and a man painted entirely in silver pretending to be a human robot. "Anytime I was competing at an international competition, I always made an effort to purchase the Lego set exclusive to whatever country I was in."

"I'm learning more and more about you," he mused.

"The sets I am hoping to find today, however, are going to

be gifts for my friends Amanda and Alice, one of the other bridesmaids. Alice hopes to become an engineer someday. Apparently, she never owned a set of Legos growing up. I *have* to rectify that with the London exclusive architectural set. It's the perfect way for her to put her talents to use."

The front window displayed a twenty-foot model of Big Ben surrounded on all sides by the Lego versions of a London police officer, Sherlock Holmes, and a gentleman in a bowler hat. They passed through the front doors. Olive spied a Lego judge in a wig behind Big Ben. He stood poised to throw a cream pie at the policeman. Olive grinned.

The ground floor had a green dragon attached to the ceiling. Yellow tables held clear tubes packed to the brim with small Lego minifigures. The line for the cash wrap extended to the center of the sales floor. Olive walked to the right. "Amanda loves anything Disney, so keep your eyes peeled for the Disney World Cinderella Castle set. We'll be building it for Clara's bachelorette party."

Olive passed a masked Lego ninja standing at a Japanese torii gate. She watched Alex's gaze dart from the five-foot Hogwarts Castle display to the Star Wars X-Wing model. A video board behind it played clips for the latest Lego film.

"Is that a model of the Roman Colosseum? The Taj Mahal? Paris?" Alex gravitated toward the wall with the larger and more complicated models of cityscapes. "I didn't realize there were sets that catered more to adults." He picked up the box displaying the Roman Colosseum. "Blimey, four thousand pieces? What happens if you lose one of them?"

"They sell replacement parts." Olive laughed. "Maybe you can take up Lego building as a new hobby. It could eventually turn into a job after tennis. There are *actual* professional Lego design masters."

"What a brilliant job that must be." Alex chuckled. He replaced the set on the shelf.

The ground floor was growing steadily more crowded. Olive gestured to the stairs leading up to the next level. She soaked in the sight of a map of the city of London displayed behind the stairs.

"The entire Thames waterfront! I see Tower Bridge, the Shard, Houses of Parliament, London Eye, and Buckingham Palace." Olive crinkled her nose. "Where is your apartment in relation to the map?" She glanced over her shoulder to the map of the Underground next to the model of the Underground car containing Lego Shakespeare and a Buckingham Palace foot guard.

"On this map, it's past Tower Bridge and behind the London Eye where that cluster of factory-shaped buildings are." Alex pointed to the eastern end of the river. "At night, with all the lights dimmed, the view is magical." He moved closer and lowered his voice. "I was originally counting on taking you on a night cruise down the Thames tonight. We would have enjoyed a similar view."

"And what's stopping us from doing that?" Olive batted her eyes. "It sounds amazing."

Alex rubbed the back of his neck. "I didn't think you'd still be in the mood after what transpired back there."

"We can't let Tessa and Sean win. Life doesn't have any do-overs." They climbed the staircase up to the second floor. She perched against the railing and stared out at the clock face of Big Ben. "There have been numerous times the last few years I wished I could have skipped over all the crushing heartbreaks and frustrations to reach the 'good part.'" Her eyes crinkled.

"When I look back with more perspective and clarity, though, I'm especially grateful for all the resilience and personal growth I've had. I've overcome every single obstacle that's come my way. If I had skipped through life, I wouldn't be the person I am today."

Alex leaned his back against the railing and looked at

Olive. "It's been an uphill battle for both of us." They shared a knowing smile.

They walked to a white wall featuring circular, clear, fishbowl-like containers of individual Lego pieces sorted by color.

"I wish I could share your optimism and positive outlook on everything. Being injured the last nine months, I've only grown more short-tempered and self-pitying." Alex put his hand into the closest bin and watched the pieces fall through his fingers. "I don't like the person I've become. I had hoped to find myself in Greece."

In a hushed tone she asked, "And did you?"

Alex shoved his hands into his pockets. "I found you."

Her heart fluttered. That was the answer she had wanted to hear. Her pulse raced. And yet, the last comment from Tessa still ran wild in her mind. She swallowed hard. "What did you ever see in a woman like Tessa?" She had to know.

"Tessa wasn't always so mean-spirited." They walked slowly toward the back of the sales floor with the Disney models. "When I was first introduced to Tessa, she had braces, stringy hair, and enjoyed spending time with my sister.

"We both turned professional the same year and shared the same coach. Neal was well known for churning out talented young tennis players." Alex looked at the Lego mosaic portrait of Sir Paul McCartney. "She was one of the few people who shared my work ethic and the drive to win at all costs."

"Was it strange to share a coach?" Olive found the Disney World set and rose up on her toes, trying to pull it off the shelf. It remained just out of her reach.

Alex used his lanky arms and handed the set to her. "At times. In my case, it was only for one season. Neal wasn't a good fit for me. He focused his efforts on Tessa. To be fair, her skills rivaled the best in the world. I can't blame him. I developed slower."

She double-checked the box and then slid it under her arm.

"Tessa found early success on the women's tour. I won my first two tournaments, but my luck didn't hold out. First, it was elbow tendonitis, then my shoulder went wonky. I was forced to rest my body." They headed to the stairs and returned to the ground floor.

"I decided to recover at my maternal grandparents' home to be closer to my sister. Tessa and I spent less and less time together. She was always too busy for me. I should've realized that we'd grown apart." Alex twisted the ring on his finger and wiped one of his hands on his trouser leg. "We'd once bonded over our mutual taste in films and music, but everything changed when she continued to win."

They returned to the display of city sets. "What happened?" She picked up the London skyline model, clenching it tightly in her hand, almost denting the thin cardboard.

Alex crossed his arms. "Companies wanted to sign the hot, new, and attractive rising women's tennis star for endorsements. By this point, Tessa had become increasingly status conscious. When Sean came along as the media darling's next top male player, she dumped me for him. I was the long-shot."

She let out a deep breath. Hearing Alex's story broke her. But in the back of her mind, she heard Tessa laughing at her. *He proposed to me.* She couldn't get those words out of her mind. Should she say anything to him?

They joined the line for the cash wrap. Olive opened her purse and searched for her wallet. She shifted her weight from foot to foot. As her feelings for him progressed over the last three and a half weeks, the ease with which Olive found herself reading Alex scared her. The relationship she shared with her parents and with her best friends invoked a completely different set of emotions and feelings. She wasn't falling for Alex anymore.

I think I'm already in love with you.

A worker in blue signaled for Olive to step up to the register and pay. Robotically she went through the motions of paying for her Lego sets. Alex hovered behind her. Outside again, she rubbed the smooth plastic handles of her yellow Lego Store bag together.

"Do you still love Tessa?" she stammered.

Alex's forehead creased. Fine lines appeared in the corners of his eyes. He licked his lips. "I'll always have a place reserved for her. Tessa and I have a long history together. As painful as it was, I'd never attempt to erase some of the happier memories."

She coughed. "But do you still love her?"

"I don't understand." Alex's nostrils flared. "Why should it matter? She's in the past."

Olive looked to the ground. Her voice turned quiet. "At the restaurant, Tessa said that you once proposed to her. Is that true or was she toying with me?"

"It's true." Alex grimaced. "I naively thought proposing to Tessa would be the solution to bring us back together. McPherson—he's the one who ruined everything."

"You're blaming Tessa being who she is on Sean?" Olive placed her hands on her hips.

"Are you defending him?" His lip curled.

"I'd *never* stoop so low as to *ever* defend him." She flinched. "He broke me in so many ways." Olive's heart was shattering. Her chest rose and fell at a rapid pace. "What if he hadn't come along?"

"I don't know. It's complicated." He ran a hand through his hair. "There can be room for both you and Tessa in my heart."

He still loves her.

"No. There can't be." She shook her head as she backed away. "She's a bully and a beast of a woman."

"Tessa is *not* a beast. There is so much you don't know about her." Alex put his own hands on his hips, his eyes fiery. He breathed sharply. "You are acting as if you and I are ready to commit to something more. There is so much I still don't know about you. We're supposed to see where this goes. It's only been three weeks."

Olive covered her nose with her hand. "I thought I read all the signs correctly."

He rubbed his temples. "I never said I was looking for anything deep, like love. I don't want to make the same mistake twice. Dating, yes. But love? I'm not even sure it exists."

"You consider me a mistake?" She breathed. "You don't believe in love?"

The second blow. Her veil of confidence was tearing at the seams. She gritted her teeth. *Stupid Olive. You should have known that, in the end, try as you might, you and Tessa are forever joined at the hip. You'll never be able to be free from her shadow.*

"That isn't what I meant." He stepped toward her. "You're not a mistake."

"Well, I *am* looking for love. I'm looking for a person to complete me. I'm looking to find the other half of myself." She wrapped her arms around herself. "If you don't want love, or even believe in it, then I'm glad this date never got off the ground." Her eyes were wide as tears threatened to fall.

"I was willing to take a huge risk. To try and conquer the emotional scars Sean left on me. I was putting everything out there *for you*. Is it wrong that I don't want to have to share your heart with another? Love *does* exist. You just have to open yourself to find it." She sniffled. "I'm no longer in the mood for dinner or spending time with you."

Alex stood frozen in place. "Maybe you're right." His tone was flat.

Salty tears fell down her cheeks. She reached into her purse and handed him the gray camera case. "Then this is goodbye." With as much dignity as she could muster, she walked to the street, hailed a black cabbie, and returned to her hotel feeling more alone and hurt than ever.

A Friend Like Me

The first in-person dress fitting for Olive occurred two weeks after her disastrous date with Alex. To this point, all her consultations with Clarissa Lee's design team had been virtual. The entire east wing of Kensington Palace had been turned into wedding headquarters.

Olive stood atop a pedestal, running her hands over the soft, silky, periwinkle-blue fabric. She loved how when she moved, the skirt shape imitated the petals of the lotus, the national symbol of India, and the inspiration for her particular dress. The masterful design work showed off her toned arms and elongated her waist with its V-neck cut top, drop waist, and asymmetrical layered skirt.

"I can see why Clara selected Clarissa as her dress designer. She is a wizard with cloth."

Amy, a member of Clarissa Lee's staff assigned to her dress, carefully reviewed the garment's fit. She held a tape measure in her hand and carefully drew out chalk lines and pinned the fabric along the hem and back seams of the dress.

"Clarissa's been Clara's go-to designer for over two years now," Amanda gushed. She snapped a photo of Olive with her phone. "After the fitting, we'll swing by Boots and pick up the photo print of you in this beauty."

"Boots?" Olive tilted her head to the side.

"Boots is a chemist." Amanda chuckled. "It's the British version of a Walgreens or a CVS."

"Aw." She shook her head. "You're sounding more and more British every day."

"I've lived here for over a year now." Amanda returned her attention to her phone's screen. "I was bound to adopt a few slang terms eventually."

"What are you planning to do with the photo?" Olive asked.

She slid it into her pocket. "I'm putting together a memory book for C. It'll be our gift to her on her wedding day."

Olive's shoulders slumped. Photos reminded her of Alex. She was still torn in two. The wounds from their disagreement were raw and painful. In spite of it all, she wanted so much just to hear his voice even if they no longer had any chance of being together.

She worried for his well-being. Had he found a sports psychologist? Being mentally strong was going to be so important for him to succeed. How was his training going? Was he still on track for a return to tournament play in late June?

Amy poked her back. "If you could please stand up straight, Miss Nakamura, this fitting would go much faster."

Olive apologized and elongated her spine. She held her hands to her side, mindful not to move. She was proud of herself for not letting her tears escape.

"When we stop by Boots, I, um, need a new SD card. The one I have in my camera is nearly full."

All the photos I took in Greece, Venice, and Austria were on the SD card in Alex's compact camera. Of all the souvenirs from this trip, those photos would have been the most valuable to me.

Why didn't I take the SD card out of the camera before I returned it to him? She sighed. It was too late to do anything about the photos now.

My sole saving grace is that I took a few photos on my phone.

"All finished," Amy said. She guided Olive to the changing area and assisted her in slipping out of the dress. "We'll have Miss Collins schedule your next fitting in two weeks' time."

"Thank you, Amy," Olive said. She changed back into her black body suit top, jeans, and a fitted lilac blazer.

"SD card, check. I have it on my list," Amanda said.

In the early afternoon, Amanda walked up as close as she could to the medieval tapestries adorning the walls within the Hampton Court Palace Presence Chamber of Henry VIII. She stared at the green and gold threads in the intricately designed floral borders.

"Doesn't it make you happy that women in this day and age aren't expected to sew and embroider to be considered 'accomplished ladies'?" She sadly shook her head. "I'd be brilliant at making knots, but embroidery would be hopeless."

Olive only half paid attention. Had Alex lived in the Tudor era, would he be an athletic prince as was Henry VIII? She remembered tennis being aptly named the sport of royalty. One of the first ever tennis courts was located on the far side of the Hampton Court palace grounds. Versailles even boasted its own court.

She pictured Alex garbed in a Tudor frock with a stately white ruffled collar, a red-and-gold embroidered tunic, and a matching red cap and feather twirling a wooden racquet in his hands.

His legs would look exceptional in those Tudor trousers and white stockings. Her body grew flushed.

"Olive, this has to stop. You're thinking about *him* again."

"That's my problem." Olive furrowed her brow. "I can't seem to stop."

Amanda took hold of her hand and escorted her to the next room for privacy. The yellow-gilded ceilings decorated with Henry VIII's coat of arms brightened up the otherwise dark tones of the room. More tapestries hung from the walls. One of her security team members discreetly stood off in the corner, just out of their earshot, as Amanda and Olive sat on a bench directly across from the room's central fireplace.

"You've been moping around for two weeks. Do you know how hard it's been for me to bite my tongue to keep from asking more details about what happened between you and Alex?" Amanda gave Olive her full attention. "Seriously, like it's killing me to see you only half-heartedly enjoying your-self. We've been through this before. You don't have to pretend with me."

Olive's walls were crumbling down. "Everything I see and do reminds me of him. I don't know if I'll ever be able to get over the heartbreak this time." She sniffled.

"Timeout." Amanda held up her hands in a "T" symbol. "Heartbreak?" She scratched her forehead. "Okay, there are obviously a *lot* of details to the story I'm missing out on. I know you two met in Athens, but after that, you'll have to fill in the blanks. Give me the *full* recap here. What happened to make you go from floating on air when you arrived to being downright miserable?"

Olive's breath hitched. The words tumbled out of her mouth. She told her closest friend *everything*. Reliving her relationship with Alex over the last few weeks exhausted her. She could feel her body experiencing the many highs and lows. All of her hopes and soddy disappointments. It took all of her emotional reserves to push through. Amanda supplied her with tissue after tissue. Her eyes were dry like sandpaper when there were finally no more tears left.

Olive studied her nails. "When Alex tried to push me away in Salzburg, I could tell he was frustrated with himself and was scared at how fast we were connecting to one another. We were of the same heart and mind." She clasped her hands together and twiddled her thumbs. "After I had time to cool off, we talked about how he has trouble trusting and letting anyone in."

Amanda nodded slowly. "And what was different about this fight?"

"At first, I was angry when he said there could be a special place for both me and Tessa. I refuse to play second fiddle to *that* woman." Olive clenched her jaw. "But love is something he isn't actively looking for. He said he wasn't even sure if love exists."

Amanda took a long look at the fireplace and back to Olive. "It's stuffy in here. Let's get some air." They headed out into the garden that was constructed to rival Versailles. "Love is so complicated."

Olive's shoulders hunched. "Is it so wrong of me to want to be the only woman he loves?"

Had the Yew hedges been taller, they could have served as a life-sized maze. They walked straight down the dirt pathway toward a fountain shooting up a jet of water thirty feet into the air.

"You love your parents, don't you?" Amanda moved her hair from in front of her shoulder to behind them.

"Of course."

"And your friends?"

Olive emphatically nodded.

"Do you love Alex too?"

Olive swallowed hard. *It's like a fuzzy dream, but if I didn't love Alex, it wouldn't hurt so badly.*

Behind them, the red-bricked palace with its many chimneys and windows stood out in stark contrast to the greenery. There were borders of early blooming red and purple flowers. They walked around the fountain. The sound of the water shooting up out of the jet and cascading back down to Earth loudly sounded in the background.

"I do love him." Olive spoke louder than intended.

"And do *you* have the capacity to love all of these people at the same time?" Amanda crossed her arms.

She could see what her friend was getting at. She sunk onto the edge of the fountain, not caring if her jeans grew wet. "Yes," she answered almost mutely.

"Let's continue to play devil's advocate... Put yourself in Alex's shoes. You think you've found the perfect person to spend the rest of your life with. You're ready to propose. Instead of it being the best day of your life, you are in for a rude awakening. Your girlfriend dumps you as if you never mattered. Not only has that person broken your heart, but they've already callously moved on."

Olive opened her mouth. "It's reminiscent of what Sean did to me." She grew lightheaded and dizzy. The air buzzed with insects.

"Uh-huh," Amanda said. "And *what* did you tell me you discussed in Salzburg earlier?"

She bit her tongue. "Trust." She buried her face in her hands.

"Ten points to Nakamura." Amanda gently put her hands on Olive's shoulders, causing her to sit up straight. "Your journey had you learning to believe in yourself again. I'm always going to be on *your* side"—they locked eyes—"but did you ever share the *full* story with Alex about what Sean did to you?"

Olive's face flushed bright red. "No."

They stood again and walked behind the fountain,

pausing in front of neatly-lined rows of English lavender. The purple flowers waved in the gentle breeze. The fragrant perfume of the lavender flowers overpowered her senses.

"From this gal's perspective, it's plain to me that both you and Alex run high on emotions. Neither of you has been able to clearly communicate to the other. He may *say* he doesn't believe in love, but that's only because he hasn't experienced it yet for himself. It's your job to show him he's wrong. Love exists and it's all around us."

"Maybe we do have a chance to be together and happy again." Olive breathed deeply. "But I don't even know where to begin. I'm still a big chicken. What if Alex doesn't pick up my call?"

"If you were to call him, he'd answer. But it is well past time for you two to kiss and make up. A call doesn't cut it. Leave everything to me." Amanda's mouth curved up in approval.

The lavender fragrance calmed her nerves, but knowing Amanda, she was hesitant to let her guard down. Her friend didn't do anything subtly. What did she have in mind?

"Call that Leo guy you met in Athens. Have him fill you in on Alex's schedule and where he practices." Amanda's hand twitched. She pulled out her phone from the back pocket of her jeans. "Michael, it's Collins. A change in plans for today's itinerary. Are you able to pick us up a little early? Great." Her eyes gleamed with mirth.

"What would I ever do without a friend like you?" Olive whispered.

Amanda sang the *Aladdin* song "Friend Like Me."

Alex rubbed his wristband across his forehead and cleared the perspiration from his vision. Olive could hear him breathing hard. His knees were bent, his eyes laser focused on his jet-black-haired coach, Adala. His racquet rolled back and forth in his hands. He tightened his grip on its handle and shifted his weight forward onto the balls of his feet.

The ball rhythmically made contact with the hard surface of the practice court as Adala bounced it. She tossed the tennis ball up ten feet into the air and brought her racket up to serve it over the net. She grunted. The ball whirled at over one hundred miles an hour into the white square outline of the service box that indicated the ball was in.

Alex shuffled to his left. His shoes squeaked. Olive clenched her hands into fists. She could hear his footwork was off. The squeaks were too close together. They should be making a nice even sound. In gymnastics, it was the same. Whether it was the sprint down the vault runway or the running entry into a tumbling pass on the floor, there was a distinct pattern of sounds feet made.

"Stop." Adala tucked her racquet under her arm. "There is no point in playing when your game is uninspiring."

"How am I supposed to regain my timing and shots without getting a full simulated match under my belt?" Alex slammed his racquet into the ground cracking the rim of the racquet's metal frame. "All we do is hitting drill after drill. It's not making *any* difference." Alex winced and stared at the mark his racquet left on the court.

"Tennis is as much a mental game as it is a physical one." Adala calmly rolled her cart of tennis balls to the side of the court. "You must take care of your body, your mind, and your spirit."

Adala waved to the glass and signaled for Olive to join them. Olive hesitated. Did Alex really want to see her when he'd lost his temper?

Leo did warn me Alex has been moody and unpredictable.

She squared her shoulders, slid open the glass door, and

stepped out onto one of the hard-surface tennis courts of the Stratford Sports Club. She could hear her pulse racing in her ears. Her footsteps echoed as she walked out into the enclosed court.

Alex looked up, eyes wide with shock. His face paled. "Olive," he murmured.

She stood with her hands clasped behind her back. "Hi, Alex."

His mouth opened and closed. His forehead creased.

His skin was pale, and his eyes dull.

He looks terrible. He's so haggard and defeated-looking.

She couldn't fathom how aged Alex appeared since their last meeting. His face was once again covered in uneven scruffy facial hair with sprinkles of silver.

He's not even that much older than me.

Adala cleared her throat. "Nakamura. Nice to see you again. It's been too long." She handed her racquet to Olive. "We'll catch up later. Knock some sense into Georgiou. If anyone can set him straight, it's you."

Olive tested the weight of the racquet in her hand. Compared to her cheap racquet at home, Adala's was heavier and had a larger head. She took a practice swing.

Finally recovering his wits, Alex sputtered, "What's going on?"

"Nakamura is your hitting partner for the day." Adala's eyes danced. "I'll be back at the end of the session in an hour or so." She left them alone.

More Than a Passing Shot

"You'll need a new racquet if you want to get some practice in." Olive's words had their intended effect. They snapped Alex out of his trance. Olive bent over and picked up his broken racquet.

"What are you doing here?" His voice came out hoarse.

"I'm here to see your tennis game." Her fingers ran over the fragmented rim and broken set of strings. "You never got back to me about my being able to watch you play, so here I am."

"But Adala..." Alex started.

She interjected. "...and I met six years ago at the Olympics. Remember. She *loves* gymnastics. Had she been one foot shorter, she might have taken up gymnastics instead of becoming a tennis player."

Alex slowly stepped toward his equipment bag to the side of the net. "Today's not going my way. I'm not worth watching or a decent partner to hit with." He unzipped the middle compartment. "I was foolish to think I could ever make it back to the tour."

"Of course, you're worth watching. You are one of the

world's top male tennis players. There are so many people that would do anything just to share the same court as you even if you are going through a rocky patch. For every great practice session there are bound to be a couple horrible ones." Alex took the broken racquet from Olive's hands and shoved it into his bag. "You just need to get in more numbers under your belt."

Alex frowned. "Numbers?"

"Gymnastics expression." Olive reached into the cart of balls and picked up a neon yellow-green ball. "It means you need more reps or, in my case, more routines. Flipping and twisting are all about muscle memory." She turned it over in her hands and tossed it up in the air.

Alex caught it. "It's not just about more practice. Everything constantly hurts. I'm tired of being in pain all the time. It's time I considered my retirement."

"If you were to leave everything behind today, would you be satisfied with what you've accomplished?" Olive picked up another tennis ball and bounced it on the ground with Adala's borrowed racquet. "Because if you are, then go ahead. Retire. But if there is any shred of doubt, even the smallest bit, then it will haunt you. You'll lie awake at night and wonder what-if."

Alex moved his equipment bag off the metal bench and sat. Olive positioned herself next to him and said, "When you are ready to retire, you *have* to be ready to do so on your own terms and be completely at peace with the decision." She put her hand on his knee and ran her finger down the length of the raised scar from his surgery. "Physical pain is weakness leaving the body. You have literally just returned to actually playing tennis. You *will* adjust."

She methodically rolled up the hem of her black workout capris to her knee. There were two reddish-purple faded vertical scars and two horizontal circular scars. "I'm living, breathing proof."

He blinked slowly. Wearily, he said, "Why are you here?" His eyes were bloodshot and puffy.

She turned her body so it faced him, picked up his hand, and put it over her chest. "Do you feel how fast my heart is racing? I'm scared and I'm nervous. I don't think I can stand it if you say you don't want me in your life 'for good.'" It beat wildly, playing a tennis match of its own.

"I'm so sorry I *ever* opened my mouth. I will never be able to apologize enough for any pain I caused you. You're the last person I would ever want to hurt." He hunched and held his head in his hands. "These last few weeks have left me stumbling through life. I thought I'd lost you."

"You've *never* lost me." Olive's lips quivered. "I am more than a passing shot!"

"Seeing Tessa unnerved me. I promised myself I would never let another person have the same hold over me. I never wanted to have my heart ripped to bits ever again." He stared intensely into her eyes. "But every time I am with you, emotions bubble to the surface that mirror the sensations I felt when I was with Tessa. This time, they are so much more intense and powerful."

He picked up her hand and slowly placed it on his own heart. "Every moment since we had our fight, I've beaten myself up, because I was too cowardly to come face-to-face with the reality that I *love* you." It beat equally as fast as if it were trying to keep up with Olive in a cross-court rally. "I *never* dared to hope I might be worthy enough or bloody lucky enough to find a woman who completes me."

Olive's eyes glistened. "I *love* you too, Alexander Georgiou."

He carefully moved her hair behind her ear. Like the moon and the stars, gravity pulled them into one another. He kissed her shoulder, moving up toward her mouth. He breathed deeply. "You're my own Greek goddess."

His breath was hot on her neck. It was like soft rain on a summer evening. She smiled softly and tilted her head. Their lips met in a gentle caress. Waves of joy resounded through her body.

Their gazes met. His molten liquid-amber eyes melted her insides. She saw passion. She saw desire. But most of all, she saw love. She was suddenly hungry for more. They deeply kissed a second time as if the extinct Diamond Head volcano was bursting back to life. Alex's lips were hot lava. She kissed him more intensely to stop the flow from escaping.

"I never knew you had such a passionate side," he whispered.

"I missed you. This is making up for lost time," Olive said.

They kissed again. Steam rose off their bodies like cold ocean meeting fiery magma. Her hands traveled down his back, taking in the defined and sinewy ridges of his muscles built from a lifetime of playing tennis. The temperature hit a boiling point. Her senses worked in overdrive. All was right in the world again.

Olive stuck her tongue out. She bounced the ball once and underhand served it to Alex. The ball flew over the net and rebounded at hip height. Alex was ready for it. His footwork, on point. From the baseline, he charged in and returned the approach shot. He wasn't going to go easy on her.

Two can play this game.

Olive shuffle-stepped to cover the corner of the court. The ball was going out wide. She moved in five feet from the net. Putting her racquet up in front of her body, she angled its head into position for a volley. With a satisfying *clink,* she felt the ball make contact with the strings of the racquet. It bounced just out of Alex's reach on his non-dominant back-hand side. She fist pumped.

"And the game goes to Nakamura. Nakamura leads the set one game to love." She triumphantly recited the score.

Alex smiled. She'd missed the radiance of his pearly whites and the laugh lines around his eyes. "This is one game I don't mind losing. Just where did you pick up skills like that?"

They walked over to the bench and put their racquets down. He offered her his water bottle. "Thanks." She drank deeply. "All my know-how comes from my mom. She played collegiate-level tennis and had ambitions to turn professional until I came along."

He ran a hand over his chin. "And your father? Does he play as well?"

"Dad is a golfer and knows zilch about tennis." She handed him back his water bottle. "Mom roped me into becoming her practice partner. We'd play on Sundays, my only day off from gymnastics. It was the perfect stress relief slash bonding activity. The only downfall is that we're both super competitive."

"If I ever meet your mother, or visit your home, I'll be prepared." He glanced at the clock on the wall by the entry door.

"You've met." She laughed as his eyes widened. "The Honolulu Open four years ago. Mom was on the hospitality committee."

"Nalani." He tapped his forehead with his palm. "I can still picture her face in my mind."

"She'll be thrilled to hear it."

They changed sides of the court. Olive and Alex played another two games. She lost both games on account of Alex having found his groove again. With the addition of a slice serve to his arsenal, all she could do was watch the ball blur past her.

On their next changeover, Alex asked, "Why haven't you attempted an overhand serve? The underhand serve is too easy for you."

Olive grimaced. "Serving is one skill I've never been able to master."

Alex raised an eyebrow. "Show me." He took a ball out of his pocket and threw it to her. She strode to the baseline, bounced the ball several times, tossed it into the air, and served. The ball landed six inches shy of clearing the net.

"I hit it into the net every single time." Olive's cheeks colored.

He moved to stand beside her and corrected her grip. "We need to work on having you toss the ball higher. Your timing is also off. There is a moment where you are dropping your shoulders too early while you are waiting for gravity to pull the ball even with your racquet."

Olive walked through the serving motion. "When my racquet is vertical, it's the same height as you," she joked.

"Being tall has certain advantages." Alex's face twitched. "When you toss the ball, aim for it to land in my hand."

The duo worked on her tossing mechanics. Every time he touched her, there was an electric charge through her body. It was incredibly intimate to share Alex's knowledge of tennis.

He's such a natural teacher. He would make an amazing coach in the future.

Adala appeared on the court an hour and a half later. Standing off to the side with her chin raised and arms crossed, she cut an intimidating figure. "That's more like it. Now you are hitting with confidence. This is the type of playing I expected when you hired me. From now on, I'll expect nothing less."

From his kit bag, Alex exchanged his racquet for a newly strung one. He removed the plastic covering. "I'm ready for a rematch, Adala. This time, *I'll* be coming out ahead."

Adala shook her head. "Enough for today. Tomorrow we can start off fresh. Today, you rest. The rest of the day is yours."

Alex sputtered. "You're letting me out of my weight training session with Ivan?"

Adala put a finger to her lips. "Don't spread the word around. Some of my other students might think I've gone soft."

As Alex packed his bag, she winked at Adala. She couldn't wait to share her evening surprise with him.

Michael opened the door to a sleek, silver 1969 Aston Martin DB6. Alex stepped out first, followed by Olive. He placed his hand on the small of her back. "Your chartered boat awaits you, Mr. Georgiou, Miss Nakamura. Have a brilliant time."

She smoothed out the skirt of her lipstick-red, A-line, puff sleeve dress. "Thank you, Michael. Cheers."

Alex let out a low whistle. "Swanky." He fidgeted with the collar of his burgundy-colored dress shirt and slid his hands into the charcoal gray trousers.

A captain in a white naval uniform awaited them in front of a white yacht. He tipped his cap to the couple. "Welcome aboard. My name is Ian, your captain for the evening. If you'll follow me, please, dinner awaits you."

They climbed aboard the watercraft and passed under a string of yellow fairy lights. The water was calm. The Union Jack flag of the UK flapped gently near the stern of the boat. Around them, Olive could see the bright lights of the eclectic O2 arena dome and surrounding skyscrapers. The red, purple, and blue hues reflected off the River Thames. The sound system of the boat played a piano soundtrack of opera arias.

She could smell the scent of freshly baked spaghetti, meatballs, and garlic bread.

The captain led them to the open deck of the boat. There was a circular table set for two. Flames danced atop the center-piece pair of white candles. A long side table held four heated trays of food, each letting off a delectable aroma of garlic, onions, and spices. A bottle of champagne sat in a bucket of ice wrapped in a red velvet bow.

"Tonight, we'll be cruising up and down the length of the Thames. However, if you two have any *other* destinations you might like me to set a course for, please let me know." The captain also explained they had full access to the kitchen staff. Both Olive and Alex assured Captain Ian that they would let him know if they required anything else.

Whitewater formed in the water around the boat. The engine roared to life. As the watercraft left the dock, it floated slowly out across the river toward Greenwich.

Alex pulled out Olive's chair. "I can't believe how much trouble you've gone into planning dinner for us this evening."

"As much as I'd love to take all the credit, it was a joint effort between me and my friend Amanda. She made all of this happen." She took her seat.

He unbuttoned the cuffs of his dress shirt and rolled up his sleeves. "Remind me to thank her." Olive took in the blue dial face of his Rolex dress watch. Lifting the champagne bottle out of the ice, he located the bottle opener and popped it open. "The operetta music, the Italian food, the boat... you've taken all the best elements from our unfinished dates and put them all together."

Alex poured each of them a half glass of champagne. She watched the bubbles float to the top and a thin layer of foam dissipate from her glass. "I'm impressed you noticed."

"How could I not? Venice in particular meant a lot to me. I wanted to be right beside you in Luca's gondolier, soaking in the gems of the city." He sat across from her. "This time, there won't be any interruptions."

From the center of the table, Olive uncovered a plate of mozzarella-covered artichokes and zucchini sticks, and placed one on her plate. She grinned. "It helps that we're in the middle of the Thames."

Alex added two appetizers to his own side plate. "Funny. We could've had the yacht drop us at my flat. It's just over there." Alex pointed to a cluster of green-tinted buildings.

To Olive, they all appeared identical. Yet through the glass windows, she could make out the black inky dots of residents moving about. The river widened.

"How is your apartment search going?"

"My solicitor's presented me with several flat options, but all are outrageously priced. There is nothing under one million pounds." Alex took a long drink from his champagne glass. "I'm looking outside the city. I've always fancied owning a cottage."

She sighed. "At least you're being proactive. I have no idea where I'm going to land."

Alex helped himself to two more zucchini sticks, leaving the artichokes untouched. "Are you looking to move too?"

"I've been living with my parents until this trip to Europe. The condo we've always lived in went up for sale and sold much quicker than any of us thought." She grasped the stem of her glass and swirled the liquid around, producing more bubbles. She could hear the gentle fizzing noise.

"And where do you see yourself setting down new roots?" Alex asked.

"Maui will be my immediate home base until I've sorted through my things, but the future?" She shrugged. "That is still to be determined. I don't want to be tied to any single location. Being here, I've been doing a lot of thinking. It would be nice to add some international clients to my business."

Alex unrolled his cutlery from his napkin. "Would you have the ability to work remotely?"

Olive nodded. "That's what I've been relying on while I've been away. It was going to be temporary, but now it might be more permanent."

"And would you consider making your home here in the UK?"

"It's a possibility." She hesitated. "But it has to be for all the right reasons, not *just* because you live here."

Alex unbuttoned the top two buttons of his shirt. "As it should." He stood and picked up his entrée plate. "I'd be cross if you didn't stay true to who you are—a strong and independent woman. It's one of the many qualities I love and admire about you."

She joined him at the side table. They uncovered the first two trays to reveal a mushroom ravioli dish and the spaghetti and meatballs she had smelled earlier. She added a heaping portion of each to her plate, skipping the salmon and shrimp dishes. Alex did not leave a square inch of his own plate bare, opting to try some of everything.

The yacht sailed under Tower Bridge with the Tower of London an arm's length away. By night, with a thin layer of misty fog, the landmark was even more haunting. Near the Royal Navy's battleship museum, the HMS Belfast, the captain slowed the yacht. This area of the river was especially crowded the closer they came to Westminster. The sound of the motor grew quieter.

Alex and Olive sat down and tucked into their dinners. The first bite of the mushroom ravioli was an explosion of flavors. It was thick and creamy. The cheese melted in her mouth. "Amanda hires the best caterers. I wouldn't be surprised if dinner was prepped by a chef from Buckingham Palace."

Alex enthusiastically twirled the thin spaghetti noodles around his fork. "And just how would she have connections to the royals?" he teased.

There was so much riding on Alex accepting Amanda and Clara. She'd feared sharing her royal connection with anyone, but Alex was no longer *just* a friend. What was Alex? Was he her boyfriend? Significant other?

I need more time to figure it all out, but Alex is the man I love. If I could fly, he'd be the wind beneath my wings.

Her muscles clenched. "My friends are, um… not your normal…" Olive chewed slowly. "Amanda, she's, er… dating Eddie. I suppose you'd know him better as Prince Edmund"

Alex's eyes widened. "The Prince of Wales?" He shook his head. "And the wedding you're in town for—"

Olive carefully said, "Clara's wedding. She'll become the Duchess of Leeds when she and David tie the knot."

He breathed shallowly, patted his mouth with his napkin, and leisurely replaced it on his lap. "When I was at school, I wasn't always the largest supporter of the royal family. Yet as an athlete who represents Great Britain, I've grown a soft spot for our heritage, customs, and traditions. The royal family is a part of all that. They *do* involve themselves in a substantial amount of charity work. I've crossed paths with the shy Princess Alice a few times."

Olive crossed her legs. "I can vouch for how down-to-earth Amanda and Clara are. I mean, they both still work for a living, do their own grocery shopping, and even use public transit. They're just like us in so many respects."

Alex doesn't have to know that recently they've both had to accept security details. Poor Amanda. She's been a magnet for the press trying to gain any insight from her about the wedding.

She's been so strong about not letting C know how stressful it's been for her.

Alex held his hands up. "We can't choose the families we are born into. I am living proof of that." He picked up his fork again. "If they are your friends, I do want to meet them. I don't judge people by their titles; I judge people based on how they treat others." He lifted his chin. "I'd be willing to wager Prince Edmund is ten times the person someone like McPherson is."

If we're on the topic of the past, let's get this over with. I'm tired of secrets.

Olive's stomach tightened with knots. "There is something I should have told you earlier about Sean." She sputtered. "Paul, my longtime gymnastics coach, is Sean's dad."

He took a bite of his food and coughed. "McPherson is the son of your gymnastics coach?"

She nodded and rested her hands on her lap. "Sean is the complete opposite of the man I still consider to be my second dad."

Alex breathed sharply.

"After college, I was thrilled to have the man I had a crush on as a kid take an active interest in *me*. But the more time we spent together, the more I lost sight of myself. I didn't have enough life experience to recognize that relationships are two-sided. I was afraid to disappoint Paul, or my parents. Anytime Sean or I had a problem, I was nervous it was because of something I had said or done wrongly."

Alex ran a hand over his chin. "I can't believe this. It must have put you in such an awkward position."

She stared out. "It did, but Paul *knows* me. We'd spent nearly forty hours a week, fifty weeks a year for seventeen years together in the gym. That's more time than I spent with my own parents. It was easy for him to see how tortured I was by

Sean's hurtful words and attitude. Paul blamed himself, but Sean's always been a troublemaker."

The boat had reached Westminster. The Houses of Parliament lay on one side and the Ferris wheel-like London Eye on the opposite bank. Loud music played from street performers standing atop Westminster Bridge. This area of London was always abuzz with activity.

She rubbed her hands over her arms. "As much as I loathe saying this, Tessa was right about my being 'emotionally stunted.' My heartbreak forced me to mature and undergo a lot of soul-searching. It helped me to understand what real love is and, ultimately, it led me to you."

"Our paths have been woven together through so many different threads." Alex appraised her. "I just hope I'm able to live up to being the man you deserve. I'm far from perfect, but I want you to know and to understand that you are loved."

She inherently knew he was speaking out of love. Together they'd both been able to overcome their own broken hearts, and as their relationship developed, it would only grow stronger with time.

Olive shivered.

"If you're cold, I can think of one way to warm you up." Alex extended his hand to her. "Shall we dance?"

She pushed her chair back with so much enthusiasm, it toppled over. They both laughed. They'd finish their dinner later. Alex led her out a few feet away from the table. They wrapped their arms around one another and swayed back and forth to a pop rendition of "Time After Time" emanating from the speaker on the boat.

In her heels, she gained three inches of height and was happily able to reach Alex's shoulders. Resting her head on his chest, she would forever remember the scent of his uniquely peppery and fresh cologne and being surrounded by the beauty of the historic buildings around them.

CHAPTER 20

Mom to the Rescue

Over the next six weeks, Olive spent as much time as she could with Alex. On Mondays, she joined him for his gym workouts. On Wednesdays, they took afternoon tea together on his break between hitting sessions. On Fridays, he joined her, Amanda, Eddie, Clara, and David to work on building the 3,428 piece Lego Creator Eiffel Tower set. Thus far, they had successfully completed the 1,685 piece Lego Creator Statue of Liberty set.

On his weekends off, Olive joined Alex in scouring the greater London area to search for a new home. With a proper work-life balance, his tennis began to improve exponentially. Olive was thrilled to see him playing with relaxed ease each and every time she stopped in to watch him practice at the Stratford Sports Club.

During the final two weeks of her London visit, wedding fever took hold. Olive was put through so many rehearsals that she'd lost track of what day of the week it was. She and Alex came to rely heavily on twice-daily video chats if they wanted to see one another.

On Clara's big day, thousands of well-wishers lined the

streets of Windsor, hoping for a glimpse of the bride in the famed golden open-top carriage. British and American flags created a sea of red, white, and blue. The noise level of the crowds reached decibels Olive never imagined possible. Even competing in a packed arena at the Olympic games paled in comparison.

Reaching the Chapel of Saint George, she would forever remember the image of Clara floating up the red carpet into the church. Her ceremony dress had a light champagne bodice with an empire waist and V-cut neckline that was tailored to perfection. With each step she took, the gold-, pink-, and orange-accented flowers and Swarovski crystals shimmered on the organza overskirt. She looked every inch the duchess.

Standing right by Clara's side, next to Amanda, Olive's eyes grew wet with tears. As Clara and David exchanged vows and officially became husband and wife, she could see the deep love and affection the two lovers held for one another. Seeing this real-life fairy tale unfold evoked joy within her and stirred her own emotions of hoping one day she could appear as radiant as one of her best friends.

Then, in the blink of an eye, three and a half months after first arriving in Athens, she was home again. One of the only motivating factors allowing her to leave the United Kingdom was knowing that in two months, mid-July, she would be once again in Alex's arms.

By then, we'll definitely know what our next steps as boyfriend and girlfriend are going to be.

Life on each of the eight Hawaiian Islands differed vastly. On the Big Island, she was surrounded by live volcanos, lush rainforests, and waterfalls. The local population was scattered and the pace of life slow. It was the most normal of the islands. In contrast, Maui was best described as what tourists pictured when they thought of Hawaii. Though it lacked a major city, it was full of pristine white sand beaches, palm trees, and resorts.

Olive stared out the window of her makeshift office. Outside it was still dark. She could make out the fuzzy silhouettes of the towering palm trees. Had she not been chatting on her headset to her client, a level-ten gymnast from the Boston area, she might have heard the relaxing sound of the waves breaking against the sand of the beach. Around her, cardboard boxes were scattered and piled as tall as she stood throughout the living room/kitchen. Her laptop computer was perched atop a square card table. A ceiling fan whirred overhead.

"I've reviewed the reel you put together of clips from your beam routine. It looks pretty solid already, but I wanted to recommend you add in a segment featuring your best individual skills focusing on form. As a beam specialist, you want to really sell yourself. College gymnastics isn't about the difficulty in a routine; it's all about clean, safe routines you are guaranteed to stick."

"Nice *Stick It* reference." The voice on the other end of the line laughed.

The corner of her eyes crinkled. *Stick It* had been one of her favorite films as a young gymnast. She was happy to hear the next generation still knew of it and could appreciate it.

It's not very realistic, but it sure is fun.

Her client asked, "What about my other events? Am I going to be asked about those? I only have a tucked Tsukahara full on vault, and I'm still working on adding a release skill to my bar routine."

Olive sighed. "It depends on the program. Some coaches will ask you to keep training your other events even if they won't factor into making the team lineup on meet day. From personal experience, if a teammate gets injured, your coach may ask you to step in and throw a simple routine so they have a score to count."

Even if she doesn't want to hear it, it's the truth. Top schools want all-around athletes.

Her client agreed to have her coach take a video at practice and that she'd send it over to Olive in the next few days. They chatted for a few more minutes. Finishing the call, she rubbed her eyes, and removed the headset.

A five-foot-six woman with a round face, tanned skin, brown eyes, and black hair braided over her shoulder, placed a coaster and a mug of hot green tea to the right of her computer. Stream rose into the air. "Thanks, Mom."

"Couldn't you schedule Hailey's meeting a *tiny* bit later?" Mrs. Nakamura sat on a metal folding chair and stirred a bowl of oatmeal atop one of the shorter piles of boxes covered in a sheet as a tablecloth.

Olive yawned and covered her mouth with her hand. "She had to call me before school."

"It may be eight a.m. on the East Coast, but it's only three in the morning here. Have you slept yet?"

Her mother knew her too well. She pinched her lips together. "Alex is going to call me on his lunch break in half an hour, then I'll nap until ten."

"I'll try and be quiet once I pick your dad up from the airport. I hope he's brought us some good vintages from Napa Valley."

"You and me both." She rolled her shoulders. They were rigid with tension. She moved her head from side to side to loosen the muscles up.

"You have more clients than you have time for." Mrs. Nakamura shook her head. "Have you received applications for your job posting yet?"

"Nothing viable." She drank the tea and let the hot liquid roll down her throat. "I'm never going to find a person who understands how the college admission process works *and* knows about sports."

Her mother's cheeks flushed. "You could hire me."

Olive rubbed her temples. "Mom, be serious."

"I am being serious." Mrs. Nakamura took Olive's hands in hers. "You'll find my resume in your inbox."

Olive opened and closed her mouth. "Mom?"

The one time I haven't checked my messages this morning.

She moved her mouse and launched her internet browser. Opening her email, she saw her mom's name as the second message from the top. Her gaze returned to her mom.

"Honey, I'm a former high school English teacher. I am the perfect person to proofread and advise on personal statements and any writing samples your clients may wish to include in their admission applications." She steepled her fingers. "I *know* gymnastics, golf, and tennis inside and out. I can learn all I need to about other sports just as quickly."

"And you want to work for me?" Her eyes fluttered.

"Yes." Mrs. Nakamura put her cup of tea down. "I'm already going insane over us having to rent an apartment until we find the perfect forever home here on Maui. It would be a big relief off my mind if my new job was working with you."

Olive closed her eyes. *She really is the perfect person for me to take on. Mom has worked with high school kids for ages. She knows what colleges expect and wouldn't need much training. This would take a load off my plate. Until I found an assistant to help with all the new business, the idea of working remotely wasn't even possible. Mom is throwing me a lifeline.*

"You're hired."

Mrs. Nakamura hugged her daughter tightly. "We can figure out the terms of my contract later. After Alex, it's off to bed with you."

She laughed. "That sounds so weird to hear you say." She

entered a few notations into Hailey's file and shut down her computer.

"While you catch up on sleep, are there any last-minute supplies you need me to run out and pick up before our girls' trip?" Mrs. Nakamura asked.

She closed the laptop, unplugged it, and placed it under her arm. The two walked to the far side of the living room where the foldout sofa sat; her current bed. "If we need anything else, I'll just get it when we land in London."

At times, she found it hard to believe she had been home a mere six weeks. Between all the client calls, and helping Mom and Dad search for a new home, where had May and the first two weeks of June gone?

"You always procrastinate until the day before. You never used to be this bad when you were younger." Mrs. Nakamura crossed her arms. "It's called saving money. Even if your business is doing well, you should be putting some money away each month in case something happens." Mrs. Nakamura was dangerous when she was in her tiger-mom mode.

"Mom, I promise I'll finish packing as soon as I wake up. We can even speak about finances too." She sat down on the sofa bed and rested her head against the closest pillow.

"Alright." Mrs. Nakamura checked her wristwatch. "Please extend my thanks again to Alex for inviting us to Wimbledon.

"I've already thanked him one hundred times, but I'll tell him again." Her phone buzzed. She swiped to answer the call. "Hi, Alex. One sec." She clutched the phone to her chest. "Will do."

Her mom brushed her forehead with a soft kiss. "I'll be leaving for Kahului in about twenty minutes."

Her mom gathered up her breakfast and entered the lone bedroom of the apartment, giving her daughter some much-needed privacy.

"Hey, stranger." She held the phone to her ear.

A throaty voice chuckled on the other end. "I'm surprised you're awake at this hour."

"Work."

"Ah." In the background, she heard Alex opening a car door and turning over the engine. "Are you and your mum all squared away for tomorrow?"

She closed her eyes. "As ready as we'll ever be."

"I'm excited to host you ladies as my first official guests at the cottage."

Only Alex would consider his newly renovated, two million pound, four-bedroom, three-bath house a cottage. I mean, it may have been a "cottage" at one point, but it certainly isn't anymore. From the video tour he's taken me on, it's more of a mini mansion.

"I'm thrilled to see you, but just be prepared. Mom has been packed for nearly two weeks."

"I can well believe it." She heard him buckle his safety belt and shift gears in the car. "Perhaps you'll find the inspiration you seek for helping you and your parents find a new home."

She opened her eyes and draped the light cotton sheet over her legs. "We'll see. The longer I'm on Maui, the more disillusioned we're all becoming. It's *so* expensive. The houses I've toured with Mom and Dad cost three times what a home on the Big Island costs."

Alex cleared his throat. "That is one of the key reasons I ventured outside of London. Money goes so much further, *and* I actually have a garden."

She placed the phone to the side of her head and lay down. "For myself, Portland and Seattle are both off the short list, but I still have Orlando to investigate. I'm thinking maybe even a long-term vacation rental may be the way to go."

"The offer for you to stay with me is always open." He chuckled. "If Wimbledon goes well, I'll be back on the men's tour beginning in the fall. You would save me the effort of finding a caretaker."

"Maybe I should follow you on tour." Her breathing was slowing. "A new city every week."

"That's always an option too."

She shook her body awake. "Alex, I'm fighting a losing battle to stay awake."

"Sleep. If we don't chat tonight. I'll see you in person tomorrow. I love you, my little pineapple."

Her body warmed every time he called her by his pet nickname. "I love you too."

London was in the midst of experiencing its first heatwave of the year. As in Hawaii, the summer tourist season was underway. Nelani Nakamura stared up in wonder at the sign demarcating the entrance to the grounds of the All-England Lawn Tennis and Croquet Club, where the oldest tournament in the sport of tennis was held annually.

Banners with the tournament's recognizable logo, containing two crossed racquets on a field of purple and green and the words *The Championships*, flapped in the wind. The queue of those hoping to procure passes to the grounds wrapped well past Olive's field of vision.

"Mom?" Mrs. Nakamura tore her gaze away from the sign. "There's much more inside. Are you ready to go in?" Olive handed her mother a VIP all-access lanyard. Mrs. Nakamura caressed the plastic covering and slid it around her neck. "Unless you care to start with a walk through the museum?"

Olive was more than amused to see her normally composed mother so flustered.

Mom is in heaven right now. She's glowing. I'm so lucky

that I am the one who has the opportunity to share the experience with Alex and Mom. I wish dad could've gotten time off work; he'd love this too.

"Honey, you are going to have to wrangle me around the grounds. To say I am overwhelmed with emotions is an understatement. I'm embarrassed to not even know whether Alex is playing in the afternoon or evening session."

"Normally you have all the draws memorized." Olive poked a little fun at her mom. "Weather permitting, Alex is scheduled for a one p.m. start on court ten. I thought we could watch Drew Russo's opening round match this morning to pass the time."

The All-England Club boasted eighteen courts, all composed of grass. Two show courts—Centre Court and Number One Court—had retractable roofs. Courts two through eighteen were scattered around the grounds with smaller grandstands. The higher a player was ranked, the more likely they would be placed on a show court. Returning from injury, Alex was ranked as the number two British player behind Henry Lee and, according to the media, was not expected to finish very highly.

The two women cleared security and had their badges scanned. Mrs. Nakamura pinched herself twice. Olive snapped a photo of her mother walking through the entrance. The worker at the entry gate said, "Welcome to this year's Wimbledon tournament. Would you two ladies prefer an escort up to the VIP concierge lounge and suites?"

"No, thank you. We'll be exploring the concessions and offerings first," Olive responded.

The worker nodded. "Should you change your minds or require assistance with finding your direction, just ask any member of our credentialed staff. We're more than happy to offer our assistance."

Immediately past the gate, thick layers of lush green Boston ivy covered the exterior of Centre Court. Guests mingled with one another. Some tournament attendees dressed to impress in suits and formal attire, and would be enjoying their own private hospitality. Others dressed casually in shorts, jeans, and T-shirts. A long queue wrapped around the corner for the retail shop and souvenir stand.

"We're really here." Her mother squealed and made a beeline for the food concession stand. She could smell the aroma of freshly-cut strawberries and clotted cream.

Mrs. Nakamura smacked her lips and searched through her handbag for her wallet. "Strawberries and Pimm's are synonymous with the tournament. That's our first stop."

Olive put a hand over her mom's. "The first round of drinks and snacks is on me." She handed her a twenty-pound note. "I tried Pimm's at a pub; you'll like it. It tasted like sparkling lemonade. The perfect refreshment for a summer day, even if it's a little early for a drink."

They reached the front of the queue and ordered a dessert to share. Strawberries and Pimm's on hand, they slowly navigated the grounds. As the morning progressed, the crowds grew and created a humming buzz of excited energy. For those only able to obtain ground passes, large-scale monitors were set just outside of Centre Court and Number One.

Visitors set themselves up in lawn chairs and on blankets atop Henman Hill, cheering on the latest female teenage sensations. In the background, vibrant green and purple floral decor spelled out "The Championships" and the year.

While Mrs. Nakamura stopped in front of the Fred Perry statue, one of the great British players of the nineteen-thirties, Olive did some shopping. She picked up a program, a charm bracelet for her mom, and a pair of hats.

Eventually, they found their way to Drew's player box and

joined Penny Russo, Alex's sister, in the stands. They were just in time to see players walk in to warm up to a smattering of light applause. As an early-round match on an outlying court, few people were in the crowd.

White chalk lines were painted atop a blanket of green grass. The players placed their belongings on the benches on either side of the chair umpire. Olive could hear the roar coming from Centre Court and Number One court on either side of courts fourteen through seventeen.

To Penny's right sat a man with salt-and-pepper hair peeking out from the brim of a Panama-style hat. He was dressed in dark-wash jeans and a charcoal gray jumper over a white collared shirt. He sat erect, hands clasped together atop his knees.

"Olive, Mrs. Nakamura, just in time. I see you wasted no time in finding the Pimm's." Penny chuckled.

"We did. The only question now is how much will it cost to import a case or two of Pimm's to Hawaii?" Mrs. Nakamura mused. "It's too tasty not to have a case in my home."

"Mom, they sell it at BevMo, but it is horribly expensive. I think it cost upward of twenty-five dollars per bottle."

"You should enjoy it for the entire duration of your stay then," the salt-and-pepper-haired man thoughtfully added.

"Granda, I'm sorry I forgot to introduce you to our guests. I've been distracted." Penny apologized.

Olive swallowed hard. This was Alex's maternal grandfather? The man who had all but raised Alex and his sister? Her muscles tensed. She wanted to make a positive impression on him. Did Penny want her to succeed?

I don't think she was distracted. Maybe she wanted to make sure Mom and I had time to settle in and find our bearings.

The chair umpire called time. The players completed their warm-ups and removed their jackets.

"No offense taken, my dear. I am just an old man who enjoys having the company of young people and the chance to enjoy a good day out at Wimbledon."

They only had a minute or two before the match was to begin. Olive took the initiative and introduced herself. "Hello, sir. My name is Olive Nakamura, and this is my mother, Nelani Nakamura. It is a pleasure to make your acquaintance."

"Charmed. I am sure." They exchanged greetings. "Alexander has spoken highly of you. You may call me Art." He shook his head at Penny and offered her an amused glance.

Drew and his opponent, a player from the United States, took to their sides of the court. Drew would serve out the first game of the match. Both players were dressed in white, the strictly-enforced dress code of the club. He wore his baseball hat backward and stood at the baseline waiting for the signal. The countdown clock in the background lit up. "Russo to start."

He bounced the ball five times, tossed it into the air, and served. It briefly brushed the top of the net and sprung into the service box. His opponent hit it off to the side and off the court. A ball boy dressed in an all-green uniform retrieved it.

"Let. First serve," the chair umpire called out. Players had two serves. If the ball bounced out, the serve was not playable. If it touched the net, however, as a let, the player had another chance at a first serve.

There was no talking or conversation when the ball was in play. Tennis was a quiet game. Penny sat in total focus, watching every move her husband made. She lived through his playing, squeezing Olive's hand every time there was a long volley.

If this keeps up, I am going to need to ice my hand by the end of the first set. Penny has a firm grip. Penny rested her other hand on the rounded bump of her stomach.

Spending the last four days with Penny and Drew since her arrival to the UK had brought them closer together. Alex had been right; his sister warmed up after Olive had been able to show Penny that she was invested in her brother and here for the long haul.

Wimbledon

Olive, her mother, and Art excused themselves as Drew's match was winding down. Having already won the first two sets, he was ahead by four games in the third set. Alex was scheduled to play a fiery Belgian teenager on court ten, located on the opposite end of Centre Court. Olive didn't want to risk being late for his match. They passed an open picnic area packed full of families with younger children running about, and a tent with green-screen backgrounds for visitors wishing to have their photos professionally taken.

Art walked with his hands behind his back. "And just how are you finding your stay here at the club?"

"This is our first trip here, but so far, it's been excellent. Mom and I have enjoyed the Pimm's, strawberries with clotted cream, the shopping, and walking around soaking in the atmosphere. I know she's keen to see the tennis museum at some point, just as I would love to try the tea service at the café." Her cheeks flushed. "And of course, we can't forget the tennis. Drew's match was so smooth. I want the same for Alex.

He deserves to do well after the close loss in the semi-finals of the King's Cup tournament last week."

Art flashed her a smile. Olive observed firsthand just where Alex's dimples came from. "One can always judge a place by its presentation of tea, and the All-England Club is no exception. In our youth, my wife and I would pop down to the club weekly." His eyes sparkled. "In fact, we met at the Wimbledon Ball nearly fifty years ago."

She lowered her voice. "I'd love to attend the ball with Alex."

He patted her hand. "Alexander has not attended in many years. It would do him well to not be such a recluse. A stunning young woman such as yourself would be the belle of the ball. Ask him to take you; I'm certain he shan't refuse you."

Mrs. Nakamura's eyes roved to a purple and white sign pointing to the museum entrance. Her mother stopped walking, fidgeted, and bit her lip. She and Art also stopped walking. Olive could tell her mother was torn. She would both want to cheer Alex on for his match, and at the same time, she wanted to explore the museum.

Mom may offer to view it later, but in reality, now that she's seen where it is, she won't want to wait.

Olive cleared her throat. "Mom, you can meet me at our seats. It's going to be a minimum of three sets, and if you factor in the warm up, you won't miss much action. Alex would be the one to tell you to make sure you have the *full* experience whilst here."

Alex's grandfather watched the entire exchange and said, "The museum is brilliant. I make a point to tour it whenever I can. I'd be thrilled to stroll through it with you."

Her mom didn't even hesitate at his offer. Mrs. Nakamura straightened her posture and took a step toward the sign. "In that case, sweetie, we'll join you when we're done." Art offered his arm to her mother. She accepted.

"Take your time." Olive grinned. "Mom can spend hours looking over the old wooden racquets and each and every exhibit. I hope you won't mind."

He inclined his head to Mrs. Nakamura. "I'm very much the same." He smiled. "My wife considers me mad as, given the opportunity, I could spend hours upon hours reviewing the same exhibits time and time again. She doesn't quite understand that there is always something new to glean from the museum."

The two excused themselves. Olive watched them make their way through the crowd and into the museum entrance inside the main retail shop. On her own, she took the long route around the outlying courts two through twelve, listening to the announcement of the scores and, cheers and groans from those watching the matches being played. Near the courts, there was a lingering scent of fresh grass.

I hope Alex never has to play on the number two court. Not that I believe in curses, but an ominous nickname like the "Graveyard of Champions," makes it a place to avoid at all costs.

Finding court ten, she flashed her credential to the usher and was shown to the seats that made up Alex's player box. Adala reclined in her chair with her arms crossed. The Swiss coach wore a white zip-up athletic jacket, black leggings, and a pair of oversized white sunglasses. Her midnight-black hair was pulled into a high, messy bun. She nodded to Olive.

"How's Alex looking?" Olive asked as she removed her purse from around her shoulder, sat, and placed it on her lap.

"He was nervous when I left him on the practice courts. But there is no reason for him to doubt himself. The last week of preparation has gone extraordinarily well, and he's played this tournament several times."

"Does he need a pep talk? I could try calling him." She started reaching into her handbag but stopped herself. "On second thought, he won't have his phone near him. I hated any interruptions during my own pre-meet rituals."

"Indeed," Adala said. "Alexander has started meditating before practices. I don't doubt he'll do the same today."

She glanced at the round, white, Rolex-sponsored clock face that displayed the time. He was scheduled to begin in less than fifteen minutes. Court ten mirrored the setup of court seventeen. However, unlike Drew's match, more than three-quarters of the stands were full. Fans waved Union Jack flags and supportive signs eager to cheer on a homegrown British player.

Adala lowered her shades and looked directly at her. "Were you aware Alexander has also taken to carrying a photo of you two in his kit bag for luck?"

She wiggled in her seat. "He has?"

Adala nodded. "It's from Athens, if I'm not mistaken. He *thinks* he keeps it well hidden under his spare clothing, but little escapes my notice."

Olive's cheeks warmed. She put her hands on them in hopes of cooling them.

Alex had made her a memory book from all the photos on the SD card before he gifted her back the Canon G7X camera. She thought she would never be more touched than when she opened that brown cardboard box. Then she saw the imposing photo collage of them hanging in the place of honor over his fireplace.

This might just top both of those moments.

She itched to know what image he'd selected. She had a photo of him taken in London saved as the wallpaper on her phone.

The crowd clapped in anticipation as Alex and his opponent, Noah Dupont, lined up at the entrance to the court. Chills shot through her body. She took in the white headband tied around his forehead, and matching white shirt, shorts, socks, and shoes. She'd never seen another player make the all-white uniform appear so appealing.

The shirt contoured to the lean, yet powerful, muscles in his chest. Each time he moved, she had difficulty looking elsewhere. Over his shoulder, he carried a bigger than normal red tennis bag packed full of spare clothing, shoes, socks, racquets, snacks, and drinks.

As he stepped out from the shade of the tunnel, the crowd roared, whistled, and shouted his name. She almost felt guilty for the Belgian player. It was obvious he would have little crowd support. Alex smiled widely. He walked with a lightness; there was no trace of nerves. His chin lifted, and shading his forehead with his hand, he searched the crowd.

She jumped to her feet and waved wildly with two hands. He immediately locked onto her. She formed the shape of a heart with her hands and pointed to him. He lifted his right hand as if he was catching it and placed a closed fist on his chest. Her pulse raced.

Several members of the crowd caught on and laughed at the exchange. She didn't care. In that moment, all that mattered was Alex knowing she was there to fully support him no matter how his Wimbledon run went.

Adala chuckled. "If you have it this bad now, wait until he wins the match."

The players retrieved their racquets from their equipment bags and took to opposite ends of the court. They warmed up by hitting the ball back and forth to one another, then went on to serving. Olive had difficulty sitting still. If Alex wasn't nervous, she certainly was.

"Time. This completes the warm-up. Dupont to serve. Love all, first set," the chair umpire announced.

Alex moved into position four steps behind the baseline, waiting to receive the serve. The eighteen-year-old Dupont tossed the ball up and grunted as his racquet came down. It was as if Alex had an early read on where the ball would be. He returned it before Olive could blink. He moved faster than she'd seen him, sure of each and every movement. In his eyes was a glint of determination.

Alex's grandfather and her mother settled into their seats as Alex was into the second set.

"He's certainly playing a fast match. It's not even been an hour yet," her mother said.

Without taking her attention off the court, she said, "The last game was maybe two minutes. He had four straight aces. He's come out on fire."

Alex ran forward and hit a strong backhand return. Dupont stood frozen, watching the ball bounce on the line a foot from his reach. His shoulder hunched, knowing that as he lost the second set, with the way Alex was playing, it would be incredibly difficult to come back in the third set.

Adala put her fingers in her mouth and whistled. "That was a money shot. About time he played more aggressively."

The crowd clapped. The chair umpire announced. "Game to Georgiou. Georgiou leads five games to love, second set."

Olive gave her full attention to her mother as Alex changed sides and walked over to his kit bag for a drink from his smoothie bottle. "Did you enjoy the museum?"

Her mom nodded. "I did. It was jam-packed, but thanks to Art, I was able to see nearly everything. I'm going to stop by it again first thing tomorrow. There are a few exhibits I'd like a closer look at."

Alex's grandfather removed his hat and scratched his forehead. "I can arrange for you to see it before the gates open to the public if you'd like."

Her mother gawked and said, "You can do that?" Olive covered her mouth with her hand.

He chuckled. "It is one of the small perks of serving on the Board of Directors."

Her mother's eyes fluttered. "It's official; I'm in heaven."

The occupants of Alex's box laughed.

Within another thirty minutes, Alex had won his opening round match in a decisive fashion: 6-3, 6-0, 6-2.

Over the next fortnight, Alex defied the odds and made it through to the championship round. The morning of the finals, Mrs. Nakamura moved about Alex's kitchen, preparing a breakfast of macadamia nut pancakes, eggs, bacon, fruit, yogurt, rice, and salmon.

Olive assisted her mom with carrying the last plate of food outside to the staging area. The bi-fold doors connecting the kitchen to the outdoor patio were propped wide open, ushering in the loud chatter of the assembled guests.

Surrounding the extra-long, red-and-white-checkered-tablecloth-covered, bespoke picnic table sat Penny, Drew, Leo, his wife Stefani, and Alex. They all clapped as the smell of the bacon and eggs wafted through the air. The overnight rain had subsided. The sun peeked out from the somewhat cloudy skies. The gentleman's final match was to be held at two in the afternoon.

Olive and her mom set the food items down on the center of the table. Olive wiped her hands on her apron. Alex placed a hand on her mom's arm and patted the empty spot next to him. "Nalani, there's plenty of room for you on the other side of me."

"Anything you say, Mr. Gorgeous." Her mother's nickname for Alex slipped out. Olive's cheeks warmed.

Leo huffed. "If Alexander is Mr. Gorgeous, what does that make me?"

"I'll have to wait and see what name comes to mind." Mrs.

Nakamura ensured each tray had serving utensils before sitting down.

"Everything is always a contest with you two." Stefani Georgiou, a curvy woman with sable brown eyes and curly, copper-colored hair rolled her eyes. She turned her body away from her husband and toward Mrs. Nakamura. "Thank you so much for putting such a scrumptious meal together."

Mrs. Nakamura's ears colored cherry-blossom pink. "After the dinner you prepared last night, it was the least I could do."

Alex tapped his fork against his coffee cup. Conversation stopped. "I'd just like to take a moment and give you all my heartfelt thanks and gratitude for coming out to cheer me on. Win or lose, I am the luckiest bloke alive."

Drew called out, "Hear, hear."

Alex held up his coffee cup. "To the defeat of Sean McPherson."

Everyone at the table followed suit, raised their own mugs, and clinked them together.

Penny and Drew nodded to one another. "We have our own news to share." She placed a hand on her bump. "We've decided to share with you that I am expecting a boy."

Alex rose from his seat and hugged his sister. He clapped Drew on the shoulder. Leo, Stefani, Olive, and her mother raised their coffee mugs again to toast the expecting couple.

"You just wait until the kiddo is born. I'm going to become his favorite uncle," Leo boasted.

Alex walked from Penny's place at the table to across from where his cousin sat. "I'm sorry to break this to you, but *I* will be his only uncle on this side of his family. As such, the responsibility of the world's greatest uncle falls to me." Alex puffed out his chest.

Drew refilled Penny's water glass from a crystal-clear pitcher.

"Leo, you can be whomever you might like to our child."

Penny helped herself to pancakes, fruit, and a slice of bacon. "But the only way to decide *who* is better suited to the title of 'best uncle' depends on which one of you can give me proper foot, back, and shoulder massages, *and* is proficient enough to perform nappy changes and midnight feedings without my supervision."

"Bring it on." Leo rubbed his hands together. "With the odd hours I keep, it'll be a cinch."

Stefani pinched the bridge of her nose. "When you complain over the lack of sleep, do not come crawling to me. Penny, please feel free to keep Leo for as long as you'd like."

Olive's mom squeezed her daughter's hand and whispered into her ear, "If your dad were here, he'd be ensuring that both men were aware of just *what* they have gotten themselves into. They're in for a rude awakening."

Olive and her mom shook with silent laughter. The endearing treatment each and every person at the table presented to one another made her especially grateful to have been welcomed with open arms into her amazing boyfriend's family.

Stefani picked up on Penny's hint and also prepared herself a plate of food. "Before this fare grows cold, don't mind if I tuck in." Leo and Alex agreed to disagree, the food capturing their attention.

Alex perched himself between the Nakamura women. "I hope my boisterous family isn't on the verge of scaring you away." He piled a hearty selection of food onto his plate.

"Not in the least. I knew when we started dating that your family was a part of the package deal. It's one of the many alluring facets I love about you."

"Just as your parents come along with you." They leaned into one another and nuzzled noses. They pecked one another on the lips, their breaths warm. She could feel the goosebumps forming on his bare arms.

Olive ran a hand over his spiky, cropped hair. "You'll be on the receiving end of a *real* kiss when you emerge victorious on Centre Court."

"And what if I lose?" He played with a lock of her hair.

She walked her fingers up his arm. "You'll still get your kiss."

"Oy! Eat." Leo threw a napkin at Alex. "You need time to digest before we leave for the All England Club."

Alex let out a raspy laugh from his throat. "I'm cracking on with it." Olive straightened and focused on her favorite macadamia nut pancakes with a side of pineapple. Everyone enjoyed their breakfasts, keeping the morning as relaxed and carefree as possible.

CHAPTER 22

A Battle on Centre Court

Tickets were sold out. The roof was open over the fifteen-thousand-seat stadium. The grass of the court had seen better days. Toward the center of the net, it was still pristine and a vibrant shade of green, yet near the baseline on either side of the court, it had worn away into patches of brown, dry dirt. An electric buzz was in the air.

Those watching from the grounds outside the stadium cheered. Alex and Sean walked past the glass windows of the clubhouse and member's balcony on their way to Centre Court. A few moments later, they emerged from the tunnel entrance to the court. Sean first, as the higher seeded player, then Alex. A pair of local teens carried their bags.

The crowd eagerly jumped to their feet. The players waved to their admirers. Olive yelled at a decibel that left Leo, Penny, Drew, and Stefani with surprised expressions. Both Alex's maternal and paternal grandparents remained sitting and chuckled to one another. Her mother and Adala discussed the previous day's women's final match won by Australian Mia Taylor.

Alone in Sean's player box, sat Tessa. She wore a sunhat

over her blonde locks and focused on her phone. Sean's parents rarely attended his matches in person unless they were being played in the States; they only traveled if it was a necessity.

Not to mention Paul is coaching four kiddos competing at Nationals next week. We're getting close to the Olympic season. All those girls are going to have to prove they can handle the pressure now if they want to make the team. Paul isn't the type of person who would compromise all his students' hard work. But I'm sure they'll be watching this live on TV.

On the court below, Alex walked to his courtside bench and rifled through his bag for his towel and racquet. Sean made his way over to the string of fans seated in the first row, screaming his name. He squeezed himself into a selfie and began signing several autographs. A Wimbledon security officer cleared his throat and reminded him that he had a match to play. Alex sat on his chair with his eyes closed, dialed in.

Alex may have won a US Open before, but this tournament is the title he's truly been after. It's the one title he wants to win more than any other.

"Fine," Sean snapped and threw the sharpie pen at the ground. He methodically took his time removing his jacket and the plastic covering his racquet.

"Time. McPherson to serve. Love all. First set," the umpire called out.

The names A. Georgiou and S. McPherson appeared on the scoreboard. The ball boys and girls moved into position. Alex jumped up and down on his toes, loosening himself up. The crowd fell into a hush and resumed their seats.

Sean bounced the ball ten times. He tossed it overhead and served it. The speed clock read one hundred and twelve miles per hour. Alex shuffled two steps back from the baseline. He let the ball bounce and returned it right back to his opponent with a commanding forehand stroke.

Sean stayed rooted in his spot and lazily sliced the ball. Alex charged forward to the net and, with a volley, directed the ball cross court. Sean was caught off balance. He extended his racquet out in the direction of the ball, but the effort was in vain. It bounced five feet away from him. The line judge stuck her hands in front of her to indicate the ball was in.

"Love, fifteen." Alex had won the first point.

"So that's how this match gets started." Olive's hands were clammy. She'd managed just fine through the first four rounds. During the quarter and semifinals, she'd begun to experience nerves. Yet nothing compared to how she felt watching him play the championship match. Her stomach was tight and on full alert.

Her mother put a hand on her shoulder. "There are more than a dozen games to go. Have some Pimm's and relax."

"Exactly," Adala added. "There isn't much you can do from up here. Everything is up to Alexander. He's played in Grand Slams before and won. The pressure isn't new for him."

Olive kept silent. *But Alex has never come this far in a Wimbledon run. It's different when you're in a hometown venue and have that hometown crowd. The crowd will no doubt rally behind Alex the deeper we get into the match. He'll need their energy. Sean is going to make this match personal and make it extra-tough. But, if anyone can defeat him, it's my man.*

Sean moved into position for the next point. Changing tactics, he slowed his racquet's head speed on the serve. Barely clearing the net, it bounced low. Alex had no chance of moving his feet to the ball in time. He conceded Sean the point.

"Fifteen all."

Throughout the first set, both players held their service games, meaning that neither player lost a game that they served. Fortunes changed when Sean missed two critical serves and double-faulted in the second to last game of the set. Alex took the game and went on to win the set 7-5.

"If they continue to play at this level, this is going to be a four-hour-long match." Olive held her face in her hands.

Adala drank from her water bottle and said, "I'd wager on a five-set, five-hour match."

"Now you understand how I felt every single time you competed. Balance beam was the absolute worst. I was so frightened to watch you flip on an apparatus only four inches wide." Mrs. Nakamura passed Olive a Ziploc bag full of almonds.

"I thought it'd be bars. You despised watching me perform my release skills and transitions between the bars."

Mrs. Nakamura shuddered. "Those two. Any skill involving a flip was a lot for my nerves to handle."

Olive snorted. "That's ninety-five percent of my gymnastics."

Alex and Sean sat on their chairs, re-hydrating and cooling themselves down before the second set in the best of five. The crowd yelled out encouragement to both players. It had taken an hour and ten minutes to reach this point.

Leo and Stefani conversed with their grandparents in Greek. Penny and Drew had excused themselves for a walk. Penny was having a difficult time sitting in the green plastic-back seats of the stadium. Olive turned backward to check on Alex's maternal grandparents.

His grandmother, Maureen, had azure blue eyes, a silver pixie haircut, and nude lipstick. One had to look closely to see any signs of aging on her face. She could pass for a woman in her late forties in place of her seventies. She stylishly wore an orange and black silk Hermes scarf atop a white blouse and reminded Olive of the actress Judy Dench.

"Rather brilliant match, is it not?" Art said.

She agreed.

"Our grandson has certainly made us proud. Yet to see him win a Wimbledon title in person would be extra special. No British man has won one since Fred Perry in 1936," Maureen dreamily said.

Olive performed the mental calculations. Her eyes widened. "I hadn't realized it's been more than eighty years."

Olive asked if either set of grandparents required refreshments. They all declined her offer.

"Second set to commence. Georgiou to serve, one set to love," the chair umpire called out.

Sean's face was bright red. From experience, Olive knew him to be angry. He was already showing signs of sloppy playing and had let out a string of choice words. He'd received an official warning for his questionable behavior. During the changeover, Tessa mouthed to him to focus and calm down. Olive gave the woman credit. Throughout the entire tournament, in the three times they'd crossed paths, Tessa had been professional.

Both players took to the court. With a new set of balls and a fresh racquet, Alex hit a slice serve to open the first game of the second set. It stunned Sean, who stood frozen, only able to stare at the ball passing by him.

"Ace!" Penny cheered.

"Wow. That's new." Olive nearly jumped to her feet.

Mrs. Nakamura clapped. "I've never seen that before either. Pretty gutsy."

Adala smirked. "We've been working on the slice serve for a few weeks. It's about sixty percent consistent. Useful when played correctly."

Olive's mom chuckled. "He's done a masterful job at keeping Sean guessing."

With his hands on his hips, Sean groaned and grudgingly moved over to the backhand side of the court for the next point. Alex tried the serve a second time with less success. In a fifteen-shot rally, Sean lobbed the ball over Alex's head when he approached the net, winning the point. Over the next three games, Sean broke Alex's serve and gained momentum. He claimed the second set 6-4.

Another hour passed. Sean and Alex continually played long rallies. Olive's neck was growing stiff from constantly watching the tennis ball change sides over the net. Both players became attuned to how the other was playing and were dripping with perspiration from the effort. The lead continually changed hands to the thrill of the crowd. The third set went to Sean 7-5.

At the three-and-a-half-hour mark, Alex won the fourth set, 6-2. As Adala had predicted, everything would come down to the fifth and final set.

It's a good thing I never took on her wager.

Her mind was riddled with other thoughts and concerns. Could Alex's body continue to handle the intense level of playing? How was his knee faring? From his body language, she could tell he was pulling deep down for any extra energy reserves. He breathed hard. His shirt was soaked through and had been changed three times.

Leo extended his legs out and stretched. He placed his hands behind his head. "I will never tease Alex again by saying tennis is an 'easy' sport. He's like a Spartan warrior out there. I'm exhausted from watching. To think he's now faced four hours of marathon running and mental focus."

Stefani removed her black cardigan. "Do not forget, Alex has also had to play some pretty long matches to reach the finals over the last two weeks."

"Even if he's exhausted, I am still going to keep on him about being my doubles partner for the US Open." Drew swirled his glass of champagne.

Penny breathed in sharply. "That remains to be seen." She frowned. "Do not *forget* our child is due at the very same time, and I won't be fit to travel."

Drew winced. "I completely forgot."

"I am counting down to the moment I can see my feet again and hold our son in my arms. My poor back has been so sore that I can barely sleep at night. And it's only going to become worse until I deliver."

The grandmothers, Stefani, and Mrs. Nakamura looked on in sympathy.

Olive was focused on her boyfriend. The fifth set was just getting underway. He stood and took his spot on the base line. His shoulders went up and down as he took a deep breath. She leaned against the railing, watching Alex glare out at Sean, jumping up and down and pounding his quads to keep himself from cramping up.

Alex rolled his racquet in his hands. He shifted his weight back onto his foot and served. Sean was in full-on attack mode, coming to the net for the first time. He hit an approach forehand shot. Alex stayed back, choosing to cover the center of the court.

He aimed for a lob over Sean's head, yet didn't hit it deep enough. Sean jumped up and slammed the ball to Alex's weaker backhand side. Alex ran to his left and slid. His feet gave way from underneath him; he fell to the ground. His racquet flew out of his hands.

Olive was on her feet and shouted, "NO!"

The crowd gasped. Alex stayed down on the grass for a moment and was slow to sit up. All the occupants of his box stood frozen, waiting to see what he'd do. Collectively they held their breaths.

"Hurry up, old man, you're holding up the match. Nobody likes a cripple," Sean yelled.

The moment the words were out of his mouth, the crowd began to boo him. Tessa held her head in her hands. Her sunhat dipped lower on her head.

"Unsportsmanlike conduct. Second code violation. McPherson to lose a point."

Sean's face filled red with rage. The chair umpire covered his microphone as Sean slammed his racquet into the ground and proceeded to argue with him. By this point, Alex was on his feet. He used the time to gingerly walk back and forth and take inventory of his body.

Olive's pulse raced. *Please be okay. Please be okay.*

The crowd clapped, and cheered, attempting to lend their support to their hometown hero. Alex bent over at the waist placing his hands on his knees. She clenched her fists. She had never wanted to see Sean suffer a defeat at the hands of Alex more than now. He straightened himself up, his face pale and forehead creased. One of the line judges passed him his racquet. He accepted it and moved back to the baseline.

Sean threw his hands up into the air and shook his head. Being given another violation risked giving up one game to Alex, or worse, disqualification. He walked a thin line. The chair umpire glanced at Alex. He signaled he was ready to resume play. Tessa stood and without so much as a glance to the court, departed the stadium.

Olive closed her eyes and sent all her positive thoughts and energy to Alex.

"Alex will push through it. He's not one to withdraw from a match. Especially when he's come this far. Even if he takes a loss to that insufferable American, no offense"—Penny took hold of Olive's hand and squeezed it—"he will see the match through to the end."

Alex tossed the ball upward; it lacked its normal height

and sailed into the net on his first serve attempt. He retrieved another ball from the pocket and went for his second serve. Again, it missed its mark—a few inches shy of clearing the net. The speed clock revealed the serve speed to be eighty-five miles per hour. Adala put her hand to her forehead and inclined her head.

Much too slow.

In painful succession, Alex lost the next three games. Sean was now ahead 4-1 in the final set. Alex couldn't move with enough agility to keep up with Sean's shots. His rival was keenly aware of his limitations. On what could be the last possible change over, Alex sat with his shoulders hunched, appearing defeated. He drank from his smoothie bottle.

Olive yearned to run down to the court and see him.

At this point, what's stopping me?

Not telling anyone where she was going, she quickly slipped out of the box and jogged down the steps of the aisle, getting as close to the lower box seats as she could. She had maybe one or two minutes before time was called. A green wall separated the sections. She pushed herself up and climbed over it, reminiscent of one of her first adventures with her boyfriend.

The members of the crowd stared as she ran down the steps.

"Alex!" she exclaimed.

A security guard yelled at her to stop. She ignored him.

"Alex!" she called out again.

He heard her voice and turned to see her panting. She reached the front row of the stands and leaned as far forward as she could, her pulse racing and stomach twisted in knots. "Security is going to take me away for this, but I had to come down here."

Alex walked over to the front row and traced the features of her face.

"I'm sorry you have to witness my soddy playing," he said in a resigned tone.

"It's not over until it's over." Olive put her finger on his lips. "I'm here to remind you to fight with every ounce of your being. This is your dream! Don't let the pain or the exhaustion stop you. Fight it. Use the anger you are feeling to ignite that fire within your belly."

A group of security guards assembled. "Miss, we can't have you down here. You'll have to come with us."

Her stomach dropped. She turned her head over her shoulder. "Just a moment."

She took hold of Alex's hands. "I love you." She kissed Alex on the cheek. "Remember what I said. Now go." She released him.

The security guards surrounded her. "If you'll follow us, please." She blinked slowly and stepped toward the security team.

"Wait!" Alex called out.

"Mr. Georgiou?" the burly lead guard quizzically said. Olive stopped moving.

"My girlfriend is my guest, as well as a guest of the royal family. I'm sure they would very much wish for her to stay and see the match through to the end."

The guard removed his cap and scratched his head. He glanced over to the royal box to see a waving Amanda, Clara, Eddie, David, and their uncle—Prince Francis.

The crowd clapped in support. The guard stroked his chin. He hesitated. "Shall I return you to the royal box then?"

She bit her lip to keep from smiling. "I'm in the Georgiou box today."

"Right then. Let's get on with it so the match can resume play."

Alex winked. "I have a match to win."

Olive sighed in contentment. "That's my man," she said

softly. The four guards escorted her as an honor guard back up to Alex's box.

Sean stood, racquet tucked under his arm, tapping his foot off to the side. "You're not even going to give Georgiou a warning for wasting my time?" he yowled.

The chair umpire kept a stony face. "McPherson to serve. Four games to one."

He threw his arms up in the air and muttered under his breath. Alex stood straighter and had an extra pep in his step. Play resumed. It was as if he had an extra dose of pure adrenaline coursing through his body. The level of his playing dramatically improved. The angle and speed of his shots picked up.

"I still can't believe you ran down courtside to see him." Her mother shook her head.

Art patted her shoulder. "I'm thrilled you did. Alexander needed a few encouraging words to climb the final few steps of his proverbial mountain."

"If those chaps had tried to escort you out of the club, my Artie would've sorted you out. After all, love is really what's at stake here." Maureen laughed.

Sean's self-control was melting away. Within thirty minutes, Alex had turned the set around, putting himself back in contention. He was now up 5-4 After the reemergence of his slice serve, Sean mistimed two easy shots. The score was 30-0. Alex was two points away from claiming the match. Sean slammed his racquet into the ground, denting it. He grumbled to himself as he retrieved a fresh racquet from his bag.

"I thought the chair umpire might disqualify him after that," Olive whispered.

Her mother leaned over the armrest. "Alex is so close to winning that unless he loses this game, I don't think it'll happen."

On the next point, Sean and Alex exchanged thirty-one

shots in the longest rally of the match thus far. He was now ahead forty to love.

"Triple championship point," Olive breathed. She sat, biting her nails.

With a mad glint, Alex recorded the fastest serve of the match.

"Ace!" Olive screamed. With a rush of exhilaration, she flew to her feet, jumping up and down and crying and hugging her mother.

Adala fist pumped and nodded in cool approval.

Alex dropped his racquet and sank to his knees in disbelief. He kissed the grass court and patted it with his hands. All around the stadium, Union Jack flags waved wildly.

Sean screamed, "How could I lose again!" He kicked his bag and bottles on his way to the side of the court. Sinking onto his bench, he hid his face with his hat.

I shouldn't be so elated to see Sean lose, but victory is oh so sweet!

Penny kissed Drew. He wrapped his arms around her while she watched her brother celebrate on the court below.

His paternal grandparents yelled out support in Greek.

In keeping with tradition, Alex ran up the steps and climbed over the very same barrier as Olive had earlier on his way up to his box. Olive stepped back as he made his way up, making room for his family to offer their hearty congratulations first.

"Well done!" His grandfather beamed.

"Alex. Alex. Alex," Leo chanted.

"Alexander the Great!" Stefani shouted.

When it was her turn, he offered her the goofiest grin of all time. "None of this would have *ever* been possible without you, Olive. Be my date for the ball tonight?"

"Of course."

He urgently kissed her, dipping her in his arms and leaving

her breathless. Olive's body was engulfed in flames. Her arms moved around the slippery nylon of Alex's sweat-soaked shirt. She saw stars and could smell the dirt from his lying on the court. Even winning an Olympic gold medal could not top this. Without a shadow of a doubt, Olive knew Alex had indeed moved on from Tessa. He loved her as deeply as she loved him. Her heart sang.

The crowd let out a series of cat calls.

Alex and Olive laughed.

Penny reminded him, "Go on and get your trophy. The crowd has waited so long to have another British man crowned as champion."

"I'll see you all soon," he promised and returned to the court where the organizers of the club rolled out a tan carpet for the trophy presentation.

The lines judges, ball boys and girls, and officials lined up. While the speeches given by everyone involved in the event might have blurred together, she would forever recall the gleeful moment Alex hoisted the winner's trophy above his head for all to see.

The roar of the crowd and galvanizing energy sent chills through her body. Tears ran down Olive's cheeks. This was everything Alex had dreamed of. He had set out to see where the season of tennis might take him, and now he was a Wimbledon champion. Both of their lives had come full circle.

Epilogue

ONE AND A HALF YEARS LATER

The beach was full of laughter. Families packed up their surfboards and headed back to their cars before the beach closed for the evening. In summer, the air outside stayed warm until the early hours of the morning. Olive and Alex walked hand-in-hand, barefoot in the white-water surf, admiring the pink and orange sun disappear behind the horizon.

"I'm extra glad this time around we rented an apartment for the three weeks we were here. Hearing all the construction noise from the remodeling Mom and Dad are doing on their fixer-upper would drive me mad," Olive said.

Alex chuckled. "I thought you enjoyed home renovations. That's all you watch when we're on the road."

She shrugged. "Watching the TV programs is one thing. Living through the reno is another monster altogether."

The water rushed against their feet, giving them a sandy massage. The palm trees swayed gently in the breeze. There was a salty scent in the air and, in the distance, a pod of dolphins jumped up and out of the water.

"Either way, after two years of searching, it was about time they found a brilliant property. I might even consider moving to the Hana side of Maui if I was guaranteed the view of the ocean your parents have," Alex said.

"It's nice, but I love the view we have from the apartment in Nafplio." Olive squeezed his hand.

"If we are being technical, that is *your* property," he teased her.

Sometimes Olive missed living on the islands she had grown up in, but being able to travel the world more than made up for it. With her mom running point in her thriving company as the Vice President, Olive enjoyed the freedom of life afforded by working remotely. Over the last year, she'd been to so many different countries with Alex that her passport would soon require more pages. He'd never again be able to hide in his hotel room and miss seeing the local sights.

Following his Wimbledon win, Alex took a brief leave of absence from play to experience the joys of being an uncle to baby Nico, Penny and Drew's bundle of joy. Leo, true to his word, learned that life with a newborn child was not quite as straightforward as he had made it out to be. Yet, with the impending arrival of his own first child, a girl he and Stefani intended to call Lyra, he would be well prepared to change nappies in world-record time.

In January, Alex returned to the ATP tour circuit. He'd made it to the semifinals of the Australian Open and the quarterfinals of the French Open. In July, he successfully defended his Wimbledon title. His career was fully revived. Currently, Alex was the number three ranked player in the world.

Sean, unfortunately, did not share the same fate. After his Wimbledon loss, he'd yet to make it past the third round of any tournament. Tessa, after signing a multi-million-dollar deal with a major car brand, had quietly retired from tennis and had filed for what would be a very expensive and messy divorce.

Alex and Olive stood together, watching the last sliver of sun disappear. The tiki-torch-inspired lights had turned on along the beach, bathing the pathway leading up toward the car park in a soft golden glow of light. Gulls and other sea birds squeaked and squawked overhead.

Olive sang a soft Hawaiian melody. "Aloha'oe, aloha'oe, e ke onaona noho i ka lip..."

"So beautiful," Alex said.

"It's a Hawaiian love song written by Hawaii's last Queen, Lili'uokalani."

"The song is beautiful, but that's not what I meant," Alex said, his voice huskier than normal. "Before I met you, there were so many times I wondered if I would ever find *the* one. I was lost and walking through life straight ahead instead of enjoying all those in between moments."

Olive could scarcely believe what was happening as he knelt down into the sand and rushing water.

"You have taught me that life has so much more to it. I discovered the piece of myself that was missing. I've never laughed so much in the nearly two years we've been together." From his pocket, he removed a small, velvet, green box. Heat flooded her body as the box opened.

"You are the only person I can ever envision myself having a future with. You've become my biggest supporter and my best friend. We've had so many special adventures together. And with the world being as vast and wide as it is, there are many more out there still to come. I love you to the deepest depths of the ocean. To the farthest star in the sky. Olive Nakamura, will you marry me?"

She stared in awe at a dainty London blue topaz and diamond ring, set on a rose gold band. She covered her mouth with her hands and nodded yes, several times. He slipped the ring onto her hand. A rush of happiness took hold. Alex popped up from his knee and spun her around in a large circle, splashing water everywhere. They both laughed and fell into the water.

Neither one cared they were wet. Olive licked her lips and breathlessly kissed him. "You are my heart. You are my soulmate. My partner in crime. You are my everything. My one and only. I love you so much, Alex."

The first star emerged in the sky, flickering brightly and fiercely, mirroring the level and intensity of their kisses. With wide, cheesy smiles on their faces, they only had eyes for one another. Together they would climb every mountain and share a future built on love, hope, and possibility.

Olive may have found her happily ever after, but just what does the future hold for Sabrina Hill?

Dear Reader

Thank you for taking the time to read "More Than a Passing Shot."

If you would like to continue reading about Olive in her early days, you can pick up your free copy of "Kona's Olympic Hopeful" at: *https://tomitabb.com/bonus-content/*

If you enjoyed this book, please take a moment to leave a review on Amazon, Goodreads, Bookbub, or whatever platform you may have discovered this book on. It helps Tomi connect with readers like you!

Love her books? Become a part of her treasured community here.

Stay connected with Tomi by scanning QR code, or by visiting her official website.

Https://TomiTabb.com

Acknowledgments

To my amazing editor Kaylee over at Sweetly Us, thank you for all of your time and patience spent in helping to shape Olive and Alex's story. From the early drafts to the finalized story, your edits have so instrumental into helping me become a better writer. To Charity, thank you for your keen eye and masterful proofreading ability.

To Brooke, my wonderful friend and cover designer extraordinaire. Thank you so much for bringing Olive and Alex to life on this gorgeous new cover! It truly looks as if they've stepped out of a scene from "Roman Holiday."

To a my friends in Greece and in Hawaii, thank you for taking the time to answer all of the countless specific questions about your wonderful cultures. I'd also like express my gratitude to Ms. L, my longtime former gymnastics coach, your love of the sport continues to live on.

To my late grandparents, I have so many memories I cherish. I miss you so much, and can not thank you enough for introducing me to the sport of tennis at an early age. Thank you to my best friend M, for being my weekly tennis partner and watching the Tennis Channel with me nightly.

Lastly to my beta and ARC teams, and to my readers, thank you for allowing me to continue to fulfill my dreams. Being able to write is something I never thought would be possible. I could not do this without you.

About the Author

Tomi Tabb writes closed-door romantic comedies filled with heart, hope, and happily-ever-afters. From royalty and bodyguards to engineers, athletes, and performers, her stories celebrate kindness, found family, and the joy of falling in love. Inspired by *Pride and Prejudice*, Tomi writes the  character-driven romances she loves to read—equal parts swoony, hopeful, and satisfying.

A California native, Tomi holds an MA in History and is putting the finishing touches on her doctorate in History, blending her love of research with her passion for storytelling. She lives with her family, one very spoiled cat, and an energetic toddler who keeps life wonderfully unpredictable.

When she isn't writing, you'll likely find her figure skating, watching tennis, or hunting down the newest pumpkin-flavored treat—one of the many reasons fall will always be her favorite season.

Website: TomiTabb.com

Also by Tomi Tabb

The Unexpected Royals

Dancing With a Royal

Jiving With a Royal

Designing for a Royal

Friends of the Unexpected Royals

Designs on Love

Engineering Love

Coasting Into Love

Set to Love

The Skaters of Sequoia Valley

The Rules of the Rink

The Sloth Zone

Caught in a Loop

The Royals of Isola Nostrum

The Great Austen Adventure

For the Love of Dinosaurs

Standalones & Companion Stories

More Than a Passing Shot

Pointe Shoes and Sugar Plums

Jingle Blades

Historical Romance

The Mysterious Mr. Marcellus